The Girl from the
Docklands Cafe

The Girl from the Docklands Cafe

JUNE TATE

Allison & Busby Limited
11 Wardour Mews
London W1F 8AN
allisonandbusby.com

First published in Great Britain by Allison & Busby in 2018.
This paperback edition published by Allison & Busby in 2019.

A CIP catalogue record for this book is available from
the British Library.

10 9 8 7 6 5 4 3 2 1

ISBN 978-0-7490-2393-5

Typeset in 10.55/15.55 pt Sabon by
Allison & Busby Ltd.

The paper used for this Allison & Busby publication
has been produced from trees that have been legally sourced
from well-managed and credibly certified forests.

Printed and bound by
CPI Group (UK) Ltd, Croydon, CR0 4YY

For my dear friend, Glynis Blackburn. An indomitable lady with a great deal of patience and a wicked sense of humour!

Chapter One

Southampton, 1912

Jessie McGonigall was a hard woman, everybody said so. She did indeed have attitude; you only had to see her walk down the street to notice her with her vibrant red hair, her tall stature and the way she strode out with such confidence – her long skirt swishing, her shawl draped around her shoulders. *Don't mess with me* was the message she gave out without speaking a word!

Her neighbours were careful not to cross her and those who had been foolish enough to do so soon realised that they'd made a serious mistake. Her red hair and Irish heritage was a force to be reckoned with in any altercation, but if she was your friend, she would walk through fire and water to defend you.

Young Daisy Brown would attest to that. She had arrived to take up residence with Bill, her young husband, in one of the council-owned two-up two-down terraced houses earlier that year and had been treated badly by a certain small band of women that Jessie referred to as the 'Coven of Witches'. There were three of them who spent much of their time causing trouble through their spiteful gossip. They had ganged up against poor Daisy making her life a misery, commenting about her old clothes and the torn but clean net curtains at her window, until one day when Jessie happened upon them where they had cornered Daisy and were berating her. Jessie, infuriated by their cruelty and seeing the girl in tears, interceded.

'Well, I can see that you bitches have found another victim! Haven't you anything better to do? You, Emily Coates, would be better spending your time cleaning that shithole of a house. You can smell the filth just walking past the door, and a good wash down yourself wouldn't come amiss! And you, Iris Jones, you would be a nicer person if you kept off the gin. Your morning hangovers make you bad-tempered and you have to take it out on somebody. And as for you, Betty Barnes, what the hell you're doing mixing with these two old biddies when you have a mind of your own, I'll never understand! Well, let me tell you all' – she cast a scathing look at them – 'Daisy here is my friend. You insult her, you insult me. Do I make myself clear?'

No one dared to answer.

'Good!' She took Daisy by the arm and walked her away to her own house, opened the door and ushered the girl into the living room.

'Sit down, love, and I'll make us a nice cup of tea.' She took a clean handkerchief from her pocket and gave it to her. 'Here, dry your eyes. Those bitches aren't worth the salt in your tears.'

Leaving the girl to recover, Jessie filled the pot of tea

when the water had boiled, placed two cups and saucers on the table and, sitting down, poured the tea, added the milk and pushed the sugar bowl over to her visitor.

'Help yourself.'

Once Daisy seemed settled, Jessie began talking to her, asking her how she came to move to Southampton.

'Me and Bill, my husband, moved down from the north thinking jobs would be better here,' she said. 'He's now working in the docks if he's lucky enough to be chosen at the call-on every day, but we don't have money for new clothes and curtains – well not yet. I try to keep the place clean and feed my hubby when he's earning – after all, he needs a good meal, working hard as he does when he gets work.'

'I know what hardship is,' Jessie told her, 'and so do those old bitches, but they wallow in it. I can see you're a cut above them. I've a spare pair of nets you can have.' As Daisy made to argue, she stopped her. 'Look, love, I don't use them, so you might as well and I've a couple of dresses we could alter. I'm taller than you, but we could shorten them. Are you any good with a needle?'

Daisy beamed. 'As a matter of fact, I am. I did work as a seamstress before I married.'

'Perfect!'

Looking across the table at her saviour, Daisy asked, 'Why are you doing this for me? You don't know me from Adam.'

Jessie smiled. 'Because I was young and just-married once and I had to count every penny, and . . . I wanted to teach those wicked bitches a lesson. They make my blood boil standing there, spewing out their filth instead of doing something useful with their lives.'

With a chuckle, Daisy said, 'You don't half have a temper on you when you go!'

Jessie burst out laughing. 'I've got red hair, so I've got to live up to it.'

When the girl had left, Jessie poured herself another cup of tea. Times were hard in the docks. The call-on every morning at seven-thirty and again at twelve forty-five was where the dockers who were not in permanent jobs lined up, praying to be chosen to work for as many or as few hours that were required. It was like a cattle market where men would call out to be chosen, pushing others out of the way to be noticed. There was no dignity here, just a desperate need to be one of the lucky ones. Her husband was fortunate to be a stevedore with a permanent position.

Jessie thought back to her hard times. She'd come over from Ireland as a child with her parents, Siobhan and Brin O'Hanneran, but her beloved father had died of consumption when Jessie was nineteen. Her mother, distraught with grief, had returned to Ireland to live with her parents, but Jessie had insisted on staying on alone. She'd rented a room and made her living, cleaning to begin with. It had been lonely during those first months and she'd just made enough money to pay for her room and scrape by on bread and dripping, with the occasional stew made from scrag-end and vegetables, but that had changed when she ended up as a cook at a working man's cafe from seven in the morning until three in the afternoon. It had been hard work, but she'd enjoyed it. She'd been confident enough by then to keep the male customers at bay and had earned their respect. Then one day, Conor McGonigall had walked in and her life changed.

Jessie walked out of the kitchen carrying three plates of steaming stew and dumplings and, with a smile, placed them in front of her waiting customers.

'That smells good, Jessie love,' said one.

'And so it should be. Didn't I make it meself?'

At that moment the cafe door opened and a tall, good-looking stranger walked in, glanced quickly around, saw an empty table and sat down.

Jessie walked over to him. 'There's beef stew with dumplings or shepherd's pie,' she said. 'What can I get you?'

The man looked up at her, his green eyes twinkling. 'That's it, nothing else?'

'This is a workman's cafe, sunshine. We serve simple food and a simple menu, but the food is good. You want a fancy menu, go to a fancy restaurant!'

He started laughing. 'I came for a meal, darlin', not a fight. I'll have the stew, please.'

She walked back to the kitchen, smiling softly. It was nice to see a new face, especially one that was so easy on the eye, but she bet the new man could be a challenge if he so desired. Well she was very able to handle that. She'd been working in the cafe long enough. Her regulars now knew she was no pushover and took no nonsense from anyone, but she was an excellent cook and popular, and so the business thrived. Her boss realised what an asset she was and made sure she was happy working for him by paying her a decent wage for these times.

Jessie filled the plate with stew, potatoes and cabbage, took it into the dining room and placed it before her new customer.

He picked up the plate, sniffed it and, as he put it down, said, 'Smells appetising.'

'That's because it is. There's sponge pudding and custard after, if you've the notion.'

'We'll see,' he said as he picked up his knife and fork.

Jessie watched him from the kitchen door between serving and was delighted when she saw how he tucked into her food with obvious enjoyment. When he'd finished she went over to the table, removed the now empty plate.

'Pudding?' she enquired.

'Why not?' he said and grinned broadly. 'I'd like some tea too, please.'

She took a mug of tea and placed it on the table together with a small bowl of sugar and a plate with the pudding and walked away.

Her boss was at the till a while later when the stranger came to pay. She heard his voice as he handed over the money.

'Sure, and that's the best meal I've had in a long time. Who cooked it?'

'Jessie, the young lady who served you,' he was told.

'Really?' the man sounded surprised. 'I may come back tomorrow.'

'You'll not find a better meal elsewhere,' said her employer. He popped his head round the kitchen door when the stranger had left. 'Another satisfied customer, Jessie!'

She was pleased with herself and wondered if the man would return the next day.

* * *

12

The new customer did indeed return the following day and sat at a table, waiting. When Jessie walked over, he looked up at her and grinned.

'Beef stew or shepherd's pie?'

She looked affronted. 'Certainly not! Today we have chicken and ham pie or sausage and mash with treacle tart to follow.'

He looked at her with amusement. 'A veritable feast for the gods. I'll have the pie to start and tart to follow.'

'Would you like a mug of tea now or later?'

'With the tart will be fine, thank you. You have a good memory.'

'Hardly,' she said sharply, 'after all, it was only yesterday you were here.' She heard him chuckling as she walked back to the kitchen.

When later she served up the treacle tart and tea, the man smiled.

'Thanks, that pie was lovely, and I believe you're the lady that cooked it, is that right?'

'It is.'

'Ah, but your husband is a lucky man.'

'I've no husband,' she replied. 'I've yet to find a man who suits me.'

Trying to suppress a smile, he asked, 'And what kind of man might that be, may I ask?'

'You may not!' she retorted with a toss of her head, as she walked away.

The young man became a regular customer during the following weeks. Jessie learnt that his name was Conor and that he, too, was Irish. They exchanged a light, teasing banter every day, which she enjoyed, and she began to wait to see him walk through the door. Although he flirted with her, that was as far as it went. Jessie began to wonder why, because most new customers who were young never failed, eventually, to ask her out. She always refused, but Conor hadn't done so.

Although the majority of the regular customers worked in the docks, occasionally a passer-by, smelling the appetising aroma, would stop by for a meal. On this particular day a man came in and walked unsteadily to a seat and sat waiting. He reeked of alcohol and loudly demanded a menu.

Jessie walked over to him. 'There's no need to shout,' she said sharply.

He looked up at her and glared.

'Don't you use that tone of voice with me, missy.'

The usual chatter stopped and the dining room became silent.

Jessie stood defiantly as she said, 'If you wish me to serve you, you'll speak to me with a civil tongue.'

'I'll speak to you the way I want to, now what's on the menu, girl?'

She took a step back. 'We have nothing in here for you, so I'll ask you to take your business elsewhere . . . now!'

He sneered at her. 'No slip of a girl is going to tell *me* what to do. I'm staying until I've eaten.'

Conor stood up and walked over to the table. Gently putting Jessie aside, he faced the belligerent man.

'You've been asked to leave, so I suggest you do so

quietly and without any trouble or I'll be forced to put you outside meself.'

The drunk staggered to his feet and lifted a fist to strike Conor, who quickly hit him in the stomach and, as the man doubled over in pain, he caught him another blow on the jaw, sending the man flying. Within seconds, two of the dockers came rushing over and, between the three of them, they picked the man up and firmly removed him into the street.

Conor stood over him. 'Go and sober up before you get into real trouble and end up in the cells.'

The man glared at the small group and, muttering angrily under his breath, staggered away.

'Thank you, gentlemen,' Jessie said as they returned, and to Conor she said, 'That was kind of you. I'm grateful.'

'Ah, for sure, I couldn't have him upset my favourite girl now, could I?' He winked at her and sat down.

Jessie walked back into the kitchen with a bounce in her step. His favourite girl, was she? But when she left at three o'clock she was surprised to see Conor leaning against the wall, smoking a cigarette.

'What the devil are you doing here?'

'I thought I'd make sure that sot didn't come back at closing time to trouble you. With that type you never know.'

'But aren't you supposed to be at work?'

'I took a couple of hours off. Now, can I walk you home?'

That had been the beginning of their courtship, and they married a year later and moved into their council house.

Conor was earning enough as a stevedore, but thinking of earlier times when the dockers were on strike, the future was uncertain so they were mindful of this and Jessie continued to work. Their marriage was, at times, volatile, but they loved one another deeply. Their one regret was that they'd never had children. It just hadn't happened and now they accepted the fact that it probably never would.

Today was their third wedding anniversary and they were going to celebrate by going to the Dolphin Hotel for dinner, and then to the local pub for a few drinks. To this end, Jessie had a bath, ironed her best dress and laid out Conor's one good suit. After all, The Dolphin was considered a smart hotel. Just before he was due home, she dragged in the tin bath and filled it with hot water she'd boiled ready for her husband, knowing he'd be covered in dirt after a long day, moving cargo onto the ships that had docked, as well as his other duties.

He walked in the front door, carrying a bunch of flowers and, taking her into his arms, kissed her thoroughly.

'Happy anniversary, darlin'! These are for my girl.' He handed over the flowers.

'Oh, they're lovely, but you shouldn't have.'

He looked at her and burst out laughing. 'Now, you know if I hadn't you'd have flown off the handle thinking I'd forgotten!'

'Ah, there, you know me too well.' She, too, laughed. 'Your bath is ready and your shirt and suit are on the bed with some nice clean underwear.'

He caught her arm and pulled her to him. With a

voice full of passion, he asked, 'Are you going to help bath me, then?'

She pushed him away, her eyes bright with amusement. 'Now then, you well know if I did, we'd never get to The Dolphin! I'll wash your back, but you keep your hands to yourself.'

He started to remove his clothing until he was down to his underwear. He leant forward and, holding her chin, gently said, 'Then I'll have to wait until later, unless when you see me all tarted up, you're not able to keep your hands off me!'

'Away with you!' She laughed, as she walked to the kitchen.

They made their way through The Ditches and walked to the Dolphin Hotel, which years before had been an old coaching inn. In the dining room, the waiter led them to a table and left them to read the menu. Jessie read it with interest. It was indeed more sophisticated than the simple fare she cooked for a living. They looked at the hors d'oeuvres, but decided to have oxtail soup to start with, followed by sirloin steak with a selection of vegetables and chips.

Conor turned up his nose at the fish on the menu.

'Sure, a man needs something more solid on his stomach after a hard day's toil,' he declared. 'Fish leaves me feeling hungry!'

To the waiter's chagrin, Conor ordered beer to drink, but Jessie asked for a glass of red wine. As the waiter walked away she frowned at Conor.

'What?' he demanded at her look of censure.

'Beer with your meal? Honestly!'

'It's what I like and what I want! I hate the taste of wine, you know that. You'll not change me, Jessie. Surely you've learnt that much in three years?'

With a wry smile, she answered. 'Oh, don't I know it! I had just hoped that for one night you might behave like a true gent.'

'Is it drinking wine I don't like just to impress that makes me a gent? I don't think so, darlin'. Treating you like a lady makes me a gentleman and not a navvy.'

'Oh, you and your silver tongue!'

His eyes twinkled as he said, 'That's what made you fall in love with me. Now don't deny it.'

'Not at all! The fact you were a good kisser was what won me over.'

'Ah well, I knew behind that independent exterior beat the heart of a wanton woman!'

'Conor! Someone might hear you. Will you behave.'

'Then leave me to drink my beer in peace, woman.'

As they ate, Jessie told him about her meeting young Daisy and how she and her husband had been struggling, and wondered if Conor could help her husband get a permanent job.

'I imagine he's doing alright at the moment, what with the sailing of the *Titanic* soon. We're working all the hours God sends to get her loaded, but when she sails, if he's still having a problem, I'll have a word. The foreman who chooses the workers owes me a few favours.'

* * *

After their meal, they walked down to The Dolphin tap bar for a drink. The pianist was playing and the mood was light, everyone singing along together, and they stayed until closing time. Walking home, arms entwined, they were still singing.

Chapter Two

It was early the following morning when Conor walked to the docks. Men were pouring in, some walking, others on bicycles, heads down, ready for the busy day ahead.

The liner *Titanic* stood proud at her moorings. It was due to sail in two days and there was still a lot of cargo to be stashed within her huge hold. Cranes began loading crates in large nets into the open space where the stevedores and dockers used a fiendish-looking large case hook on a wooden handle to help them grasp the goods and stack them safely, making sure that they were solidly placed and couldn't move.

There was an order to handling a ship's cargo. The lightermen conveyed the goods between ship and quayside, then there were dockers in gangs, usually about eleven or twelve in each, who worked together with a gangmaster, helping to load and unload under the supervision of the stevedores, the most skilled workers.

It was a dangerous occupation. Sometimes the nets,

full of cargo, tipped and failed to hold the goods. Many a man had suffered serious injuries as the contents spilt out. Sometimes there were fatalities. Every penny by every man was well and truly earned, but when there was a shortage of vessels, there was little work and families suffered. The pawnshops were busy during such times. In the worse cases of hardship, the only forms of assistance were private charities and the Poor Law, offering help only after a means test, which was humiliating and was the last resort for many.

Today, the noise level during loading was high: the movement from the cranes, the tractors' engines as they moved the goods, the voices of the gangs calling to one another and the stevedores, yelling their instructions.

On board the liner, the waiters were setting up the tables in various dining rooms, the stewards and stewardesses prepared the cabins and, in the galley, butchers hung their meat in freezers, while the chefs prepared the menus for the voyage, making sure that all their ingredients were being loaded, checking each delivery on the quayside against the long list in their hands. Vegetables and fruit came on board. Barmen saw to the bars and checked the stock that had been delivered. Floral displays were being made up for the public rooms. The air of excitement was palpable as you walked up the gangway.

There had been so much publicity about this beautiful passenger liner. 'The ship that was unsinkable'. The passenger list was formidable with many wealthy passengers crossing on the maiden voyage. This only heightened the stress levels of the dockers to get everything right. It wouldn't do for the cargo to move out of place during the voyage, it would make the ship unsafe. To this end, Conor was even more watchful for any mistakes.

It was a long day and the men were weary and dirty from working in the hold. They took a short break for lunch to eat a sandwich before returning to work. They worked under lights when it grew dark, which made their job even more dangerous. Conor called a halt until the morning. He wasn't risking his men's lives for the White Star Line!

Jessie looked up as she heard her husband open the door and saw just how weary he looked.

'Sit down, darlin'. I've a kettle boiling for a good strong cup of tea, then I'll fill the bath.'

Conor slumped down on the old settee, removed his boots, lit a cigarette and, leaning back, he closed his eyes for a moment.

'That was a long day, Jessie, I wondered if we'd ever get home. In the end it got too difficult and dangerous in the hold as the light wasn't enough to be safe, even with the ones we'd set up, so I called a halt.'

'You were right to do so. Why put your neck and others' on the line? Nobody will thank you for it.' She poured the tea. 'It must be wonderful to sail on the *Titanic* as a passenger,' she added wistfully.

'The ones with the money sail in splendour, right enough, but those in steerage are less fortunate; but then, if you have money in this world, you lead an entirely different life.'

'Ah well, let's hope those trying for a better life in America will find what they're looking for. Sure, it's a mighty big step to take to leave your country for the unknown.'

'We both did it!'

'Yes, but it was only across the Irish Sea, not the Atlantic; now that *is* an adventure.'

'Not one I'm interested in. I'm happy staying here.' Jessie didn't say a word and Conor frowned. 'I'm hoping you're not having any dreams of emigrating?'

'Not really, just wondering what it would be like, is all. I'll get the bath ready,' and she disappeared.

Life was hard enough in this country, Conor thought as he drank his tea. He was lucky having a permanent job, but that could all change in a flash, he knew that. Times were hard enough as it was. If that happened in America, what would you do? Where would you go? It was a big country, with millions of people. At the very worst, here they could return to Ireland if they had to, at least there they both had family. No, America was not for him!

A few doors away, Daisy Brown was seeing to Bill, her husband. He'd had a bath and was now sitting down to a tasty stew with dumplings. Ever since the *Titanic* had docked, he'd been employed and was a happy man. It was grand to be earning money and not having to worry how to pay the rent and put food on the table. Knowing that he could be out of work again when the ship sailed, he'd put aside a few shillings whenever he could in a glass jar towards a rainy day, as he called it.

As his wife cleared the dishes, he noticed she was wearing a new dress and frowned.

'Have you been shopping?' he asked, nodding towards her new apparel.

'No, of course not! Jessie McGonigall gave it to me with another. I just had to take up the hem.'

'We don't need charity, Daisy!'

She was furious. 'This isn't charity! Jessie is my friend and she offered. I've not had a new dress since we came here and the ones I had were threadbare. Do you want to see me walking around in rags just to satisfy your stupid pride?'

His cheeks flushed with anger. 'Don't you think I know what you've had to suffer with me not always able to get work? It breaks me up not being able to provide for my wife.'

At his stricken look, her anger melted away. 'It's not your fault, Bill. All dockers' wives understand the difficulties when their husbands don't get picked in the morning. There's no shame in that and there's no shame in me accepting a gift from a friend. If the tables were turned, I'd do the same for her.'

He let out a deep sigh. 'I'm sorry, love. I'm just so tired – not that I'm complaining, of course. To be honest, when we moved south, I thought life would be easier and it isn't. I feel I've failed us both.'

She knelt beside him. 'Life is difficult for all the likes of us, Bill. The poor of the land, wherever they live, have to struggle, it seems to me. In this country it's the rich and the poor. But money isn't everything.'

'You're wrong there. With money you can be miserable in comfort!'

She had to smile at the thought. 'Maybe, but I'd rather be poor with you, Bill, than rich without you.'

He gathered her close to him. 'Oh, Daisy, I do love you, but you deserve better than this.'

'Something will turn up, you'll see. Now come on, off to bed. You've another long day ahead of you.'

As her husband slept, Daisy lay trying to think how they could improve their lot and eventually fell asleep with an idea that she would discuss tomorrow with her friend Jessie.

It had been a hectic day in the cafe and Jessie was feeling weary as she walked home. To her surprise, Daisy was waiting on her doorstep for her.

'Jessie, do you have a minute?' she asked.

'Sure, I do, come on inside we'll have a chat over a cup of tea.'

The women eventually settled and, as Jessie poured the tea, Daisy spoke.

'I've been thinking of a way for me to earn extra money, but I don't know how to go about it and I wondered if you could help. As I told you, I used to be a seamstress before I married, and I wondered if I offered my services, you know, doing alterations, making dresses, mending, would there be anyone interested, do you think?'

Jessie thought for a moment. 'Well you could always advertise, put a notice in a couple of shop windows. Like the paper shop in East Street and a couple of shops in Canal Walk. It won't cost you much to do that. A few pence, that's all. It's worth a shot.'

'Would you help me to word it?'

'Of course I will. Just let me find a pen and paper and we'll see what we can do. Then you need to buy blank postcards to write out your advert.'

The two of them set about the task in front of them and after a while were pleased with the result.

PROFESSIONAL SEAMSTRESS
All work undertaken.
Alterations. Mending. Garments made.
All enquiries. Daisy Brown. 25 Union Street.

The women were pleased with the result and, after drinking her tea, Daisy rushed off to buy some postcards and visit a few shops to advertise her work when she'd written upon them, thanking Jessie profusely.

When she was alone, Jessie thought about her friend and hoped she would find some customers, knowing that once the *Titanic* sailed, jobs would again be short if there were not many ships in dock. But then she remembered that Conor said he would have a word with a foreman he knew. She so wanted to help the couple. But now it would be interesting to see how Daisy's plan worked out. She poured another cup of tea. Conor would be late, she was sure. The *Titanic* sailed tomorrow and all cargo would have to be stowed by tonight. She'd made an extra pie in the cafe that morning and brought it home to save her cooking again. All she needed do when her husband was ready to eat was warm the pie in the black-leaded stove in the living room.

* * *

It was indeed late when Conor eventually arrived home. His clothes were ingrained with dirt from the hold, his face black and, when he removed his flat cap, there was a white area of his forehead that the cap had covered. It looked very strange.

Jessie had the bath all ready for him in front of the stove.

'Now you strip off, darlin', and soak in the hot water, I've a glass of the black stuff for you and you can drink that as you soak off all that dirt.'

He took off all his clothes and lowered himself into the hot water with a deep sigh and took the tall glass Jessie handed to him.

Taking a good gulp of the Guinness, he sighed. 'You have no idea how good that tastes and how much I needed it tonight.'

'Oh, I can see that just looking at you. Well, is the ship ready to sail?'

'As far as my men are concerned it is. We've done our job, now it's up to those on board. We'll be on duty early as the passengers arrive for embarkation at nine-thirty, then at noon the ship sails.'

'Ah, I'd love to watch her leave,' said Jessie, 'but I'll be busy. It'll be a sight to behold right enough. You'll have to tell me about it when you get home.'

The following morning, trains brought in the passengers. Crew took their baggage and helped them find their cabins. The band on the dockside was playing a selection of the favourite tunes of the time. Streamers fluttered from the ship to shore. Relations stood on the jetty waving goodbye to friends and family, some in tears, others laughing and calling out. The railings of the ship were crowded with passengers as the ropes were let go and hauled inboard. The four funnels let out their unmistakable roar as the ship slowly moved away from its moorings. Cameras flashed as the press took their pictures that would be front page news in the morning.

Conor stood and watched. He wished Jessie could have been here to experience the excitement. No matter how good he was at describing the scene to her, the atmosphere had to be seen to be understood. He turned away, eventually, to continue with his work.

Busy in the cafe, Jessie heard the sound of the *Titanic*'s funnels echo across the dockyards and into the streets at noon. There is no sound like a liner about to sail; it can make the hairs on the back of your neck stand up. There was a sudden wave of conversation from the customers as they talked about the ship, the pride of the White Star Line making its maiden voyage – the excitement of it all.

In the docks, tractors were removed, the quayside cleared ready for the next arrival, whenever it was due. The men queued for their pay now their job was finished and in the morning many of them would be standing in line at the call-on, praying to be one of the chosen.

The following morning, Jessie handed over her halfpenny to the newsagent for a copy of the *Daily Mirror* with a picture of the liner sailing out of the docks, showing the crowds waving her on her way. Conor had described the event as best he could and now seeing the pictures she could envisage the scene more clearly. She saw the passengers lining the ship's rail and noted the high fashion of the women waving and smiling, and for just a moment she felt envious. How great it must be to have money, to be wealthy. Not to have to work long hours to be able to pay the bills and put food on the table. Many of them had servants to do the housework, see to the washing, even look after the children, she'd been told. Now that she could never understand! Why would you let another woman bring up your child? She'd never do that.

Just for a moment she was overcome with an emptiness that occasionally gnawed away at her. She would love to have a baby. In the early days of her marriage it was a deeply rooted need, but gradually when month after month she found she wasn't pregnant, she put away the longing. Hid it way back in a recess of her mind, until it was only occasionally that it did appear . . . like today. She allowed herself to wallow in the need again, just for a moment, and then, getting to her feet, she shut it away for another time.

The town settled down after the sailing of the *Titanic* until the sixteenth of April when news that the ship had sunk hit the news and the headlines! Paper boys rushed about, selling their papers, calling out as they did so, '*Titanic* sinks after hitting an iceberg. Read all about it!'

The *Daily Mirror*'s headline mistakenly reported that no lives were lost, due to a wireless report that had been misunderstood. But when the news eventually broke about the loss of life, the relatives of the crew, many from

Southampton, crowded outside the White Star Line's office in Canute Road, waiting for further news . . . traumatised by what they might hear. The long wait began.

It was five days later when eventually lists of survivors were posted on boards outside the office. It was then apparent the huge scale of the loss. Weeping women were led away by family or friends. Whole streets in Northam and Chapel were draped in black crêpe. More than five hundred houses in the town had lost at least one member of their family. Of the 1,500 who lost their lives, 815 were passengers.

Although no relations of Jessie's were on board, she knew several crew members who used the cafe when they were in dock and she was upset wondering if any of them had been lost. It was as if a black cloud had settled over the town as stories filtered through. The ship had hit an iceberg . . . there were not enough lifeboats. Then they heard about the *Carpathia* going to the rescue. This gave a grain of hope to those who had no definite news.

Those men still working in the docks who had stowed goods away in the ship's hold were as shocked as everyone else. They, too, had seen the passengers embark.

'Those poor people,' said Conor that night after dinner. 'So many children and women. At least they would be first in the lifeboats, but still . . .' He drew on his cigarette. 'So much for your poor buggers hoping to make a new life in America, Jessie.'

She shook her head. 'It doesn't bear thinking about, yet I can't get it out of my head. Neither can anyone else. It's the only conversation in the cafe, because almost everyone who comes in has lost a relative. I hardly know what to say to them.'

'There's nothing you can say, darlin', just feed them well and smile. For God's sake, there are so many sad faces, so smile; it may spread a little cheer.'

Chapter Three

Despite the tragedy that had happened, life had to go on. Young Daisy Brown had gleaned some success from her advertisement and she came in to see Jessie and to tell her about it.

'Well isn't that grand, Daisy. I'm really happy for you.' But something was obviously bothering her neighbour. 'What's the matter?' Jessie asked.

Daisy looked furtive as she answered. 'I have had two ladies who want work done and a fair bit at that.'

'So?'

'They're a couple of the local prostitutes! You'll have seen them waiting to do business in Canal Walk just by the Horse and Groom.'

'Their money's as good as any other,' Jessie remarked, 'so what's the problem?'

'Bill. He'll have a fit if he finds out!'

With a laugh, Jessie said, 'Don't tell him, then. No doubt they'll come for fittings when he's at work?'

'But what if he's at home after not being picked in the morning? He's working today, but you know there's no guarantee that he'll be working every day.'

'He might not know they're a couple of brasses and, if he recognises them, you tell him your clients are none of his business, just like who he works for is none of yours!'

Daisy looked shocked by the very idea.

'Now you listen to me, girl. We wives stick with our men through thick and thin, but we must stand up for our rights. Don't be a doormat or you'll be treated like one! That's what my mammy taught me. They are customers to be treated with respect. After all, Daisy, they're working girls earning a living just like everyone else.' She burst out laughing. 'Well, maybe not quite like anyone else.'

'They want mending done and each wants a dress made for them. It's good money and they didn't quibble when I told them my price.'

'There you go, then, you're in business. Who knows, Daisy, maybe one day you could have a shop of your own!'

'Oh, for goodness' sake, will you behave.'

'Ah, Daisy love, we all of us must have a dream, something to strive for.'

'What's your dream, Jessie?'

She sat back in the chair and thought for a moment. 'My own business, maybe, and a small house with a garden, not too big, enough to grow flowers and vegetables and a lawn.' She hesitated. 'And a baby in a pram.' There was such a note of longing in her last statement that Daisy knew instinctively not to remark on it.

Jessie rose to her feet. 'I have a million things to do before Conor gets home. Now you just get on with your ladies and enjoy the money.'

With Daisy's predicament at the forefront of her mind, Jessie spoke to her husband that evening. 'Remember you said you'd have a word with the foreman about getting Bill from next door some work on a more permanent basis?'

'Yes, I remember.'

'Could you do it soon? They really need the money and if you could help it would be a blessing.'

He looked fondly at his wife. 'Why are you so concerned about them, darlin'?'

'I've known hardship and how it can destroy you. They're a lovely couple. I'd just like to help them out, is all.'

Putting his arm around her he kissed her cheek. 'I'll see the man tomorrow.'

Two days later, Daisy knocked on Jessie's door, her eyes bright with excitement.

'I've just come to tell you that my Bill has been taken on as a member of a gang. Isn't that marvellous? No more worry about the bills and, even better, he doesn't need to see my customers!'

'That's great news, Daisy. I'm really pleased for you.' She gave the girl a hug.

'Must be off,' said Daisy. 'I've work to do.'

* * *

It wasn't long before, 'The Coven', as Jessie called them, realised that two of the ladies of the night were visiting Daisy and, not knowing the reason, began their twisted gossip. As Daisy left her house one morning to shop for food, the three women stood together and, with expressions of distaste, began to question her. Iris Jones was the first.

'You thinking of going on the game to earn some money now, are you?'

Daisy was puzzled and more than a little shocked by her accusation.

'What on earth are you talking about?'

The woman leant over Daisy, who stepped back to get away as the odour of stale gin assailed her nostrils. 'We saw two brasses go in your place. We wondered if they was givin' you instruction, you know, on how to please a punter.'

The girl was horrified. If these vile women were to tell her husband, she knew her business would be over before it began, but she remembered Jessie telling her not to be a doormat and she glared at them.

'How dare you! It's none of your business who comes to my house and if I hear you've been spreading rumours, ladies – and I use the term lightly – I'll report you, Iris Jones, for libel and you, Emily Coates, for not cleaning your house, which must be rat-infested due to the filth you live in. She just glared at the third woman and walked away. But she was trembling from head to foot. As she rounded the corner, she leant against the wall, afraid her shaking legs wouldn't hold her any longer.

Now she *was* in a state. If Bill got to know how her customers earned their money, there would be ructions in the house. He was aware she'd advertised and that she was sewing for two ladies and had been pleased to see his wife so animated about her work and earning more money. He'd been really proud of her and told her so. But if he knew the truth . . . there was only one person she could confide in.

Jessie was surprised to hear the cafe bell tinkle as a customer walked in. Breakfasts were over and it was far too early for lunch, so who could it be? When she walked out of the kitchen, she was very surprised to see Daisy Brown standing there looking worried.

'Sorry to come to your work, Jessie, but can I have a word?'

Seeing the girl's hands were shaking, Jessie sat her down, poured two cups of tea and sat at the table with her.

'Daisy, you look terrible. What on earth is the matter?'

The girl told her of the women who had waylaid her and what was said, then she told her how she'd reacted.

Jessie roared with laughter and slapped Daisy on the back.

'Good for you, girl! That showed them, and I bet it took them by surprise.'

'But what if they let on to my Bill? I'll have failed before I've started, 'cause he won't have those women in his house, I can tell you that for a fact.'

'Drink your tea, love. I'll have a word when I go home. I know a few things about those old biddies that they wouldn't want known, so stop your worrying.'

But when her neighbour had left, Jessie was livid that the three useless and vindictive creatures were in a position to do harm to her friend. Well she'd soon put a stop to that!

* * *

Jessie strode purposefully along Union Street and knocked on the door of Iris Jones's house. Iris looked flummoxed to see Jessie standing there.

With her green eyes flashing with anger, Jessie glared at the woman.

'I hear you've been interfering with the affairs of young Daisy Brown, Iris.' As the woman opened her mouth to speak, Jessie carried on 'Now, I'm sure you wouldn't like your neighbours to know that you go round the market every morning, begging for money, the money you tell the people is for your poor starving children – which you don't have – when it's really to buy the gin you pour down your miserable neck!'

The woman paled.

'The police might be interested to hear how you behave. They don't like beggars, as you well know, so I suggest you keep your evil thoughts about Daisy Brown to yourself. If I hear you even *murmured* anything to her husband, I'll have you. Understand?'

'Yes,' said Iris in barely a whisper.

'I didn't hear you, Iris!' said Jessie loudly.

'Yes!' This time her utterance was clear. Then she slammed the door.

With a broad grin, Jessie moved along to Emily Coates' house and banged on the door.

When it was opened, the rancid smell seemed to rush out as if wanting to escape. Jessie stepped back. 'Jesus Christ, Emily, this place is a health hazard!'

'What's it to you?' the woman snapped.

Jessie grabbed her by her filthy shawl and put her face close to the other woman.

'If you give Daisy Brown any more grief, I'll have someone from the council down here to fumigate this place and, when they see the state of it, you will be out on your ear.'

'I didn't say nothing, it was that Iris Jones what did it,' she said as she grabbed the shawl out of Jessie's hand.

'But you were there ready to put in your two pence given the chance, of that I'm sure. Now, I don't want to hear any more. Understand?'

'Yeah, I understand, now bugger off!' She turned and went inside.

As Jessie entered her own home, she was chuckling to herself. She'd not bothered to go to Betty Barnes' house as she wasn't a worry, she just stood and let the others spread their gossip. No, she wasn't a concern, but she felt sure the other two would keep quiet after her visitation.

But the following morning, Jessie was faced with a problem of her own.

Chapter Four

On the dot of seven o'clock, Jessie opened the door of the cafe and locked it behind her. Her employer always came in later, leaving Jessie and the young girl who helped start work on their own, preparing and cooking the food for the day, before opening at eight o'clock. She and her helper, Nancy, who had arrived shortly after Jessie, were busy in the kitchen when George Ames let himself into the premises. He popped his head round the kitchen door.

'Jessie, can I have a word with you?'

Wiping her hands on a cloth, she went into the cafe. Looking at her boss, she saw his usually florid face was worryingly pale.

'Are you alright, George?'

'Come and sit down,' he said, motioning to a table and chairs. Then he began, 'I'm going to have to sell up, love.'

This was the last thing she expected and for a moment she was speechless. 'Blimey, George, that came out of the blue! But for heaven's sake why?'

'I haven't been feeling well and went to the doctor's . . . well to cut a long story short, I've got a dicky heart and I've got to rest, so I'm moving back to Bradford to live with the old folk.'

'Oh, George, I'm so sorry.' She didn't know what else to say she was so shocked. It also meant she would be out of a job. 'How will you manage, financially?'

'Oh, I've got a bit saved – after all, this is a good business.' He looked at her with a thoughtful expression. 'Why don't you take it over, Jessie?'

'What?'

'The building is on a lease; the rent isn't bad and, let's face it, you know as much about running it as I do. I'll sell you my equipment at a decent price, which you could pay back monthly.'

This completely threw her, but then she began to think about it. 'Let's get today over and when we close we'll talk some more. Meantime, perhaps you'll write down some figures, the rent, how much for the equipment, so I'll know what it would entail.'

The rest of the working day went by in a blur and they were extra busy, so Jessie didn't have time to think until she shut the door after the final customer had left, then she sat down with George and the notes that he'd made. After, she went home to discuss the situation with Conor.

They sat together poring over the figures. With them both working they had some savings, enough to pay the rent for three months, but if Jessie took over, she'd have to stock up with fresh food to cook and pay the bills herself. If business was quiet, that could cost them the rest of their savings.

'What if the business fails?' Jessie said, frowning with concern.

'Come now, darlin', you keep that place going. Without your cooking and personality, George would be quids out of pocket, even if he had another cook. The men like you and are used to you; they wouldn't enjoy a change, that's for sure.'

She looked wistful as she said, 'It's been my dream to have my own business, but it's a serious decision to take. All our savings would be gone; we'd have nothing to fall back on if it went pear-shaped.'

'What are you worried about? I'm earning, and my job is as safe as it can be in the docks. If the cafe failed, which it wouldn't, my money would still be coming in. It's up to you, Jessie, but I'm all for it.'

She stretched and yawned. 'I'll sleep on it and make up my mind in the morning. Come on, let's go to bed.'

Curled up in the arms of her sleeping husband, Jessie thought deeply about her customers. Many of them worked in the docks; others were crew members from any of the other ships that docked there. A few were from the liners, but mostly from cargo boats. There was the passing trade too. But most of the days the cafe was busy with her regulars and Jessie knew this was mainly from the fact that she had a reputation as a good cook.

She slipped out of Conor's hold and, getting out of bed, looked out of the window, the full moon lighting the shabby houses, the narrow street, and she recalled talking about her dream to Daisy. Now she'd been given a chance to take that first step to realising that dream. What a fool she would be if she turned it down!

The next morning, as she cooked Conor's breakfast, she told him of her decision.

'I've decided to accept George's offer.'

'You've made the right decision, Jessie love.' He rose from his chair and gathered her into his arms. 'You are an amazin' woman, Jessie. You're a brilliant cook. You're a bright and clever being, so you are, and I love you.' He kissed her. 'And I'm a lucky so-and-so to have you as me wife. I'll see you tonight, now go and be a businesswoman! But don't get too full of yourself that you won't share me bed at night, because that I won't agree to!'

'Ah, there's no fear of that, Conor McGonigall. Where else would I find such a good kisser?'

He raised his eyebrows as he said, 'Well I certainly hope my other skills as a lover are equally appreciated?'

She gave him a playful push. 'Go on with you, fishing for compliments. I've not left you, so you must be doing something right!'

At the end of the day she sat with George and told him she would accept the offer.

He beamed at her. 'Thank goodness for that. I'd have dreaded having to close up until another buyer could be found. Now then, I'll have to give a month's notice, but I'll put your name forward. Let's have a fresh pot of coffee to celebrate, but I think we should keep this all to ourselves for now. We don't want to make waves with the customers and have to face a lot of questions as to my reason for leaving.'

'What *will* you say when the time comes?'

'I'll say I've decided to retire, that's all.'

As they drank the coffee and chatted, Jessie cast an eye around the dining room. It could do with a lick of paint. When she made some money she'd have it done to smarten up the place. Perhaps she'd make a few cakes to sell as well. The men might like to buy one to have later in the docks with a cup of tea. The odd picture on the walls would brighten the room as well. A million thoughts went through her mind as she sat considering renting the cafe.

They bought their meat at the local butcher in Canal Walk. She'd insisted on that when she took the job. Not any old meat for her customers. Cheap cuts from a good butcher was the way to keep the bills down and this had worked well, so she'd not change that. Once a week she'd go to the market for vegetables and buy in bulk for the week ahead. But the changes to the interior would be taken slowly. Men didn't take kindly to too much change at once, this she knew. She began to feel really excited at the prospect.

But in a small community, news soon spreads and somehow the grapevine learnt of George's impending departure, but not the reason why. Neither of them had said a word, but someone had found out. Her customers were delighted when they questioned Jessie and she told them she planned to take over.

Then one day a stranger came in for lunch. He was rather smartly dressed as opposed to the usual customer in their working clothes and Jessie wondered who he was.

It soon became clear when, after he'd eaten, he asked to speak to the owner.

Jessie became watchful as the two men talked, but when she saw George becoming angry, she began to worry about his heart and she walked over to them.

'Everything alright?' she asked her employer.

'No, it isn't!' snapped George. 'This gentleman wants to take over the cafe and I've told him the place already has a new buyer, but he's insistent and is going to see the company that owns the premises.' George looked doleful and added, 'I had to tell him nothing had been signed when he asked.'

The man looked at Jessie. 'You're an excellent cook; perhaps you'll come and work for me when I take over?'

'Not in a million years,' she said and walked back into the kitchen, her cheeks flushed with anger. She was in despair. She had yet to sign any contract to take over the business, so had no redress if the company decided to sell to another buyer. If this man offered to pay a higher rent, then her dreams went down the drain as there was no way she and Conor could afford to pay more. There was nothing she could do about it, but she certainly wouldn't work for the man who took away her chance of a lifetime.

When the stranger had left, George went into the kitchen. 'I'm sorry, Jessie, but there's nothing I can do to stop him. Cheeky bugger even gave me his business card! As if I would ever need it.'

'Can I have it please?' He handed it over. It read LARRY FORBES. DIRECTOR and listed a Southampton address.

'I don't want it because this is out of my hands, unfortunately,' said George.

'I know. Now you're not to worry, it isn't good for you. We'll just have to wait and see what happens.' But as she walked away, she was fearful of the outcome.

Two days later, she received a letter from the company who owned the building. It told her there had been an offer on the premises with an increase of the rent. It stated that if she was prepared to make a counter-offer, they would consider it and gave her a week to respond.

She put the letter aside with a deep sigh. There was no way she could top the offer; they didn't have the funds. But she hated being beaten by that self-satisfied man who'd offered her a job when he took over! She was even more incensed when he walked into the cafe later that morning, smiling.

'Good morning. Jessie, isn't it?'

'No, it's Mrs McGonigall,' she said, giving him a hard stare.

He ignored this. 'I just thought I'd pop in to let you know I intend to have this business. It's a small gold mine, full every day with your regulars. You have built a fine reputation, *Mrs McGonigall*! We could do very well together. I'm prepared to double your salary to make you stay.'

'Thanks, but I'm not interested,' she said as she walked towards the kitchen.

'I think you should know that I hate to lose,' he called after her. Then he turned and left.

Standing in the kitchen, Jessie fumed to herself. This

man, this stranger, was going to walk in and benefit from the years she'd spent building the business and that infuriated her. Well, she wasn't going to let him get away with it! She went into George's office, found a large piece of paper and started writing on it. Then with a satisfied smile, took it into the dining room and placed it on the counter.

As each of her customers arrived she quickly told them what had transpired and that she too would leave if the new man took over. They were in an uproar about this and all of them signed the petition she had prepared saying they would no longer use the cafe if someone else took over. By the end of the week there were so many signatures that Jessie had to make out another two pages to be signed. She then enclosed it in an envelope addressed to the stranger from the card George had given her, with a letter explaining that she felt he should know that if he did take over the cafe, he'd have very little business to start with and would have to build a new clientele.

Two days later, Larry Forbes walked into the cafe, his anger apparent to anyone who looked at him. He strode up to Jessie, who had just served a customer.

'I suppose you think you're very clever,' he said.

She stared at him. 'Not at all. I thought it only fair to inform you of the situation. You thought you'd be buying a going concern, when in truth you wouldn't be.'

The dining room was silent, the customers listening to the angry exchange.

'I'm not sure that the men who signed that bit of paper

wouldn't still come in anyway. They must have somewhere to eat.'

Before Jessie could answer, one of the men spoke up.

'You're wrong there, mate. We only come here for Jessie's cooking. She leaves, so do we!' There was a murmur of agreement from all the other customers.

Forbes studied the men's faces. They all stared back at him. He turned on his heel and walked out.

Jessie was overcome with emotion. 'Thank you all,' she said and, before the tears began to flow, she fled into the kitchen.

The following day, George heard from the owners that the new man had withdrawn his offer, so they would be drawing up a contract for Jessie McGonigall to sign. She received a letter, explaining the situation, with a date and time for her to visit their office. Both were delighted, as were the men who used the cafe. Jessie thanked them profusely as she told them the good news.

'Ah, Jessie love, you cook a bloody sight better than my old woman. Without a lunch here, I'd be starving to death!'

Although she was thrilled with the outcome, she knew that in Larry Forbes she'd made an enemy.

On the allotted day, she chose her best dress, put on her hat and gloves and presented herself at the owner's office and signed the contract. She would take over the day George left, so the business could carry on immediately, without any closure.

After she signed the papers, she thanked the man profusely.

He shook her hand. 'This wasn't personal, Mrs McGonigall. We are business people, after all. But congratulations, we know how hard you've worked. Your customers will be happy, I'm sure.'

That evening she and Conor went to The Dolphin tap bar to celebrate. He lifted his glass.

'To Jessie McGonigall, businesswoman of the year!' He leant forward and kissed her. 'Well done, darlin'. I'm really proud of you. This is the start of great things!'

Grinning broadly, she said, 'In time, we'll have our own house too, see if we don't!'

'Nothing you do would ever surprise me, Jessie. I'm only too happy to be part of it. Just don't overwork yourself with your plans to improve what you have, that's all.'

Chapter Five

It was now late September and Jessie was pleased with herself. Business had been good and she'd made money, despite having to pay off George for the equipment. Now she decided to have the dining room painted. One of the locals started after she'd closed on Saturday. He, Nancy and Jessie had moved and stacked the chairs and tables into the centre, and the man began washing the walls down in preparation.

In the morning, she and Conor went along to give a hand with the painting as the place had to be ready for business the following day. They all enjoyed applying the fresh magnolia to the walls and white to the ceiling, laughing and joking as they worked, but it was almost midnight when they finished.

Jessie made a mug of tea and some sandwiches to eat before they put back the tables and chairs ready for business. Then they stood and looked at the outcome of their work.

'Bloody hell!' Jessie declared. 'The place looks twice as big!'

'It's grand, darlin,' her husband agreed, 'but I'm fair knackered. I think we could all do with a good night's sleep.'

Jessie, aching in every bone of her body, agreed. She paid the man and locked up.

The following morning when her customers arrived, they were all very complimentary.

'I hope you ain't put up the prices, Jessie, to pay for this?' one teased.

Laughing, she said, 'Not yet, Charlie, but maybe at the end of the year by a few pence. The cost of living doesn't stay the same, you know!'

'Ah well, a few pence ain't a great deal for a good meal.'

At the end of the day as she counted the takings, she let out a deep sigh of contentment. *How lucky I am*, she thought. *I took the opportunity and it's paying off.* With the money she was making and Conor's wage, she was managing to put a few shillings away towards her next dream, their own house. But a month later, those dreams were in tatters.

It had started as a normal day, and it wasn't until she'd taken her last orders that the cafe door opened and one of the docks police walked in.

This was not unusual, as those on duty would often pop in for a mug of tea during a break or before going home.

'Hello, Jim! Be with you in a moment . . . nice mug of tea?'

But Jim continued to walk towards her and she realised that something was wrong from the set look on his face. He took her by the arm and walked her into the kitchen.

'What is it?' she asked fearfully.

'It's Conor, Jessie. There's been an accident.'

She felt the blood drain from her. 'Is he . . . is he. . . ?'

'No, love, he's not dead, but he is seriously hurt. One of the loads slipped the net and fell on top of him, I'm told. He's in hospital.'

She staggered and grabbed hold of the countertop to stop from falling.

Nancy, her helper, pushed a chair forward for her to sit on and passed her a glass of water.

'I must go to him,' Jessie exclaimed as she took a sip.

'I can manage on my own, Jessie,' Nancy ventured. 'There's only three meals to serve. You go to your man.'

Jessie removed her apron, donning her coat and hat before rushing out of the cafe and catching a tram to the hospital. Once there, she rushed up to the reception.

'My husband, Conor McGonigall, was brought in after an accident in the docks,' she gasped.

The nurse looked at some notes on her desk and said, 'He's in surgery, Mrs McGonigall, take a seat in the waiting room. I'll tell the doctor you're here so then he'll come and see you when he comes out of theatre.'

Jessie made her way to the waiting room, feeling sick to her stomach, praying silently that her man would be all right.

It seemed an eternity before she heard footsteps and a man in a surgical gown entered. She got to her feet.

'Mrs McGonigall?' She nodded. 'Please, let's sit down.' Once seated, he said, 'Your husband has had a lucky escape. He could have been killed this morning, but, fortunately, it appears he saw what was happening and almost managed to get out of the way.'

'Almost?'

'Yes, the heavy crate still caught him, but only half of it, so I'm told. But he has sustained several serious injuries.'

'Like what?' Jessie unconsciously crossed her fingers.

'He has a fractured pelvis, several broken ribs and a broken leg, but, mercifully, no head trauma.'

'Is he going to die?' She could hardly utter the words.

The surgeon took her hand. 'No, Mrs McGonigall, he isn't going to die, thankfully; however, he's going to need nursing for some considerable time. We will be keeping him here for a while, of course.'

'Will he ever be able to work again?'

'Let's get him better first, then we'll talk about that.'

'Can I see him?'

'He's still in recovery and, of course, unconscious. I suggest you go home, have some strong tea and something to eat. Come back this evening. When he's awake he'll be anxious to see you, I'm sure.' He rose to his feet. 'Try not to worry. Your husband looks a strong, fit man and that will be a great help to getting him back on his feet.'

On her own, Jessie felt the tears well in her eyes. Conor! Her rock in all things, now lying injured and incapacitated. It was so foreign to the picture of him in her mind. The vibrant man, striding into the living room after a heavy day's work. Tired but able. And now . . .

Daisy saw her walking up the street and realised from her demeanour that something was wrong. 'What is it, Jessie?' When she heard, she ushered Jessie into her house and made her a cup of tea and a sandwich. 'I know you don't feel like eating, Jessie, but now of all times you need to keep up your strength. Don't you worry about when you come back from the hospital tonight, I'll have a meal keeping warm for you and you can tell me how Conor is. Now, is there anything I can do?'

'No, Daisy love, you've done more than enough already.'

'What about the cafe?'

'Nancy is finishing off for me; she has the keys and will open in the morning ready for when I go in. I still have a business to run, and now more than ever I need to do that as we no longer have Conor's money. I'll be able to visit him in the afternoons and evenings as thankfully my business hours fit in with that nicely.'

Putting an arm around her friend's shoulders, Daisy said, 'Look, Jessie, you've had a dreadful shock. I suggest you go home and climb into bed and try and get some sleep. You've been up early and working, now you'll need to be fresh for this evening's visit.'

It was sound advice and, to her surprise, once she was enclosed in the warm bedclothes, Jessie slept solidly for two hours.

The alarm clock she'd set just in case she slept rang loudly, making her wake with a start, then she remembered why she was in bed in the afternoon. She lay for a moment gathering her thoughts. She'd need to take pyjamas for Conor and some toiletries. She'd better pack a couple of towels too, just in case. She got out of bed and walked downstairs to make a cup of tea, pull herself together and pack Conor's bag.

* * *

Eventually, Jessie arrived at the hospital, asked which ward her husband was in and made her way there, her heart pounding. Outside the door to the ward, she took a deep breath. The last thing Conor needed was a wife in tears. She pushed open the door, asked the sister which bed was her husband's, and was ushered to one with the curtains pulled round.

'He's asleep,' she told Jessie. 'Just sit quietly and I'll bring you a cup of tea in a minute. Mr McGonigall needs to take his medication soon.'

Jessie looked down at the pale features of her man. It nearly broke her heart. He had a few scratches and a few stitches on his cheek. But the bruises were beginning to show and he looked as if he'd certainly been in the wars, as her mother used to say. She kissed him on the forehead, then sat beside him taking his hand.

'Oh, Conor!' The words slipped out as she gazed at him and the tears gathered in her eyes as she shook her head in disbelief. Everybody knew that such accidents happened when cargo was being loaded, but, of course, you never expected it to happen to one of your own. Jessie knew how careful and watchful Conor was, so it obviously took him by surprise . . . or so she assumed. He began to stir.

'Conor,' she said quietly.

He opened his eyes. 'Jessie?'

'Yes, my darlin', I'm here.' She stood up so he could see her clearly. 'How are you?'

He tried to move and moaned. In a faint voice, he said, 'I feel as if a bloody ship just sailed over me.'

'A load slipped out of the net and fell on you, I was told.'

He frowned. 'Oh yes, now I remember. It came over

the hold too quickly and when the crane driver tried to slow it, the bloody thing tipped. Jesus! I remember seeing it hurtling towards me and I tried to dive out of the way.'

'Just as well,' Jessie said, 'otherwise you wouldn't be here now.'

The curtain was opened and the doctor appeared. 'I hear you're awake, Mr McGonigall. How do you feel, or is that a silly question?'

Conor managed a sardonic smile, but his voice faltered as he said, 'I can't find any part of me that doesn't hurt, Doctor, so what's the damage – and please give it to me straight!'

'You have a fractured pelvis, a couple of broken ribs and a broken leg. It could have been much worse.'

'Frankly, as the crate fell I thought I was going to die, so I figure I got off lightly.'

Jessie smothered a cry of anguish at his words. 'Oh, Conor!'

He gripped her hand. 'Now don't fret, darlin' I'll recover eventually, won't I, Doctor?'

'Indeed, you will, but it'll take time and you'll have to learn to be patient.' He turned to Jessie. 'Another five minutes with your husband, Mrs McGonigall. We mustn't tire him.'

Jessie could soon see the exchange with the doctor had wearied Conor and she rose to leave. 'I'll be in tomorrow,' she said and kissed him.

He was fighting to keep his emotions in check, but he managed to smile at her. 'Now, you're not to worry, I'll be fine.'

Jessie walked away hurriedly, but once she was outside the ward, the tears flowed. At least Conor was alive, and she was grateful for that, but how long before he'd be well enough to come home?

* * *

The following morning in the cafe, Jessie had to answer numerous questions as word had spread of the accident. Eventually, Nancy, seeing how it was distressing her employer, went into the cafe while Jessie was in the kitchen.

'Now you all listen to me: stop asking questions! Can't you see how upset Jessie is? For goodness' sake think and pass the word round to the others that come in!'

There were murmurs of apology as she walked away.

But it had the desired effect, and the morning passed with Jessie able to work and shut her mind to her problem until closing time. Then after clearing up, she packed some sandwiches to take to the hospital in case Conor hadn't fancied hospital food. But just as she was leaving, Larry Forbes arrived.

'Mrs McGonigall! I've just heard about your husband and called in to say how sorry I am.'

She gazed at him with suspicion. What was this man up to now? 'Thank you.'

'If there's anything I can do, you only have to say.'

He gave a benign smile, but the ice-cold expression in his eyes chilled her.

'Thank you, but I'm fine,' she said, and she walked away muttering, 'the only thing you can do, Mr Forbes, is leave me alone!'

Chapter Six

For the next few weeks, Jessie's life followed a pattern. She would go to work, hurry home to freshen up, then go to the hospital to see her husband, returning to an empty house. That was the worst part. Daisy would pop in for a quick chat to see if Jessie needed anything, for which she was grateful, but the evenings would drag and she would clean her house from top to bottom, then black-lead the stove to within an inch of its life, to stop her from fretting and worrying about the future. Once Conor had recovered, would he return to work and would he still be able to keep his job as a stevedore? If not, how would he feel? Conor was a proud man. After being in charge he'd find it difficult to work in a lesser position, but maybe he'd have no choice. Would he have to join the dreaded call-on each morning? All these thoughts tormented her and interfered with her sleep, which made her even more tired as the days passed. To make matters worse, she'd had another visit from Larry Forbes, who stopped by for a mug of tea.

As she served him, he looked up and studied her closely.

'Good morning, Mrs McGonigall, I can see that your husband's accident is taking its toll on you too.'

She looked startled. 'What do you mean?'

'You have dark circles under your eyes and you're much quieter than usual. If you're finding it all too much I'd be happy to give you a good price for the cafe.'

Glaring angrily at him, she said, 'You never give up do you, Mr Forbes? Don't waste your time coming in here to see me. I have absolutely no plans to leave my business, now or in the future!'

He was unfazed by her anger. 'Just so you know, should an emergency occur and you need to offload it, that's all.' He rose from his seat. 'I'll leave you to get on, but remember I'm only trying to help.'

'Like hell! You don't fool me for a moment, but don't bother calling again; it would be a waste of time!'

He just smiled at her, then he left.

While Jessie was going through her rough patch in life, young Daisy was making her pocket money sewing for Doris and Maggie, the two prostitutes. Although she'd been a bit wary of taking them on as clients, to her great surprise she found them likeable and amusing, and as they got to know her, they would sometimes gossip about their way of life and their clients. It was a different world to the one Daisy inhabited and it did intrigue her, but they had embarrassed her more than once with their chatter.

'How can you take a stranger to your bed?' she once asked.

'You get used to it,' Doris told her. 'It wasn't easy to begin with, but in time it's just another punter. You get on with it and takes their money.' She laughed. 'While they're humping and grunting, I'm doing my shopping list, mentally. With some, it's over in five minutes. Money for old rope, really!'

'Do you ever get someone you fancy?' she asked shyly, but curious to understand.

Maggie joined the conversation. 'I had a sailor the other night who was *gorgeous*. He was just missing his wife and having his oats. Now he *did* know his way around a woman's body. I had a lovely time. He actually made me come!'

Daisy felt her cheeks redden and changed the conversation.

As she let the girls out after their fitting, Iris Jones and Emily Coates were standing by their door, having a chat and a cigarette. They looked at the girls with disdain.

Doris saw the look. 'Got your eyeful, have you? Bet it was many a year since you two had a tumble,' and they walked away laughing.

Daisy smothered a smile and walked back indoors. Ever since Jessie had spoken to them, the two hadn't said a word to her, except to glare whenever they saw her, but she was still very careful not to get into conversation with them, knowing how unpleasant it would be, and still not trusting them to keep their mouths shut when they saw her husband.

Thanks to Conor's intervention, Bill was still working in a gang, but the gang leader had been changed and the new one was demanding a cut of the men's wages if they wanted to stay working, which didn't please them. They dared not argue for fear of being kicked off the gang, but it made for bad feelings as they worked, and every night when Bill came home, his indignation grew.

'He's a bloody crook!' he exclaimed. 'The man earns his own wage and now has some of ours too. It just isn't right.'

'Calm down, love,' said Daisy. 'At least you've got more regular work; you don't have to line up every morning any more.'

'It's the only thing that keeps us from complaining and that bugger knows it. He struts about like a cockerel. It makes me sick!'

'We all have to put up with some things in life, Bill; you just have to get on with it.'

He looked surprised at her outburst. Daisy had changed during the past months. It was ever since she started earning her own money. She had grown in confidence, whereas in the past she would agree with everything he said. Now, if she didn't agree with him, she said so. He wasn't sure if he liked it or not – however, here, she was right. After so long worrying about getting work, he knew he'd have to put up with the change – like it or not.

It was now almost Christmas and Conor was allowed home at last. His ribs and the fracture to his pelvis had healed, but the knee on his broken leg was giving him trouble and he was still having to walk using crutches so as not to put any weight on it. It would take time, he was told, and he'd been given exercises to do before returning to the outpatients' ward of the hospital.

He was not a patient man, and now he was at home time seemed to hang. In the hospital it was always busy, but at home Jessie was working and he felt lost. One day he hobbled down to the docks to see his old mates.

By the time he got to the dock gates he was feeling exhausted, so he stopped in at the police hut on the gate and sat inside talking to the constable on duty that he knew.

'How's it going then, Conor, my old mate?'

'Too bloody slow. I can't wait to be well enough to get back to work.'

The man frowned. 'After such an accident, do you think that's a possibility?'

'What do you mean?'

'Come on, Conor, you know how physical your job is. You need to be strong and really fit to do it. Will you still be able, is all?'

Frowning, he said, 'I'll just have to wait and see, I suppose.' Standing up, he said, 'I'll let you get on. Good to see you again.'

'You too, Conor, take care now.'

The cafe wasn't far away and Conor carefully made his way there. At least he would see Jessie and there would be people to talk to.

He was greeted warmly by many of the customers who knew him and, of course, Jessie made a fuss of him, giving him something to eat while he waited.

'Conor doesn't look too bad, considering,' Nancy said.

'No, he's recovering, but it's slow and he doesn't know how to fill his time. You know what men are like.'

Conor sat enjoying his food and the chat from the various customers. One or two came over to his table and sat for a moment. But they all asked the same question.

'Will you be able to take up your old job when you're well?'

It was a thought that terrified him. His upper-body strength was fine, but it was his leg that was his main concern. He needed to be nimble in the depth of a ship's hold and he wasn't at all sure if he would be able to be so, and the waiting to find out was wearing him down. He didn't say anything to Jessie, but no doubt she, too, was worried about his future. Thank God she had the cafe or they really would be in Queer Street.

He sat drinking his tea and looked around. He was so proud of his wife. The cafe had been smartened up, the food was delicious and business was good, but he found it difficult to accept that Jessie was the main breadwinner now and not him. He'd worked hard to earn his place as a stevedore. He was good at his job. The bosses trusted him as did the men who worked with him. But what of the future if he was unable to bring in the money when he recovered?

When Jessie had finished for the day, she suggested now that Conor had rested perhaps a slow walk along to the pier might be nice. It would give them a chance to sit quietly and take in the sea air, especially as they had hardly been out together since his return home, and they could catch a tram ride back.

They were well wrapped up against the cold and sat in a shelter out of the wind. She snuggled up to him to keep warm.

'This reminds me of when we were courting,' she said. 'Remember how we would come along and play the machines, then have an ice cream in the summer?'

He put his arm around her. 'That I do. I thought I was the luckiest man alive to have such a beauty by my side.'

'So you were! There was many a man who had asked me out and I'd turned down.'

He gazed at her fondly. 'Any regrets, Jessie?'

She looked into the face of the man she loved and caught the uncertain tone in his voice. It broke her heart. Conor, who ever since she'd known him had been certain of everything. She'd so admired his strength of character, it had been one of the things that had drawn her to him, and now, for the first time, he was vulnerable and it showed.

Leaning forward, she kissed him. 'Not for a second! Now I think we should make our way home. Best get the next tram or we'll both catch our death of cold.'

She helped him to his feet, handed him his crutches and they set off.

It was the week before Christmas and in Southampton, all the windows of the shops were suitably decorated. Jessie had put up decorations in the cafe and had a typical Christmas menu on offer as one of her two choices, knowing that some of her customers wouldn't be having this over the holiday.

There was turkey with all the trimmings, roast potatoes and vegetables, and her home-made Christmas puddings, which she'd been making the previous month, served with custard. With each cup of tea, a free mince pie. This made her even more popular with her customers.

One of her favourites came to pay his bill. 'Oh, Jessie love, that was a wonderful spread. Don't know when I last had turkey at Christmas.'

She knew that the man worked hard in one of the local warehouses and that he had three small children. She was aware that he struggled to make his wages stretch to feed and clothe his family. He only came into the cafe once a week, as he couldn't afford to do so more frequently.

'You come in here and see me on Christmas Eve,' she told him. 'I'll have a few things to help your wife over Christmas, but not a word, alright?'

For a moment he was overcome. 'I don't know what to say,' he began.

She put a finger to her mouth. 'Shh, you say nothing, now off you go.'

It was Christmas Eve, and after she and Nancy had cleaned and cleared the cafe, Jessie had given her customer a parcel of food for his family and was now making her way home through crowded streets. People were bustling about doing their last-minute shopping. Walking through Canal Walk, she looked at the butcher's shop with its turkeys and chickens hanging from hooks in the windows. Christmas trees leant against the wall outside the greengrocers. Bundles of holly and mistletoe lay beside them and cut logs in sacks for the fire, to save on the cost of coal. The pawnshop was busy where those who were short of money had taken various goods in for cash, yet there was an air of festivity despite all this. The human spirit seemed to rise above its problems at such a time.

She had invited Daisy and Bill to join them on Christmas Day, but they had all decided after dinner tonight to go across the road together to the Builders Arms for a drink, knowing the pianist would be playing, which meant a good old sing-song was on the cards.

The place was fairly packed, but folk made room for them to sit so Conor could be comfortable. Paper decorations hung from the ceiling, colourful baubles rested between the bottles on the shelves behind the bar, the landlord was wearing a smart shirt and bow tie for the occasion and the pianist was playing all the favourite songs of the day. One of the locals stood by the piano and started singing. 'I'm Burlington Bertie', to great applause, then 'Knees Up Mother Brown' was sung lustily by all. But when last orders were called, the pianist started to play 'Once in Royal David's City' and the night was finished on a festive note.

Folk poured out of the pub onto the street, still singing, many of them somewhat unsteady on their feet and fuelled by too much beer. None more so than Iris Jones, who staggered out of the snug bar, singing at the top of her voice, words slurred beyond recognition, arms waving as she staggered from side to side. She suddenly saw Jessie and her neighbours, and headed towards them.

'Well if it ain't bloody Lady Jessie McGonigall, who thinks she's a cut above everybody!'

'Shut your mouth, Iris, you're drunk.'

'S'right I am, I'm celebrating Christmas.' She gazed blearily at Daisy, then at Bill. 'Does he know yet?'

'Know what?' asked Bill.

'That's enough, Iris!' Jessie tried to shut her up, but Iris was in her own drunken haze.

'Your missus sews clothes for a couple of the local

brasses, but you mustn't know!' She put a finger alongside her nose. 'Shh, don't say I told you.' With that, she headed for her front door, opened it and fell in.

Bill turned to his wife. 'Is she telling the truth?'

She had no choice but to answer, 'Yes, they are my customers.'

'You have invited two brasses into our home?' He was livid.

Jessie went to say something, but Conor frowned at her and shook his head.

'We'll see you both tomorrow about noon. Night, now,' and he ushered Jessie away.

'This isn't your business, darlin', you can't interfere. Leave them to sort it.'

But as they opened their front door and walked inside, they could hear raised voices from their neighbours.

'Oh dear, that's ruined Christmas for them, I'm afraid,' Jessie remarked.

Chapter Seven

Closing his front door behind him, Bill turned to his wife. 'You have some explaining to do!'

'Alright, I will. I have two very good customers and, yes, they are a couple of prostitutes, but their money is as good as anyone else's!' She stood defiantly before him and added, 'They are decent women, Bill, honestly.'

'Decent? How can you say that when you know how they earn their money? No *decent* woman would sell her body.'

'Who are you to judge? I certainly don't, and when they come here they are just two ladies wanting work done for which they pay me and for which I'm grateful.'

'Ladies? Well, I won't have them in my house, so you tell them not to call again. They're not welcome!'

Daisy put her hands on her hips and glared at him. 'I'll do no such thing! This is my chance to use my skills and I'm enjoying it, besides, the money is useful. If you were to lose your job, we would still have money coming in. Let's face it, your new gangmaster is a crook, you said so yourself. Who knows what he'll end up doing?'

This silenced Bill, because he'd been thinking the same thing of late. He still remembered the mornings standing in line for the call-on and not being chosen, the days they'd not had much to eat, wondering how to pay the rent. His small stash of money in the jam jar wouldn't last for ever if he lost his job.

'Well, I'm not happy about it, Daisy.'

Sensing the change in his attitude, her tone softened. 'I know, and I respect your feelings, but we have to earn what we can for the bad times. You know as well as I do that things change.' She put her arms around him. 'They are just two women who are doing the same thing, trying to survive, but in a different way, that's all.'

He looked concerned. 'I just don't want anyone to think this is a knocking shop, that's all.'

'Bill Brown! How could you say such a thing? As if anyone who knows us would even consider that.'

He just shrugged.

'Come on, love, I'm tired. Let's go to bed,' she said. 'It's Christmas Day tomorrow and we're going next door for our dinner, and you know Jessie, she's a marvellous cook, I'm really looking forward to it.'

He rose to his feet and, taking her hand, led her up the stairs. 'Can I have my Christmas present tonight?'

With a chuckle, she said, 'Only if you've been a good boy, that's what Father Christmas says.'

'I'm not sleeping with bloody Father Christmas!'

'No, you're not.' She laughed. 'That wouldn't be any fun at all.'

* * *

Jessie had been up early preparing the food, putting a small turkey in the oven. Over breakfast, she and Conor exchanged gifts. She took his gift to her with childish excitement. Tearing off the wrapping and letting out a cry of delight at the beautiful shawl inside. She swished it round her shoulders, the warm autumn colours matching her Titian hair.

She stood up and, looking in the mirror at her reflection, said, 'Oh, thank you, darlin'. It's lovely.'

He beamed at her. To see his wife happy was his greatest joy.

She handed him a parcel from beneath the Christmas tree in the corner. 'This is for you.'

He removed the wrapping to find a warm, dark-grey jumper. 'Just the thing for the cold weather, thank you,' he said. 'I love it,' and he kissed her.

'I wonder how those two next door are feeling this morning after last night's revelations? Daisy knew Bill would go mad if he knew about her customers being prostitutes. Would you mind if it was me in that situation?'

He thought for a moment. 'No, I don't think so. After all, she's just trying to earn extra money. I've seen the girls working in Canal Walk, most of them seem alright. They're trying to earn a living, like everyone else. Let's face it; it's a bloody hard way to earn a crust.'

'I'm not at all sure Bill sees it that way. Well, we'll soon find out. Now come on, we need to clear away and get dressed. There's lots to do before they arrive.'

When Daisy and her husband knocked on Jessie's door later that day, she ushered them in. She looked at Daisy and raised her eyebrows in a question. The girl looked back at her, winked, smiled and said, 'Merry Christmas!'

Jessie let out a sigh of relief. Christmas Day was going to be alright, after all.

The men drank beer and the girls had sherry from a half-bottle Jessie had purchased, while the turkey cooked. Then they went into the kitchen after a while to see to the roast potatoes and the vegetables.

'So . . . how did you get round him?' asked Jessie.

'I did what you told me: stood up for myself instead of being a doormat! Eventually, he came round to my way of thinking.' She beamed at her friend. 'It worked, to my surprise.'

'Well done, you. I could have killed that Iris, letting the cat out of the bag like that.' She started laughing. 'I bet she's got one hell of a hangover this morning.'

'Serves the old bitch right! She could have caused me a load of trouble.'

Jessie added more water to the pot with the Christmas pudding steaming away and they returned to the living room.

It was late that night when they called it a day. Everyone was full up from the feast Jessie had prepared and they had all had their fair share of alcohol. Their spirits were high as they gathered outside. Jessie glanced along the street at Iris's front door and saw it was partially open. She walked along and, pushing it wider, called out.

'Iris. Iris, are you there?' There was no answer. Jessie stepped inside and put on the light. The fire was out and Iris was asleep in the chair beside it. She walked over to her to waken her. 'Iris, wake up, let's get you to bed.' There was no response. She went to take her hand; the woman's arm was limp. Jessie felt her face. It was cool.

'Oh, Iris!' She turned to Daisy, who'd followed her. 'The poor woman's gone to her Maker.'

Conor went to the pub where there was a phone and asked the landlord to call the police, which he did. They arrived and by then most of the inhabitants of Union Street were stood watching. Eventually, a doctor was called who pronounced the woman dead and a funeral car came to take the body away. Neighbours stood watching, murmuring softly at the sight. Some were sympathetic, others, remembering her vicious tongue, had no sympathy at all.

As the car drew away, Jessie and the others went back to her place where she made them all a pot of tea. The festive spirit was no longer in the air, just one of shock. They sat at the table and Jessie poured the tea.

'I know she was a miserable old woman,' she said, 'but that's no way to die, all alone in the dark. There is one thing: she was so drunk that hopefully she just sat in the chair and fell asleep.'

'There'll be an inquest,' said Conor, 'then they'll know more.' They drank their tea in silence, all with their own thoughts and, shortly after, Daisy and Bill went back to their own house.

Alone as she washed up the cups and saucers, Jessie couldn't help but think about Iris and she smiled. The last time they saw her she was singing at the top of her voice and was blissfully happy in her drunken state. That really wasn't a bad way to leave this life, she thought.

* * *

71

Boxing Day was spent quietly in the McGonigall household. Jessie taking advantage of a rest before returning to the bustle of business, Conor resting his leg and contemplating the days when he'd be fit again.

It was mid afternoon when Jessie said she'd just walk along to the cafe to check on her stock for the following day and Conor said he'd go with her for the exercise.

The streets were quiet as all the shops were shut, as were the pubs until the evening. There were no trains chugging into the docks, no sound of ships' funnels announcing their departure, no whistles – no noise at all, which seemed very strange, but it was pleasant strolling slowly and unhindered for a change, stopping to gaze into the shop windows, commenting on the contents.

They arrived at the cafe and stood outside to look at it with a sense of pride. They had kept the name 'Ames Cafe', after all. George had run it for many a year, to change it seemed pointless. It was now part of the history of the street.

Unlocking the door, Jessie kept it open to let in some fresh air, then opened the back door too. She warmed some water, and then poured it over some green soap into a bucket to mop the floors.

'Can't have my customers coming into a place that smells stale,' she remarked as Conor watched her.

'Can I do anything?' he asked.

'Yes, there's a washing-up cloth in the kitchen. Pour some water in the sink and add a bit of disinfectant to it, but not too much or the place will smell like a hospital, then wipe down the tabletops.'

On finishing their chores, Jessie made a pot of tea and sat making a list of the goods she needed to buy the next morning. As she finished, she looked up and saw that Conor was looking at her with a strange expression.

'What? Why are you looking at me that way?'

'I'm just thinking how competent you are. You never cease to amaze me and at this moment I feel surplus to your needs!'

She was stunned. This was Conor McGonigall, the man who had captivated her and with whom she had fallen in love because of his strength of character, his attitude to life, his certainty. He was her rock and she needed him.

Her eyes flashed and her nostrils flared in anger. 'How bloody dare you sit there and say that to me! Yes, I can run this place without you, yes, I am competent, but so are you or have you forgotten? You've had an accident and yes, you were injured, but they didn't bloody well remove your brain or not that I'm aware of. I need you, of course I do. How could you ever doubt it?'

A smile crept over his features, and then he began to laugh.

Jessie, still angry, glared at him. 'Perhaps you'll tell me what you find so funny?'

'Oh, darlin', you are such a firebrand. I love a woman with spirit!'

Her eyes narrowed as she looked at him convulsed with laughter. 'You survived the accident in the dock, Conor, but I'm not sure you'll survive the thrashing you will get if you don't stop laughing at me!'

He rose to his feet and limped around the table, pulling Jessie to her feet and holding her close. He kissed her, but she didn't respond. He looked at her, and then he held her by her chin, gently but firmly and he kissed her again and again until eventually she gave in. Returning his kisses with so much passion he could feel the stirring in his loins.

He released her. 'You'd best stop, darlin', else I'll take you here on the floor now, in front of the window.'

She placed her hand on his crutch and, with a chuckle, said, 'Best we go home now, then, Conor. It's obvious we need each other, wouldn't you say?' Laughing, she walked towards the door, ready to leave.

'I knew you were trouble the morning I walked in here and I'm so happy I was right. You are a minx and I love you.'

She tossed her hair out of her eyes and opened the door. 'Then let's see you prove it!'

Chapter Eight

Jessie was up early as she had to go to the butcher to buy fresh meat for the daily menu. When Nancy arrived, she told her what had happened to poor Iris.

'It was a shock when I realised she was a goner, I can tell you. But it was so sad. All alone in her chair, the fire out, especially at Christmas when families are together. But she doesn't seem to have any relatives. Well, best get on.'

The day went well. Her regulars were happy to return to their normal routine. Jessie was her usual buoyant self, exchanging banter with the men as she served them.

Ever since the sudden death of Iris Jones, her friend Emily Coates had been very quiet and Betty now kept herself to herself, which was a great relief to Jessie and especially Daisy, who no longer had anything to fear from the gossips now that Bill knew about her clients. Peace reigned in the street. Now everyone was waiting to see who would move into Iris's house once the council had cleaned it. Iris had no family, it appeared, so the contents of the place had been removed and disposed of. Her funeral was being held in a few days' time.

As she was making a cup of tea in her kitchen, Jessie was thinking about the woman, wondering what her life had been like before she knew her, wondering what had made her into the sad and vicious person she'd become. She still couldn't get over the fact that Iris had died alone, with no one to mourn her and, with this in mind, she called on Daisy to come and have a cup of tea, saying she had something to discuss with her.

'What's on your mind?' Daisy asked as she sat down.

'It's Iris's funeral next week,' she began. 'It seems she has no family, so no one will attend. It's bad enough that she died alone, I just can't bear the idea that she'll be buried and no one gives a damn, so I've decided to go and I wondered if you would come too?'

Daisy looked at her in astonishment. 'Jessie McGonigall, you are a strange one. That woman didn't have a nice bone in her body, yet you are worried on her account.'

'I know, but it's enough that it'll be a pauper's funeral, that's as bad as it can get – except for no one to be there.'

'Beneath that tough exterior, you are just a softy. I'll come with you, if you want me to. It's the least I can do. What about the cafe?'

'I'll wait to see what time the funeral is. If it's when the cafe is open, I'll go in early and cook, then I'll hire a girl to help Nancy.' And so it was decided.

As it happened, the funeral was in the afternoon as there had been a plethora of other services beforehand. It was a bitterly cold January day as Jessie and Daisy stood and listened to the brief sermon given by the vicar. His voice seemed to echo round the empty church. There were no hymns and before very long they were standing beside the open grave, collars pulled up around their necks, hats pulled down, trying to keep warm, both holding a small bunch of flowers.

'Ashes to ashes, dust to dust,' the vicar intoned, and Jessie felt the tears prick her eyes.

She stepped forward, picked up a handful of soil and threw it in the grave on top of the coffin. 'Bless you, Iris. I hope you will be happier now.' She crossed herself and walked away, waiting for Daisy. They left their flowers by the grave.

Daisy wiped her eyes. 'Never did I think I would feel pity for that old woman,' she said, 'but that was so sad.'

'Come on, love, we both need a drink,' said Jessie, and they walked away, took a tram as soon as they could and found a pub.

'I think it very fitting that we should both have a gin and tonic,' said Jessie. 'After all, it was the old girl's tipple; it seems the right thing to do.' And they did.

'All we need now is to make old Emily take a bath and we'd have done a good job,' said Jessie.

Daisy turned to her. 'If you think I'm going in to clean that cesspit of a house with you, you've another think coming!'

'Don't be daft! We'd probably catch the plague. No, I was just thinking aloud. I don't understand how a woman can live like that, that's all. Come on; let's have another drink before we go.'

* * *

But on the way home, Jessie began to think about old Emily. She was alone. The same thing could happen to her and that thought distressed her. The old girl should be somewhere where she could be cared for. So that night she wrote to the council.

Two days later, there were sounds of ructions coming from Emily's house. The old girl could be heard swearing and screaming at the top of her voice. Then two men came out of the house, carrying her between them. Not an easy job as she was struggling. They put her in the back of a van and one climbed in with her. The following day, the house was cleared and fumigated before the decorators arrived.

While all this had been going on, Conor was at the outpatients' department at the hospital, waiting to see the doctor, who examined his leg and made him walk around the room, then sit down.

'It seems to have healed well, but, of course, the muscles are weak. It will take time and exercise to get them back, but eventually you'll be fine.'

'Can I go back to work?' Conor held his breath.

The man frowned. 'I am signing you off, but do you think you can do your job just yet?'

'Doctor, I've been out of work for weeks. I need to be earning again.'

The doctor read his notes. 'You're a stevedore, I see, which means you need to be active. I think you're pushing it a bit, to be honest.'

Conor just looked at him, then said, 'If you'll sign me off, I'll be on my way and thanks for everything.'

Seeing the determination on the face of his patient, the doctor knew that to argue would be fruitless. He signed the paper and handed it to Conor.

'Just be careful, is all I'm saying, Mr McGonigall.'

Conor put the paper in his pocket, rose from his seat, shook the doctor by the hand and left. He then made his way to see his boss.

John Irving greeted Conor warmly when he entered his office. The men shook hands.

Conor handed him the note from the doctor. 'I've been signed off, boss, so when can I return to work?'

Irving read the note. 'How's the leg?'

'All healed now, thanks. I can't wait to return to normal.'

'You were a lucky man that day, Conor. You could have been killed. I'm really pleased to see you've been given a clean bill of health, but the only thing is, I don't have a place for you at the moment.'

'What?' This was the last thing he expected to hear.

'I'm really sorry, but I have a full complement of men. I can put you on the list. You're a good man, but I just don't need another stevedore, unless we get really busy and, at the moment, I have enough men to cope with the incoming ships. Obviously, we get the ordinary dockers that we need at the daily call-on.'

Conor was at a loss for words as he'd expected to be taken on immediately.

Seeing his consternation, Irving said, 'I had to find

someone to take your place, of course, but I can't now give him the sack to make way for you, as he's done a good job. You'll just have to wait. As soon as I have an opening, you're top of my list. I can't do more than that, I'm afraid.'

There was nothing more to be said so Conor took his leave. Outside, he sat on a bench, lit a cigarette and wondered what he was to do. How long would he have to wait to be called? Was it weeks? Obviously not days. He went into the nearest pub for a pint of beer, then he walked home.

Jessie had returned before him so when her husband walked in, knowing he'd been to the hospital she asked him how he got on.

'The doctor signed me off.'

'Oh, Conor, that's marvellous. You must be relieved.'

'Yes and no. I went to see my boss, but he hasn't a job for me at the moment.'

'What? But I thought you were on a permanent basis.'

'I was until I had my accident and they had to fill my place, and now they don't need me – well, not until they get busy. At the moment he has enough stevedores, apart from the dockers which, as you know, are taken on daily when needed. I am top of the waiting list.'

'That's good, isn't it?'

'Not if I have to wait very long, Jessie. I could still be out of work for some time.'

She could see how depressed he was and she knew he had longed for the day to be signed off from the hospital, but now he'd lost his position, which had been a matter of great pride to him.

'Never mind, love, it may not be for long and we still have money coming in from the cafe. We aren't destitute.'

'That's not the point!' His eyes flashed in anger. 'I'm the man of the house. Now I'm fit I should be earning.'

Jessie stood in front of him. 'Now you listen to me, Conor McGonigall. Don't you give me all that bullshit about being the man of the house. You may think you're fit enough to work, but, frankly, you need more time. Time to walk, to exercise, get the strength back into your leg. Maybe this is a blessing in disguise.'

He glared at her. 'You just don't understand!' He got to his feet and shoved her out of the way. 'I'm off to the pub.'

She let him go. She knew her husband well enough to know his pride had been hurt. He was disappointed at not being able to return to the hierarchy of his workplace, among his peers. She knew this made him feel less of a man. She also knew he'd come home legless having drowned his sorrows and the next day she'd have to find a way to rebuild his confidence. But how the hell was she going to do that? A knock on the door stopped her train of thought. She opened it and Daisy stood there.

'Have you heard about Emily?'

'No,' said Jessie. 'Come in.'

Daisy walked in and sat down. 'Old Emily was taken away today and the council arrived shortly after. They took all the furniture away on a cart to be burnt. Oh, Jessie, the smell was awful. They fumigated the house and soon it will be painted and decorated. She's not coming back.'

'How do you know?'

'I asked one of the men. They're taking her to some old

81

people's place to be cleaned up and there she'll stay. Some charity home, as far as I can tell. She went kicking and screaming. Her language was awful!'

'Well at least she'll be clean and fed, and if she dies, she won't be found like Iris!'

Daisy looked at her friend and suddenly realised. 'You sent for them, didn't you?'

'Yes, I did. It's the best thing that could happen to the old bitch!'

With a chuckle, Daisy got up from her chair and hugged her neighbour. 'You are a sly one, but that old lady won't thank you. However, I do, on her behalf. I've got to go, see you tomorrow.'

Jessie made herself a pot of tea and, as she sat drinking it, she started laughing. In her mind, she could see how Emily would put up a fight if anyone tried to get her into a bath! It cheered her considerably.

Chapter Nine

A week later and Conor was still depressed and restless. Jessie knew that he'd been looking at the situations vacant in the local paper, but he'd been working in the docks all his life, it was all that he knew, and he pushed the paper away. He decided to wait a couple of weeks and if he didn't hear from his boss, he thought he'd join the call-on in the hope of getting some work. It wouldn't be easy for him to do so after being a stevedore with responsibilities, but he was anxious to get back to work, so he'd have to swallow his pride.

Bill Brown was walking into the docks to join his gang when he happened to glance across at the men huddled together hoping to be chosen for the day's work. To his surprise, he saw Conor standing among them. He didn't have time to stop and have a word, but knowing what it was like to be in his shoes, he felt for him. Being a stevedore was a good position, one that many aspired to, so he knew that Conor must be desperate to be standing there.

If any of the other dockers recognised Conor, they didn't say so. All of them were fighting to be chosen. A daily wage was enough to put food on the table, and friendships were forgotten in the pushing and shoving that followed to catch the eye of the gang boss.

Dave Jennings cast his eye over the men, looking for the strongest to add to his gang. He only had three vacancies. He spotted Conor McGonigall. He had worked with him on many a shipment and knew his capabilities. He knew, also, that he'd been in an accident and the fact that he was here meant that he was desperate, which suited Jennings. Desperate men wouldn't argue too much about handing a percentage of their earnings over to him on pay day. He pointed to him.

'McGonigall! Over here.'

Conor pushed his way to the front and waited for the other two men to be chosen, then they made their way to the ship they would be working on. He kept his head down knowing that today he'd be taking orders instead of giving them, which would stick in his craw, but at least he was working. When he saw that Bill Brown was part of the gang, he thought it ironic. After all, he'd been the one to get him the job, although Bill was unaware of this fact. They nodded to each other and then the work began.

The men began loading the cargo into the nets before the cranes carried them from the quayside over to the ship's hold. It was heavy work and, by the end of the day, Conor's leg ached. But despite that and the fact he was working as an ordinary docker, he felt happier than he'd been for some time. He felt he'd regained his manhood. He was once again earning. He and Bill walked home together.

They chatted about everything except the day's work. Bill didn't bring up the subject and thought he'd wait until Conor did first, but the Irishman didn't mention it and so Bill took his lead from that. They parted at their front doors.

'See you tomorrow,' Bill said.

'Indeed, you will,' answered Conor as he'd been told he would be needed for the week.

Jessie was in the kitchen when she heard Conor return. She walked into the living room and saw her husband wearing his work clothes, covered in dirt. She was at a loss for words.

Conor burst out laughing at her surprise and, picking her up, he spun her round, and then put her down. 'Close your mouth, darlin', or you'll catch a fly!'

'What on earth is going on?'

'I'm working again. Not as a stevedore, for the moment anyway, but I was at the call-on and got taken on for a week. Make us a cuppa, darlin', I'm parched, then I'll take a bath.'

She went into the kitchen to fill the kettle. At least Conor looked happy for once and she was grateful for that, and if he had swallowed his pride and taken a lesser position she had nothing but admiration for him, knowing just how hard it would have been for him. She put the kettle on the hob and filled some large saucepans with water to warm, ready to start filling the bath, then sat down to wait.

'I'm working in the same gang as Bill next door,' he said. 'I don't like the gang boss, Dave Jennings. He treats his men like cattle – without respect. That's no way to get them working happily. A happy workforce is a good workforce. There is such an air of resentment; you can feel it as he shouts his orders. He also takes ten per cent of their wage – Bill told us, remember?'

'Don't the men say anything?'

'Don't be daft, love. One wrong word and he'll replace you. Nobody can afford to say anything.'

This concerned Jessie, knowing Conor's short fuse. He commanded respect and he'd earned it over the years. She couldn't see him lasting very long under those circumstances.

Conor, eventually, had his bath and sat down in clean clothes to eat his meal. He put his leg up on a stool to rest it, but Jessie had noticed how swollen it was and had soaked a towel in cold water, rung it out and made him pull up his trouser leg so she could wrap it round his limb. She didn't make a fuss: having told Conor he needed to take his time to let the muscles grow strong again, she knew he wouldn't want to be reminded of it.

He didn't comment either, except to thank her and, by the time they retired to bed, the swelling had subsided.

The following morning in the cafe, as Nancy and Jessie were preparing the vegetables, the postman delivered a letter addressed to her. She was puzzled as she opened it as she wasn't expecting any mail. She read it and let out a cry of surprise.

'What is it, Jessie? Is something wrong?' Nancy added, seeing the look on her employer's face.

'The lease of the shop has been sold,' she said. 'They are writing to inform me, and the new owner will be calling on me soon.'

'Is that bad news or good?'

'It all depends. If the rent is still the same it doesn't matter, but a new owner may have new ideas for the premises. I do have a contract, so it shouldn't make much difference. We will just have to wait and see.'

A few days passed and no one came to see her, so Jessie imagined all was well until, just as she was about to lock up on the third day, Larry Forbes arrived.

'I'm sorry, but we're closed!' she said sharply.

He stepped inside. 'I don't want anything to eat, Mrs McGonigall, thank you.'

'Then what *do* you want?'

'That really is not the tone to use when talking to your landlord,' he said.

'My landlord? What on earth are you talking about?'

'Didn't you get a letter saying the lease of the premises has been sold?'

It suddenly all fell into place. She glared at the man facing her. 'You bought the lease?'

He pulled out a chair and sat down. 'Yes, I did. The property is now mine. You are now *my* tenant.'

She just shook her head. 'By hook or by crook, eh? You just couldn't take no for an answer. Very well, Mr Forbes, you obviously came here to say something.' She drew out a chair and sat opposite him. 'Speak up!'

'The monthly rental will stay the same.'

This surprised Jessie, who thought the first thing he'd do, was to increase it.

'However, I will expect ten per cent of your weekly take.'

This she wasn't expecting. 'Like hell you will!'

He shrugged. 'Take it or leave it. The choice is yours. In the small print of your old contract, it stipulates that all arrangements are only applicable to the present owner. If the lease is sold, changes can be made by the new owner. If you want to keep your business, you'll agree. After all, had I put up the rent you would have had to pay the amount, busy or not. At least this way if you have a quiet week then it won't be so costly.'

Jessie was livid, knowing that he could do such a thing legally. She gave a wry smile. 'I have to hand it to you, you are a clever bastard and a devious one. I have no choice, as you well know.'

'Then let's shake on it.' He held out his hand.

Jessie looked at his hand with distaste. 'We don't have to go *that* far; I've said yes, that's enough.'

'Not quite.' He took a sheet of paper from the inside pocket of his jacket. 'Here is a new contract for you to sign. It's for six months, not a year, saying the rent is the same but agreeing to the new proposal. I'll wait while you read it; it won't take long.' He handed her a pen and sat back.

Inside, Jessie was fuming. She wanted to stuff the paper down his throat, but she controlled her temper. This was not the time. The contract was laid out clearly, but stipulating that the new agreement began the following week. She read through the agreement, then, picking up the pen, she signed her name with a flourish and pushed it across the table.

Forbes got to his feet. 'Oh, just one more thing. I'll have someone from my office work at the tills taking the money, keeping a record of the daily take, totting up at the end of the week.' As Jessie made to argue, he continued, 'After all, it would be so easy not to enter the odd meal here and there . . . with you being so busy, you know. It'll be one job less for you to have to worry about.'

Jessie erupted. 'Well I'm not paying their wages and that is *not* negotiable!'

'No, I'll do that, Mrs McGonigall, have no fear. He's working for me, not you. Good day to you.'

Nancy came rushing out of the kitchen, having been listening intently. 'Oh, Jessie, that man is a devil. Didn't I tell you!'

Jessie lit a cigarette and handed one to her friend. 'He's got me over a barrel and he knows it. But not a word to the customers; I don't want them knowing. We'll just carry on as usual, but if there is some way out of this mess, I'll bloody well find it. I don't intend working for that man a minute longer than I have to.' She decided not to share her dilemma with her husband. It wasn't his problem, it was hers. But she thought it ironic that now both of them would be handing over a percentage of their hard-earned money!

Chapter Ten

At the end of the week, Conor stood with his colleagues, waiting for his pay packet. Jennings handed his over and Conor read the front showing his daily earnings and the total, plus the ten per cent taken out. He looked up at Jennings, feigning ignorance of the deal.

'What's this? I'm short here.'

Jennings just gave him a cursory glance. 'It's what I charge for the privilege of being in my gang, instead of waiting in the call-on. You work well and I'm offering you a place, but you have to pay for it. Any problem with that?'

The offer of a place was too good to turn down at the moment, so Conor swallowed his anger. He would accept hoping that he'd soon be back in his old position. It was money coming in, after all.

'No problem,' he said and walked away. He was furious that he'd let the man get away with this duplicity, but vowed when he was back as a stevedore, he'd shop him and let the authorities know what was happening.

* * *

That evening after a bath and a meal, Conor and Jessie went across the road to the Builders Arms for a game of darts and a drink, but Conor noticed that Jessie was far from her usual exuberant self. As the game finished, they sat down.

'Something wrong, darlin'? You're very quiet tonight.'

'No, just tired,' she said. 'It's been a busy week. I'm looking forward to a lazy Sunday.' But all the time she was contemplating having a stranger standing at her till, making a note of every penny that was passed over, watching her every move.

On Monday morning, as was usual, Jessie and Nancy arrived early to prepare and cook the food for the day. Just before eight o'clock, there was a knock on the door. A young man stood there waiting to be let in. Dressed in a smart suit with waistcoat and stiff collar and a tie, he looked so out of place that Jessie had to hide a smile.

She opened the door. 'Yes?'

'I'm from Mr Forbes,' he said somewhat arrogantly. 'I'm here to be in charge of the till.'

'No, mister – wrong. I am in charge here, my friend, nobody else. You are here as a cashier to take the money and be polite to my customers, so change your tone of voice or you'll be leaving with my foot up your arse! Do I make myself clear?'

There was a look of dismay and surprise on his face.

'Right,' he said. 'Can I come in?'

'I suppose so.' She stood aside, locking the door behind him and walked over to the counter. 'Here is the till. The bills go on this spike as they're paid. There's a five-pound float, check it now and, as you'll be the only one taking the money, any shortages, I expect you to make them up.'

He looked astonished, then angry. 'I wasn't advised about that by Mr Forbes,' he protested.

'Really?' said Jessie. 'Well, I'm telling you. After all, any shortages will be through an error on your part, not mine, and I can't afford any mistakes. And another thing: if we get really busy, I expect you to earn your money and remove empty plates from the table and take them to the kitchen.'

'Mr Forbes didn't say anything about that either,' he said angrily. 'I'm not here to do menial tasks!'

'This is a business; there is nothing menial about working here. We work hard for our money and I have a reputation to uphold. You will not be allowed to undermine it! Here's a cloth. After you've checked the float, wipe down those tables. We'll be open in ten minutes and I'm busy.' At his hesitation, she added, 'If we are not ready for service, there won't be any money for you to take. Any questions?'

He saw the anger in her eyes and decided this was perhaps not a woman to cross. If he returned empty-handed, his boss would be furious. He reluctantly took the damp cloth.

Nancy was giggling quietly when Jessie returned to the kitchen. 'That told him, Jess! Arrogant little prig. Today may prove to be interesting when the men come in.'

Indeed, it was. Seeing a new person at the till and a smartly dressed young man at that, Jessie was ribbed unmercifully.

'Does your husband know about this, Jessie? Sneaking a man in on the premises? And a posh one, at that!'

Jessie laughed. 'Come off it, Jim. He's far too young. I like a real man, not a boy.'

Henry Marshall, the young man in question, felt his cheeks redden at the joshing and was already regretting being sent here to work. He'd been lambasted by the lady who ran the place, made to do a menial task and now he was the butt of the jokes coming thick and fast. He was not comfortable at all. But the smell of food invaded his nostrils and, as plates came by one by one, it made him feel hungry.

At first, Henry stood at the till taking the money with an imperious air, which really annoyed Jessie. But as it got busy, she took the opportunity of demoralising him.

'Clear that table, young man and wipe it down,' Jessie ordered time after time. 'Come along, we'll need it again in a minute. You're costing me money and Mr Forbes won't like that when I tell him!'

He had little choice with all the customers watching him. As he worked, he began to sweat with the heat of the cafe and his collar felt as if it was choking him. Taking out the handkerchief from his top pocket, he wiped his forehead.

'What's it feel like, working for a living?' asked one of the customers, grinning broadly. 'Dressed like a kipper and all.'

Henry looked at the man with undisguised distaste. 'There's no reason to be rude!' he said.

Then he became flustered as the others laughed at his discomfort.

Halfway through the day, Jessie handed him a sandwich and a mug of tea as he stood at the desk.

He was absolutely parched, and he thanked her and

drank from the mug. Looking at his fob watch, he saw he had at least another hour to go before he could cash up and wondered how he would survive such a dreadful day.

Eventually, it was closing time and Jessie locked the door. Henry started counting the cash in the till and totting up the bills. To his great relief, there were no discrepancies.

Jessie came out of the kitchen and stood by the counter. 'Well, everything alright?'

Henry, having recovered his equilibrium, said, 'To the penny.'

Jessie made no comment except to hand him a bag, telling him to put the money and bills inside *and* a copy of his tally for the day. 'Make sure you date it,' she ordered. 'We don't want any mix up.'

When he was finished, he looked at her and said, 'I'll be here again in the morning.'

'If I were you, young man, I'd wear something less formal. You saw how busy we were. You don't need a waistcoat, and that stiff collar is too much in the heat of the cafe. I can't waste time on you if you pass out on me. Understand?'

'Yes, Mrs McGonigall. I understand. Good day to you.' He waited for her to unlock the door and left the cafe. Outside, he walked a few paces, then stopped and breathed in deeply. 'Thank God for some fresh air,' he muttered. But as he strolled away, he knew he couldn't possibly do this indefinitely. Just the thought of tomorrow was bad enough. All he wanted now was to go home, change his clothes and sink into a hot bath to ease his aching bones.

* * *

While all this had been going on, Daisy Brown had been dealing with Doris and Maggie, her customers, who had come along for a final fitting. By this time, the three of them had become good friends, exchanging personal problems, as you do. Daisy had been telling them how Bill's foreman stopped ten per cent of all his men's wages.

'That's bloody criminal!' Maggie exclaimed. 'Christ Almighty! The poor buggers don't earn a fortune. Why don't they all refuse?'

Daisy looked at her in surprise. 'It's obvious. They'd lose their jobs – that's why. You should see the men at the call-on each morning. It's pathetic how they have to scramble to be chosen to work. Lots of them have kids to feed as well as rent to pay. It's inhuman, that's what it is. But does Dave Jennings care? Does he hell!'

Doris and Maggie looked at each other on hearing the name, but made no comment until they were outside.

'Isn't Dave Jennings one of your punters?' Doris asked her friend.

'Yes, nasty piece of work. Treats me like dirt, but is eager enough to lay me down.'

'I bet he treats his men the same,' remarked Doris. 'Pity we can't help Daisy's husband, though. She's a good girl and talented. If only she could find someone to back her, she could open her own business.'

'Yes, and pigs might fly!' They left for Canal Walk to start work.

The following morning, Henry Marshall walked reluctantly towards the cafe, dreading what lay ahead. But he'd taken

Jessie's advice and wore a lighter jacket over his trousers, a shirt with a softer collar and had dispensed with his waistcoat. He'd been told to report to Larry Forbes at the end of the day and he wondered what he'd have to say about his attire. Forbes was a stickler about the appearance of his staff.

As Jessie let him in, she noticed the changes as he walked over to the till and checked the float. Everything was ready for service in the cafe, so she didn't need to give the new cashier a job. His relief was noticeable. But as the day progressed that changed and he found himself clearing tables as they became vacant, letting the waiting men take a seat.

As he watched Jessie serving, he had to admire her. She was fast and efficient, but she still made time to talk to her customers and he could see how popular she was with the men. He just couldn't understand why his employer would want to be involved with this business. It was unlike any of his others and, at the end of the day; he left the cafe and made his way to the office of his boss.

Forbes looked him up and down and frowned. 'Why are you not dressed as usual?'

'It's so hot in the cafe, sir, that my stiff collar nearly choked me by the end of the day. Mrs McGonigall suggested I dress more comfortably because she had no time to look after me if I passed out.'

Trying to hide a smile, Forbes said, 'Yes, that sounds just like her. How was business?'

'Brisk! The customers start coming at eight o'clock and sometimes she has a queue outside at midday waiting for a table.'

His employer raised his eyebrows in surprise. 'Really?'

'She's an amazing woman, Mr Forbes. I've never seen anyone work so hard and so efficiently. Here are the takings for the last two days.' He handed over a slip of paper.

Forbes was impressed when he read it. 'This is better than I thought. Thank you, Marshall, you may go.'

Henry hesitated. 'Could you tell me how much longer I'll be working there?'

The other man's eyes narrowed. 'As long as I need you.'

The young man heard the steel in Forbes's voice and knew better than to argue.

'Thank you, sir.' He turned and walked out of the room. He didn't know who the tougher boss was, the man he'd just left or the lady he'd been sent to assist.

Larry Forbes sat back in his chair and chuckled softly. Jessie McGonigall was quite a woman. He liked a female with spirit and she had plenty of that, but she had to learn her place. He lit a cigarette and, as he puffed away on it, he could picture Jessie McGonigall berating his young man. It might be interesting trying to tame such a woman.

Back in Union Street, the new arrivals had moved into Iris Jones's council house after it had been cleaned and decorated. The Williams family, Maisie, Percy and their two boys, Jack and Tommy, seemed harmless enough. The boys were five and seven and the husband worked as a porter at the Great Western Hotel. They arrived with furniture piled on a handcart with suitcases on the top. It was very clear to those who watched that they didn't have a great deal, but they were friendly and quiet. The inhabitants breathed a sigh of relief after the previous owner who had done nothing but cause trouble.

Maisie would take the boys to school in the morning after her husband left for work and spent her day cooking and cleaning. They soon became a familiar part of the street and everybody settled down once again.

Jessie would stop and talk to the boys who would be playing outside after she came home in the afternoons, and sometimes she'd play hoops with them or, to their delight, hopscotch. She soon became their favourite and for her they were a delight, and went some way to fill the gap in her life. The family were soon accepted by their neighbours and settled in.

Chapter Eleven

Conor was having a bad day. His gang were loading a cargo ship and his leg was aching, making him limp a little. Jennings noted this and how it slowed Conor's progress.

'You need to speed up, McGonigall! You're not on a fucking holiday!'

Conor froze, his temper rising. The other men fell silent as they worked, wondering what would happen at this tirade, remembering how Conor used to be a stevedore, giving orders and knowing his reputation for getting the job done, but, more importantly, how well he treated his men, and the respect with which he was held.

Swallowing his anger, Conor glared at Jennings. 'Don't worry, the job will get done and you will still get your ten per cent!'

Jennings was puce with rage and quickly looked around to see if anyone other than his gang was within earshot. 'You watch that Irish temper of yours, or you will be out on your ear!' He walked away.

Bill Brown wandered over to his neighbour and quietly had a word. 'Be careful, Conor, he's a wicked bugger and doesn't like to be crossed.'

'I don't care, but he had better keep off my back. I will not be spoken to like that by anybody.'

Bill went back to work, but he was worried for his friend.

During the rest of the day, Jennings continued to pick on Conor, who ignored him and just carried on working, knowing if he let the man get to him he'd end up thumping him and that wouldn't do at all. It would play right into his hands. But when he finished work, he glared at Jennings as he left, vowing to get even with him at the first opportunity.

Two days later, the opportunity arose. The crane was lifting a net full of cargo into the hold and Conor saw that Jennings hadn't seen it swinging towards him, as he had his back to the load as it came over. As the net was lowered, Conor grabbed Jennings and threw him onto the deck on his back as the load passed over their heads.

Jennings paled as he saw how close he'd been to being injured, or worse. Conor knelt astride him and clutching his hook by its wooden handle, pressed the steel against Jennings' throat. The man's eyes widened in horror.

Conor smiled softly 'You need to keep a sharper eye out – you're not on a fucking holiday! You could have been killed if I hadn't had my wits about me. If I had a mind to finish the job, I could do so right now!'

Jennings spluttered in fear, but Conor shut him up. 'I would say that saving a life – twice – would entitle me to collect *all* my wages in future – wouldn't you agree?'

The man, unable to speak, had no option and nodded. Conor pulled him up onto his feet. 'Good, now we understand each other,' and he climbed out of the hold, leaving Jennings shaken to the core, his throat bruised from the pressure of the hook.

Conor continued to work without any more trouble for the rest of the day, which gave him great satisfaction. But he knew he'd made an enemy of Dave Jennings.

At the next payday, Conor took his pay packet from Jennings and quickly read the front to see if all his wages were inside. When he saw there had been no ten per cent stoppage, he looked at Jennings and grinned. 'Looks fine, just as it should be.'

As he walked away whistling, he could feel the hostility oozing from the gang boss, but as Bill joined him on his walk home, he didn't mention what had happened. That was not to be common knowledge.

That night in Canal Walk, Maggie took Dave Jennings to her room, where he vented his anger on her as he roughly abused her body, leaving her sore and bruised. When she complained afterwards, he slapped her face with considerable force, then threw his money on her bed and left.

The next day when Maggie went to Daisy's house to collect a gown, Daisy was shocked at the bruises on Maggie's face. 'What on earth has happened to you?' she asked.

Maggie lowered her aching body into a chair, tears brimming her eyes. 'It was that Dave Jennings; he's one of my punters. He was in a vile temper and was rough with me. He slapped me just before he left, when I complained about his treatment.'

'Oh, Maggie!' She didn't know what else to say. But later that day she confided in Jessie.

'You should have seen that poor girl! Bill works for Jennings, as does Conor. Bill said he was a dreadful man. He's a bully. He needs a good sorting out, to my mind. How would he feel to be set upon, I wonder?'

When Jessie told her husband that night, he wasn't surprised, but he was angry.

'The man's a bully. He has no regard for anyone but himself!'

'Well, you be careful of him, Conor. A man like that is dangerous.'

It was now February and bitterly cold. But as Jessie read the papers and saw that the body of Captain Scott and his party of climbers had been found dead in the Antarctic, she wondered whatever made them contemplate such a journey. It was cold enough here, she couldn't imagine how anybody would go to such an inhospitable place of their own free will. But she was more sympathetic when reading about the suffragettes, she was all for women's rights. She said as much to Conor that evening.

He looked at her in astonishment. 'Bloody hell, Jessie! As if you don't already have that. Look at you, running your own business and, if I recall, the very first day I met you, you were your own woman.'

'But don't you see, darlin', not all women had the chance that I had, and for those poor souls, I welcome the likes of Emmeline Pankhurst.'

'Maybe so, but she's trouble and so are her band of followers, you see if I'm not right.'

Jessie remembered his words as she read about Mrs Pankhurst's trial after the explosion at Lloyd George's golf villa. Fortunately, no one was hurt, but Pankhurst accepted full responsibility. Jessie didn't agree with this. She thought it foolhardy and dangerous. Perhaps Conor was right about the woman.

Things were running smoothly for Jessie in the cafe. Henry Marshall had eventually settled into his job and began to lose his autocratic ways as the weeks passed. He began to enjoy the banter of the men and was now no longer embarrassed about their teasing. Jessie began to warm to him and now made sure he had a meal after the lunchtime rush, before he cashed up for the day.

As he relaxed, he would chat about his boss whenever Jessie gently probed him for information. It seemed that Forbes, unmarried, was a shrewd businessman who'd worked hard to achieve his status. He now had several business interests, which paid well. Jessie could admire anyone with a work ethic. But she still didn't trust him.

At the end of the month, Forbes paid her a visit just before closing time. When Jessie saw who had walked in, she was immediately on her mettle.

'Mr Forbes! What brings you here?'

'I thought we could have a chat over a cup of coffee to discuss business.'

Her eyes narrowed as she looked at him. What was this bastard up to now? She went into the kitchen and returned with two mugs of coffee and sat opposite him. 'Well?'

He grinned at her. 'There's no need to be so hostile, Mrs McGonigall. I've only come in to say how well you've been doing. The figures that Marshall has given me have been very satisfactory.'

'Don't even think of asking for a bigger percentage because I'd rather close the cafe!'

He sipped his coffee and stared at her over the rim of the mug. 'I have no intention of doing so, but I thought as things are working out so well, we might have dinner together to go over the figures, maybe find a better agreement for when your contract finishes.'

This was so unexpected that Jessie was speechless for a moment. Then she started to laugh. 'You are joking, of course.'

'No, I'm serious. I admire the way you run this place. I like successes – and in a woman, what you've achieved is extraordinary, especially in this day and age.'

'Good heavens, are you paying me a compliment? Be very careful, this is very much against your nature.'

'You have no idea as to who I am or my nature.' He looked at her, a challenge in his voice. 'Perhaps it's time you found out.'

'No, thanks, I'm not that interested. I'm happy with things as they stand. Now if you would kindly drink up, I want to close. It's been a long day.' She rose from her chair and waited for him to move, fingering her shop keys as she did so.

Getting to his feet, he said, 'One day you might change your mind.'

'I wouldn't put money on it if I were you.' She opened the door wide. 'Good day to you, Mr Forbes.'

Walking into the kitchen, she looked at Nancy. 'That bugger only invited me out to dinner!'

Nancy looked astonished. 'No!'

'Yes. He wants to discuss our next contract, or so he says. Whatever it is, he's wasting his time.'

Larry Forbes walked along Oxford Street, a set expression on his face. *That woman is so sure of herself*. He wondered what had given her such strength to be able to stand on her own two feet so well. But he didn't take kindly to anyone who challenged his position, especially a female; nevertheless, she intrigued him. His invitation to dinner had been a ploy to try and get behind that hostility. She must have a weak spot somewhere. There had to be a way of bringing her to heel and he was determined to find it.

Although the men who worked the docks were used to working outside in all kinds of weather, the cold made their jobs more difficult. They were forced to wear heavier jackets to keep warm, but it made moving the cargo a cumbersome job and if the ground was slippery from either rain or ice, it became hazardous. Like today.

The previous night had been so cold that the quayside was icy and slippery underfoot. The men were aware of the danger and walked with care in their hobnailed boots, but, nevertheless, one or two ended up on their backs as they tried to move the cargo.

Jennings railed at them as they fell. 'Watch your bloody feet; you should be used to these conditions. Now get a move on or we'll be behind. If you can't keep up, I'll get a crew who can!'

The men muttered beneath their breath. The atmosphere was charged with their anger.

'Speed things up, McGonigall! You of all people should be able to cope with this, *once* having been a stevedore!' He said this with such derision that Conor felt his hackles rise.

The men were standing on the quayside waiting for another load to be moved and Conor turned to Jennings. 'I was a better boss than you'll ever be!' He glared at the other man. 'You have no idea how to handle your men and you haven't the intelligence to learn, either. You're an ignorant bully, but you haven't the guts to face up to a man, you only take out your frustration on a poor helpless woman. Paying a prostitute doesn't give you the right to beat her up!'

The other men stopped work and listened.

Jennings was stunned into silence and, looking around, saw that all of the men were listening to the angry exchange. This enraged him and, with a cry of anger, he threw a punch at Conor, sending him flying onto his back.

Conor was back on his feet in a flash, his Irish temper, which he'd managed to keep in check, now unfettered. He landed a punch on Jennings' chin, sending him reeling. He pounced on Jennings again, throwing another punch, putting him on his back, cheered on by his workmates who were enjoying the fact that their boss was getting what they considered to be his just deserts.

It was Bill Brown who put a stop to it by pinning Conor's arms to his side. 'Enough! You don't want to kill the bugger; you're in enough trouble as it is.' He hauled Conor off Jennings.

Conor had no choice but to stop. The gang boss scrambled to his feet. He glared at Conor. 'Get off the dock. You are no longer working for me. Now get out of here, and you other men get back to work – now!'

There was muttering as the men did as they were told, but all of them had enjoyed the fracas and a few had secretly hoped to see Jennings end up in the water.

Conor collected his tools, but when he picked up his metal hook, Jennings took a few steps backwards, remembering how the steel had felt on his throat once before.

Conor walked out of the dock gates and made for the nearest pub for a pint and a cigarette to calm down. Later he'd have to tell Jessie he'd been fired, and he wasn't looking forward to that one bit.

Chapter Twelve

Jessie was surprised to see Conor sitting in his chair drinking a cup of tea when she arrived home that afternoon. 'What are you doing here? Are you sick?'

'No, I've been fired.'

'You what? How did that happen? I thought you were settled in the gang.'

'Jennings and I had a falling-out.'

She sat in a chair opposite him, glaring. 'You lost your temper, that's it, isn't it?'

'He pushed me too far Jessie. I won't be treated like dirt by anyone, least of all by a man such as him. The man's an ignorant pig, so he is!' He then told her what had transpired.

Listening to Conor, she could see why he'd lost control, and when she heard how Conor had brought up Maggie the prostitute and her treatment at Jennings' hand, she could understand why blows were exchanged.

With a sigh, she said, 'Well that's that! You've not heard any more of going back as a stevedore, then?'

'No, I'll go along in the morning and see John Irving. He said I was top of the list, but that was ages ago. I can't understand why he's not been in touch.'

But the following morning Conor discovered that John Irving had retired and a new man had taken his place, someone he didn't know. He was told to go into the office where a Mr Brian Gates would see him.

The man behind the desk looked at Conor over his glasses. 'What can I do for you, Mr McGonigall?'

'I wondered when my job as a stevedore would be vacant again. Mr Irving had me at the top of his list, but I've not heard anything.'

'I'm sorry, Mr McGonigall, I don't understand. Can you explain?'

Conor told him about the accident and how his place had been filled and he was told he would be called as soon as a place came vacant.

'You are now fully recovered?'

'Yes, sir. I've been working in a gang until yesterday, waiting to be recalled.'

'Yesterday? Why yesterday?'

Taking a deep breath, Conor said, 'I was fired by the gang boss.'

The man sat back in his chair and stared hard at Conor. 'What was the reason for your dismissal?'

'I'm afraid Dave Jennings and me had a falling-out.'

'Please explain what you mean.'

Conor knew there was no way out for him. 'We came to blows and he fired me!'

'You hit your boss?' Gates looked appalled.

'I know it sounds bad, sir, but Jennings is a bully; he's also a crook. He takes ten per cent of every man's pay for his own pocket and no one dares refuse or they'll be back to the call-on again. I was a good stevedore; I looked after my men. I have a good reputation – ask anybody. I admit, I lost my rag, but he had it coming!'

The man frowned. 'I see. How long has Jennings been taking this money?'

'I don't know when it began, but ever since I've been working for him and before that, I know for a fact.'

Gates appeared to be deep in thought. 'I don't have a vacancy for you at the moment and I'll have to look into your serious accusation, McGonigall. I'll be in touch with you. That's all I'm prepared to say at the moment. Good day to you.'

Conor left the office wondering what would happen next.

Brian Gates sat behind his desk, deep in thought. He was an honest man and lived life by the rules. To hear that a gang boss was cheating his men angered him. He'd come up the hard way working as a docker, then a stevedore, before being promoted to a desk job and eventually making it to his management position. He knew how hard it was for men to make a living and then to have some of their wages docked illegally stuck in his craw. Well, he wouldn't have it!

He went to his filing cabinet and withdrew two files. One was Jennings'; the other was Conor's. He took them back to his desk and started to read.

* * *

Two days later, Bill Brown called in to see Conor after work to tell him he'd been sent for by Brian Gates and asked about his wages.

'I told him the truth and how long it had happened to me. He asked me to keep my visit to him quiet. What's going on, Conor, do you know?'

Conor explained. 'So, Gates *is* looking into it? I wondered if he would. He was surprised when I told him about Jennings and he didn't look pleased, I have to say.'

'Bloody hell, Conor, Jennings has no idea. Wait until he finds out. I wonder what will happen to him?'

'He'll lose his job, I would think.'

Bill frowned. 'If he does, I would say you'd better watch your back!'

'What do you mean?'

'Well it's bloody obvious where the information came from with you being fired and all. None of us dare say a word in case we lose our place.'

After his neighbour had left, Conor had time to consider his position. If Jennings was fired, he'd be out for blood. He decided to keep all this to himself; he didn't want to worry Jessie.

The next payday, as the men lined up to receive their wages, Brian Gates stood watching, unseen, at a distance until the last man was paid, then he moved forward.

'One moment, men!'

Everyone stopped. Jennings frowned. What the devil was his boss doing here?

Gates went over to the line of men. 'Show me your pay

111

packets please.' He took them one by one and read the front and saw the wage that everyone was entitled to and noted the ten per cent that had been written in pencil below and the new total. He looked at Jennings and, holding out the pay packets, asked, 'Can you explain these discrepancies to me, please?'

Jennings was flustered. 'It's just a little arrangement I have with my men, sir.'

'And what would that be, might I ask?'

The man knew he was in deep trouble. 'The men kindly offered to hand over some of their wage to ensure they maintain their position permanently.'

'Really?' He turned to the men. 'Did you make an offer to do this or were you *told* to do so?'

'We were told!' They said in unison. Knowing that at last the thieving gang boss had been rumbled.

'Right. I want you all to go home and write the date that this practice started for each one of you. Bring it to work tomorrow morning when a new gang boss will be taking over. Jennings! With me, to my office.'

The men stood and watched Jennings walking behind his boss towards the dock gates, then they all started talking at once.

'I reckon Conor shopped him!'

'It's about bloody time they caught that bastard and it looks as if we'll get our back pay.'

They all left the dock, chattering away and laughing at what had transpired.

Brian Gates walked into his office, followed by Jennings. He sat at his desk and left Jennings standing. Gates stared at the man in front of him, a look of disgust on his face.

'You have worked as a docker, you know how hard it is to get chosen and then how hard you have to work for not a lot of money. Yet, knowing this, you had no compunction at taking part of their hard-earned wage. How despicable!'

Jennings started to argue.

'Enough! You have committed a fraud! I will have to put this before the board and let them decide whether they will get the police involved. But for the moment, you're fired. When the men give me their dates tomorrow, the amount of money they are owed will be repaid by you, to the penny. You have your own pay packet?'

Jennings nodded.

Gates held out his hand. 'I'll take that for now as the first contribution towards the money the men had to part with.'

Jennings had no choice but to hand it all over.

'You will not work in the docks again, Mr Jennings. I'll see you are blacklisted. You will be hearing from me once the board have met. Good day to you.'

'You can't have me blacklisted!' Jennings, puce with anger, glared at the man behind the desk. 'I've worked all my life in the docks; it's the only life I know.'

'You should have thought of that before you cheated your men. Now get out!'

Lumbering towards the door, Jennings turned. 'You haven't heard the last of this!' He stormed out of the room, slamming the door behind him.

Gates sent for a messenger boy and, giving him an address, sent him on an errand.

* * *

113

Conor was sat reading the paper when there was a knock on the door. When he opened it, he was surprised to see an errand boy standing there.

'Mr McGonigall?'

'Yes, that's me.'

'I was asked to give you this, sir.' The boy handed over an envelope, then left.

Conor sat down and opened the envelope, filled with curiosity. He read it slowly, then read it again and started laughing. He grabbed his jacket and rushed out of the door, almost knocking over his neighbour in his haste. Bill started to say something, but Conor kept walking.

'In a rush, Bill. I'll see you when I get back.'

Conor had a bounce in his step as he walked down Bernard Street towards Canute Road. It was Friday and the workers were pouring out of the dock gates on their way home. Some walking, others on bicycles. Sometimes four abreast, like a swarm as they rode through the dock gates, splitting up as they reached the road.

There was the usual cacophony of sounds particular to the docks. The whistle of a goods train, a shrill hooter for close of business, the roar of a funnel as a ship is due to sail. Among this, the cry of the paper boy. 'Read all about it!'

Conor listened to it all. It was music to his ears as he made his way to a building, whistling as he did so. He entered and made his way to an office on the first floor and knocked on the door.

'Come in!'

Chapter Thirteen

Brian Gates looked at Conor. 'Sit down, Mr McGonigall. You may not have heard, but today I was in the docks when the men received their pay and I discovered what you told me of Jennings taking ten per cent of their wages to be true. Why didn't you report this to me sooner?'

'Like everyone else, I needed to be working, earning a wage. I'm not sure I'd have been believed either. Jennings has been a gang boss for a long time. I couldn't take the chance.'

'For your information, Jennings has been fired and blacklisted.'

Conor made no comment, but he thought that now Jennings would certainly be out for his blood.

Gates continued, 'I don't have a vacancy at the moment for a stevedore, but I do for a gang boss. I've read your record and can see you were good at your job and popular with your men, so I'm offering you Jennings' job. Are you interested?'

Conor was stunned. This he wasn't expecting. 'Thank

you, Mr Gates. I would be more than happy to accept.'

'Good. You start on Monday morning, taking over the job in hand. I'm putting my trust in you, McGonigall, so don't let me down.'

Conor rose from his chair and shook hands with the man opposite. 'Thank you, sir. I'll do a good job for you, you have my word.'

Once outside the building, Conor paused to take a breath. *What a bloody turn-up*, he thought. The men would be pleased, he knew that, but Jennings . . . that was another matter.

The man in question had been lingering on the doorstep of a pub waiting for it to open. He was seething with rage. 'That bloody Irishman has done this,' he muttered. 'He shopped me when I fired him, I'm sure of that. Well, he won't get away with it.'

The landlord unlocked the door of the pub and Jennings hurried inside. 'A pint of beer and a whisky chaser,' he ordered. It was the first of many.

Jessie was sitting in the kitchen making cakes with Jack and Tommy, the Williams children, when Conor walked in. He stood and watched for a moment. Ever since the family had settled, Jessie had made a fuss of the children and, knowing how much she had wanted a family, Conor had been pleased for her. The boys obviously adored her. She would offer to give them tea to give Maisie, their mother, a break, but also to fill a need in her. Today, they were making scones. The first lot were coming out of the oven.

'Just in time, darlin',' she said. 'The boys have been baking, haven't you?'

They nodded shyly.

'Oh, that's great,' Conor said. 'I could do with a cup of tea and a scone; they're my favourites.'

The boys beamed.

Jessie put some jam and cream on the table, placed the scones on a plate, took the kettle off the top of the stove, made a pot of tea, put plates and knives on the table and, looking at the boys, said, 'Right, let's sit and have tea. Remember, jam first!'

She looked at Conor and smiled. It looked like any family sitting together. Alright, she thought, the boys were on loan but that would do. It wasn't a bad second best.

While everyone tucked into the food, Jessie looked at her husband. 'Where have you been? I thought you'd be home when I got back.'

'I was in the docks,' he said. 'I've a new job. I'm taking over from Jennings. I'm the new gang boss!'

Her eyes widened in surprise. 'How did that come about?'

'I'll tell you later,' he said, nodding towards the boys.

When eventually they were alone and the children had been sent home with scones for their parents, Conor told Jessie what had happened. She looked perturbed. 'I'm happy for you, Conor, but what about this man, Jennings? What will happen to him if he's blacklisted?'

With a shrug, Conor said, 'Who knows?' He kept his concerns to himself.

* * *

On Monday morning, Conor arrived in the docks early to check on the work that was scheduled for the day, wanting to be prepared, then he waited for the gang to arrive.

Bill, surprised to see Conor there, rushed over to him. 'I didn't have a chance to tell you yesterday: Jennings has been fired.'

'Really?' Conor feigned surprise.

'I wonder who we'll get today?' Bill remarked. 'I hope it isn't some miserable bugger.' He was so concerned about the new gang boss; he forgot to ask Conor why he was there at all.

The other men eventually gathered, looking around wondering who they'd be working for and surprised too to see Conor there, although no one said anything.

Conor stepped forward. 'Good morning, men. I'm your new gang boss and I want this work cleared today.'

For a moment the men were stunned, then they rushed forward and shook Conor by the hand, delighted for his promotion. He smiled at them all. 'Now, let's get down to it. You all know what we have to do, so let's not waste any time. We'll show the bosses how a good gang works.'

The atmosphere was entirely different. The men worked well together, joshing with each other, yet getting the job done.

Brian Gates, unseen by the men, watched and noted the camaraderie and left after a while, pleased with his decision to put Conor in charge.

Dave Jennings woke that morning with a blinding headache and hangover, which didn't improve his disposition. He made some tea, lit a cigarette and wondered what to do next. He was out of a job, couldn't find one in the docks now he was blacklisted and he was enraged at his position. He decided he needed to eat, but there was nothing in the house, then he remembered that McGonigall's wife ran a workman's cafe. He got dressed and left his house.

Jessie heard the tinkle of the bell over the door of the cafe as it opened and went into the dining room to see who had walked in.

A big, surly man was standing there. 'Good morning, can I help you?'

'You serving breakfast?' he asked.

'Yes, take a seat. What would you like?'

'Eggs, two, bacon, sausages, tomato and toast with a strong mug of coffee while I wait,' he snapped as he sat down.

Jessie walked into the kitchen and gave the order to Nancy. 'You do the toast as I cook the rest, but make a strong mug of coffee first,' she said. 'I think my customer has a hangover, looking at him. He reeks of alcohol.'

'He's not drunk, is he?' Nancy asked nervously.

'No, he isn't, but I'll take the coffee to him when you've made it.'

Jennings looked around. Not a bad place. The smell of bacon wafted through from the kitchen. Nice-looking woman, he thought as Jessie placed the coffee in front of him and walked back to the kitchen. He watched her. Her skirt swishing just above her ankles from beneath the long white apron she wore. Her Titian hair worn twisted onto the top of her head to keep it tidy as she cooked.

119

He'd heard one or two of the men in the docks talking about this cafe and the tasty meals served, but he'd not been in the place before and, as other customers appeared, wanting breakfast, he thought, *So the bastard Irishman had another wage coming into the house apart from his own. On to a nice little earner, no doubt,* which only infuriated him more.

After he finished his meal, he paid his bill and left without a word of thanks.

'Miserable bugger,' Jessie muttered. 'I hope he doesn't come in again.'

Jennings went into a newsagent and bought the local paper, took it to the park and sat looking at the situations vacant. Having been a docker all his working life, there was little he was qualified for apart from manual work. He pored over the adverts, getting more frustrated as he did so. Eventually, when the pubs opened, he made his way to the nearest one.

At the end of the day, Conor and his men lay down their tools. The daily work had been completed and their mood was light, with not having Jennings standing over them baying his orders, reprimanding them for one thing or another. They'd worked hard and well together, and now were looking forward to the rest of the week.

One of the men stepped forward. 'Mr Gates wanted us to bring a list of the dates we started paying Jennings his cut.' The others agreed and all held up a piece of paper. Conor collected them and said he'd see they got to the office. On the way home, he took them into his headquarters and walked up to the receptionist. He asked for an envelope, put the papers inside, licked the envelope closed, wrote Gates's name on the outside and handed it over.

'Mr Gates is expecting this,' he said. 'Will you see he gets it today, please?'

Walking home, Conor felt happy. Today he'd been in charge and the men had worked well. They all seemed pleased about his promotion, which was a bonus, and he felt that Brian Gates would be pleased too. He'd go home, have a bath, have something to eat and take Jessie out for a drink to celebrate. But when he turned into his street, he found the neighbours in a state, gathering together, planning to go on some kind of hunt. Jessie was standing with the others, listening to a police constable.

'What the hell's going on?' he asked his wife.

'The boys have gone missing,' she told him with tears in her eyes. 'They came home from school, had their tea, went outside to play and haven't been seen since. We've all searched our houses and sheds, but nothing and it's beginning to get dark.' She grabbed his arm. 'Oh, Conor!'

He held her to him. 'Now, darlin', you know kids. They have gone off on some adventure not realising how worried everyone would be. They can't have gone far. They'll be found, mark my words.'

'The police are doing a house search in nearby streets and houses,' she told him, 'but Maisie and her husband are beside themselves. She collapsed, and the doctor and Percy are with her now. Where would the boys have gone, do you think?' Jessie asked. 'Think. If you were them, where would you go?'

Conor thought for a moment, wracking his brains searching for a clue, trying to think of something the boys had said. Then he remembered they had been talking about fishing the other day and he'd told them how he used to go by the pier, with a bit of string and a worm on a hook, when he was a boy and how interested they were with the whole idea. He looked at Jessie and told her.

'Would they know the way?'

'Yes, because Maisie and Percy have taken them there, walking *on* the pier. Come on, it's a possibility. Let's go and take a look.'

They shut their front door and rushed away.

The walk seemed endless, although it wasn't very far, and when they eventually reached the pier, Conor stopped. 'They wouldn't have any money to go onto the pier,' he said, 'so let's look around below.'

They walked to one side and searched, but found no one, then as they were walking down the other side, they heard someone screaming and started to run. They saw Jack up to his waist in water, screaming in fear and when they got to him he pointed and they saw Tommy, out of his depth, floundering in the water. Conor dived in as Jessie strode into the water to pick up young Jack, her skirt soaked as she lifted and carried him back to dry land. She held him close, talking softly as she tried to comfort the child.

'It's alright, Jack. Conor will get him, you see.' But the boy just sobbed, clinging to her as he watched.

Conor soon reached the lad and pulled him to the bank,

talking as he did so. 'It's alright, Tommy. I've got you, you're safe now.'

The boy was pale, coughing and spluttering, and obviously suffering from shock.

'Come on, Jessie, let's get him home. Hopefully the doctor will still be there. He needs to look at the lad, and if he's gone, we'll just have to get him back.' They started running, each carrying a child.

Passers-by looked at them in astonishment. Conor was soaked to the skin, Jessie's skirt was wet and clinging to her legs as she ran, and the boys too were wet through.

Fortunately, as they reached Union Street, the doctor emerged from the Williamses' house and, on hearing his name called, stopped. He then saw Jessie and Conor with the boys. When Conor quickly explained, they rushed into the house so he could examine Tommy.

Maisie jumped to her feet when she saw her sons, crying and calling their names, taking Jack from Jessie. She held him tightly to her after wrapping a blanket round him, as the doctor began his examination of the other child.

After what seemed an age, he declared that, apart from having a fright and being cold, he would be alright. He then examined Jack and suggested Percy put the boys in a bath to warm them, and then to bed. He'd call in the next day to see that they were alright.

Conor helped Percy warm some water on the stove and fill the tin bath, while Jessie and Maisie undressed the boys, peeling off their wet clothes, then they placed Tommy and his brother in the warm water, his father talking continuously to them, trying to keep the children calm as he and Conor washed them. Then wrapping them in towels, Percy dried one as his wife dried the other.

Conor saw the tears in the man's eyes as he looked at him. 'I can't thank you enough, Conor.'

Brushing this aside, Conor said, 'I think you should give them a hot drink, then get them into bed. Stay with them until they fall asleep. They've had a bad scare and they'll feel secure if you're there. I'll let the police know they're safe.'

Jessie made a pot of tea to calm Maisie, who was still weeping. Putting an arm around her, Jessie said, 'It's alright, Maisie, they are safe now. Try not to let the boys see you upset, it'll only frighten them even more.'

Eventually, everyone settled down. The boys, now exhausted and back with their parents, soon fell asleep.

Conor returned with four glasses of brandy, sent over by the landlord of the Builders Arms. They sat down and drank it slowly. It was just what they needed. Conor told them about finding the boys after remembering a conversation with the children.

Maisie spluttered. 'If you hadn't remembered . . .'

Jessie interrupted. 'But he did! So, put those thoughts away, Maisie. They're two boys on an adventure, but after today, they won't ever do it again; they'll be too scared. Thinking about what might have been is a waste of time and what's more it'll drive you crazy – so bury it!'

The sharpness of her voice seemed to get through, and Maisie nodded. 'You're right, of course. I must stop being silly. I can't thank you both enough.'

'You can stop that, too,' said Jessie. 'We're neighbours. You would do the same for us.' She stood up. 'Now, I must get a bath ready for Conor because a dip at the pier certainly wasn't enough to clean him, as you can see!'

They all looked at Conor and laughed. The daily dirt was somewhat streaked, but still very evident. It was enough to break the tenseness of the atmosphere and they were all able to relax a little.

After Jessie had changed out of her wet clothes, she boiled the water for Conor's bath as he sat wrapped in a towel and glanced over at him. 'I don't know about you, darlin', but I feel as if I've been run over by a tram.'

He let out a deep sigh. 'I know what you mean. What a day! But thank God it all worked out alright.'

'Talking of work, how did your first day go as gang boss?'

He sat and told her about it until at last he was able to lower himself into the warm water and feel the tension leave his body. What a day it had been, but thank God he was able to get to Tommy in time. The look of terror in that boy's eyes would stay with him for a long time.

The incident was reported in the *Southern Daily Echo*, naming Conor and Jessie as the saviours of the boys, which was an embarrassment to them both. The boys, however, were thrilled to read their names in the paper until their father spoke sharply to them, explaining how they had caused the police to spend time searching for them and the worry they had caused.

Jessie was overcome by the plaudits handed to her by her customers and soon stopped it by telling the men they would have done the same and brushing their compliments aside, as did Conor in the docks when his gang read the report. But there was one man who was not pleased when he read the paper.

Dave Jennings read about the incident. There was no sympathy for the boys' near catastrophe, only outrage that Conor had been named as a hero, and his wife. All it did was fire his anger for the man who was responsible for his downfall and he vowed to get his revenge.

Chapter Fourteen

Things slowly got back to normal in Union Street. Jack and Tommy were a couple of subdued boys for a while, but children are resilient and before long they were outside playing as usual. However, now they didn't stray from the street.

Watching them play as he stared out of the window, Conor turned to his wife. 'Those boys should be taught how to swim.'

Jessie looked at him in surprise. 'I doubt you'd ever get them back in the water.'

'That's the point, don't you see? They'll always fear the water until they are able to swim. I'd be happy to teach them when the weather gets warmer. We could all go to Leap Beach, take a picnic, make a day of it. Me and Percy could take a dip and encourage the boys to do so too.'

'Well, we'll just have to wait until then, the water's too cold now.'

'You're right, of course, but I'll mention it to Percy

when I see him. I don't fancy another dip meself at the moment. I remember how cold it was. Fair took my breath away as I dived in, so it did.'

Conor was well settled as the gang boss and looked forward to going to work now that he was in a position of authority. Giving the orders instead of taking them, earning a living which, to him, was so important in not having to live on Jessie's money alone. It had restored his manhood, in his mind.

Dave Jennings had managed to get work as a labourer on a building site. He wasn't a happy man. This world was alien to him. The docks had been his life; he didn't know anything else . . . until now. Every night he'd return home feeling belligerent and it was eating away at him.

That night he went to the Horse and Groom in The Ditches to drown his sorrows and towards the end of the evening, well into his cups, he walked out of the pub. Looking around at the girls waiting for a punter, he walked up to Maggie, who was standing with her friend Doris, and took her by the arm.

She looked to see who it was and paled as she saw it was Jennings. She pushed his arm away and glared at him. 'I'm not interested, thanks!'

'What do you mean, you're not interested? Who do you think you're talking to?'

'You, you bastard! You hit me the last time I took you home. I don't want your custom, so push off!'

Hearing the argument and having been warned about

this man by Maggie, the other girls who were waiting gathered round her.

'Leave her alone or we'll call the Old Bill,' said one.

Jennings gave a derisory laugh. 'The police? Don't be so bloody silly! The coppers will take you in for soliciting.' He made to grab hold of Maggie again, but she pulled a long hatpin from her hat and pointed it at him.

'You touch me again and I'll stick you with this!'

He stepped back. 'You wouldn't dare.'

She laughed at him. 'Go on, then, try me. I'd love to get my own back on you, you wicked bastard. Call yourself a man; you're just a bully.' And she made to jab him.

He leant away from her and, in his drunken state, he staggered.

The women jeered at him, calling insults, loudly demeaning him as a man until he was humiliated and slouched away. All the way home, he cursed to himself. There was only one person who was responsible for his state and he muttered his name constantly all the way home.

The following morning, Jennings was asked to drive a van loaded with building materials to a shed in the docks. He'd driven trucks before and, of course, knew every nook and cranny of the area. He delivered the goods and, as he climbed into the driver's seat, he saw Conor in the distance, walking towards some crates waiting to be loaded. He turned on the engine, put the van into gear and moved off.

Conor, intent on his mission, didn't see the van approaching him at speed and it was only someone yelling at him to look out that made him turn round. He just had time to dive out of the way, but he saw the face of the driver as the vehicle passed by.

A couple of the dockers rushed over and helped him to his feet. 'Christ, that was a close call!' said one. 'You alright, mate?'

Conor brushed away the dust from his clothes. 'Yes, thanks for the warning.'

'Bloody idiot driver! There's a speed limit in the docks and he was driving like a maniac. Did you see who it was?'

Shaking his head, Conor lied. 'No, no I didn't.'

'Well I saw the company name on the van. It was Kennedy's. You should report him; he could have killed you!'

As he walked away, he thought, *That was the general idea*, but if Jennings was that intent on causing him damage, and failing, would he try again and if so, when and how? Well he wasn't just going to sit around and wait.

The next day, the gang only worked a morning shift and Conor went home, washed and changed, then made his way to Kennedy's site. He found a spot where he could watch the comings and goings without being seen and settled himself.

In the late afternoon, a lorry drove into the yard. It was full of workers whom Conor assumed had returned from a job. The men all alighted and, saying their goodbyes, took off in different directions on their way home for the day. Conor spotted Jennings and followed him at a distance to see where he lived. Eventually, they arrived at a shabby house in the Chapel area, where the surrounding houses looked decrepit with dirty net curtains at the windows that hadn't been cleaned for an age.

Conor waited until Jennings had closed the front door behind him, then after a while he walked to the gate, which was hanging off its hinges. Empty beer bottles were piled up in a box against the front wall. He knocked on the door and waited.

Inside the house, Jennings had just opened a bottle of beer when he heard the sound of someone at the door and frowned. Who the hell was that? The milkman had left a pint on the doorstep and wasn't due to be paid until Friday. It was too late for the postman and, not having any friends, no one else ever came to call. He ambled along the passageway with its worn carpet and opened the door. Before he knew what had happened he'd been sent flying backwards and Conor McGonigall was kneeling over him.

'I saw you driving that van, Jennings. You tried to kill me, you bastard!' He caught the man by the front of his jacket and lifted his head, then he punched him in the face several times.

Jennings, taken by surprise, was in no position to fight back, although he tried, but Conor was fit and strong and he gave the man a severe beating. Getting to his feet, he looked at the bruised shape on the floor. 'Let that be the end or one of us will die and I can assure you it won't be me!' He kicked him viciously in the side, then left.

Jennings staggered to his feet and groaned. His face felt as if it was on fire and he was in pain on his side where he'd been kicked. He limped to the kitchen and, running the tap, soaked a cloth in cold water and held it to his face. After a while, he did it again and lowered himself gingerly into a chair. He'd been taken completely by surprise. He'd hardly registered who was at the door before he was on his back. He removed the cloth and saw there was blood on it. Heaving himself to his feet, he looked at his refection in the wall mirror. His eyes were swelling, his nose was bleeding and he was sure it was broken. He knew that he'd not be able to work for days and what's more he probably needed to go to the hospital, but there was no way he could get there today. He took a slug of his beer, soaked the cloth once again and, sitting back in the chair, covered his face.

Conor rubbed his bruised knuckles as he made his way home. He knew that he'd damaged his adversary, but would this be enough to teach the man a lesson? Was his hatred even stronger than his common sense? He had no way of knowing, so he'd have to keep his eyes open for a while. He would, however, keep what happened today to himself. If Jessie thought he'd been in a fight she'd be livid, and he certainly didn't want her to know about the incident at the docks.

Weeks passed and nothing was seen or heard of Dave Jennings. Conor began to believe that he had at last got through to the man. He was certain he'd broken Jennings' nose and hopefully that would have taught him his final lesson. His gang were working well and were busy most days depending on the shipping that docked with cargo to unload and reload.

It was now June, and Jessie was wondering what would happen when her contract was to be renewed next month. Larry Forbes hadn't been near and her young cashier, Henry

Marshall, had been called away to do another job for his boss. When he told Jessie, it was with regret in his voice.

'I have to leave after this afternoon, Mrs McGonigall. Mr Forbes needs me on another job.'

'Oh, Henry, I'll be sorry to see you go,' She was sincere in this. It had been an education for the young man who had arrived with ideas above his station. He had been arrogant and condescending to begin with, but soon had been taught a lesson in understanding that people from all walks of life have to earn a living, and that here, there was no discrimination in her cafe. It had been a lesson in life for young Henry and one he would never forget.

The customers heard this was his last day and all had a kind word as they left, many teasing him, but now he could understand it wasn't malicious, just good fun.

After he'd finally cashed up, Jessie asked him if he had any idea what would happen when her contract ran out, but he couldn't tell her anything

'I'm not in a position to know such things, Mrs McGonigall, I'm afraid, or I would willingly tell you.'

She thanked him for his time there. 'Call in any time, Henry. You'll always be welcome,' she told him as she let him out of the cafe.

She and Nancy sat and shared a pot of tea at the end of the day, when they'd cleared away. Jessie looked around the place. She was so happy here. Since she'd taken over, business had increased with some sidelines she'd introduced, like home-made cakes and sandwiches to take away; these had done well. Yes, she was content with her lot.

* * *

Sitting at the desk in his office, Larry Forbes was deep in thought. In front of him lay the contract for the workman's cafe, due for renewal in a month's time. He was in a dilemma. Jessie McGonigall was like a thorn in his side. Her attitude towards him was an irritation, yet she intrigued him and what's more, he found, to his chagrin, that she was devilishly attractive, something he'd tried to ignore.

All his business life, he'd been the one to call the shots. She was the first person to stand up to him, which both irritated him, yet earned his reluctant admiration. She had a good business brain and was fiercely independent, which in these times was unusual. Most women knew their place and were content, but not Jessie McGonigall. She was a suffragette without even knowing it! A feisty woman like that would make life very interesting, not only in business but in a more personal sense. He had to admit that he desired her and if he were really truthful, had done so from the moment he first met her. Together they could make a great team. But . . . it would have to be on his terms. He sat back and considered his position: he wasn't bad-looking; he was wealthy. He'd had women in the past – he was a man with needs after all – but none of them had interested him enough to make their relationship permanent. But Jessie – now that could be different. Of course, there was a problem: she was a married woman. Maybe if he offered her enough . . . ? It was an intriguing thought.

Chapter Fifteen

Jessie was walking around the dining room of the cafe at the end of the day, making sure all was ready for the morning, when the door opened. She turned, about to say that she was closed, when she found herself staring into the eyes of her landlord.

'Good afternoon, Mrs McGonigall.'

She just stood and looked at him for a moment, then she noticed he was carrying a bottle of wine. 'Mr Forbes. What brings you here?'

'Do you have any glasses on the premises?' he asked.

'I do.'

'Then would you mind bringing two to this table?' He pointed to one nearby and, pulling out a chair, he sat and looked at her unflinchingly.

Somewhat intrigued, she walked into the kitchen and returned, putting the glasses on the table. He took them and motioned for her to sit down. Then from his pocket he took a corkscrew and opened the bottle. Pouring the wine into both glasses, he handed one to her.

'What are we drinking to, or is that a secret?'

He gave a laconic smile. 'That all depends.' He took a sip and swallowed. 'Try it, it's a very good wine. I prefer red; I think you will approve.'

Jessie did so. It was smooth and rich with the aroma and taste of dark fruit, but with a flavour she'd never experienced before and she thought it must be expensive. But what else would it be? She eyed his suit, its fine material – obviously handmade. His expensive watch, pristine white shirt and silk tie. It was the first time she'd studied anything but his face. She had to admit he wore his wealth with style.

'Well, do you like it?'

'Yes, I do. It's very smooth . . . like you!'

He laughed quietly. 'I'm not sure if that's a compliment or not.'

She leant forward. 'Get to the point, Mr Forbes. What do you want?'

'That's what I like about you, Jessie. No messing – cards on the table. No games.' He sat looking at her, his eyes twinkling with amusement.

She waited, silently.

Eventually, he spoke. 'You have a fine business brain. You know how to deal with the public. You are a woman ahead of your time and you don't even know it. If you so desired, there is nothing you couldn't accomplish with the help of the right person.'

She didn't react to his remarks, just slowly sipped her wine and stared at the man sitting opposite her, but her mind was working furiously. *What's this bastard after? He's here for a reason, yet* . . . and yet, she was intrigued. In

136

this mood, he was a different man. Beguiling, even. 'And?' she challenged.

'I think we could do business together and be very successful. You could do far better than this.' He motioned to the room in which they sat. 'Not that I'm denigrating the work you've done here, the improvements, your reputation. You worked hard to achieve all that. But I see you in a class above all this. You have the looks, you have the skills – you could do anything you wanted, really.' He leant toward her. 'Jessie McGonigall, you are worth far more than a workman's cafe!'

'I totally agree with you, and one day I'll have something even better!'

'But how long will you have to wait? Do you have the finance to furnish your ambition?'

'Not yet.'

'If you had, what would be your next move?'

She sat quietly thinking. 'I would like a small hotel. One with about ten rooms. I would employ a chef to do the cooking and the staff to maintain it and I would be in charge.'

'That's a big ambition in this day and age, a woman in such a position.'

'It doesn't mean it can't be done,' she said with a note of defiance.

'I agree, but it would take a great deal of money, more than I imagine you'd be able to raise.'

Jessie knew that he was correct in his assumption. The bank would hardly finance her without collateral. Her skill and ambition were the only things she had to offer. But she wasn't going to back down.

'It will just take time to save,' she said.

'What if I offer to back you financially?'

Jessie was taken by surprise. 'Why on earth would you do such a thing?'

'Because I think you'd be successful.'

Her eyes narrowed as she looked at him suspiciously. 'What would be in it for you, Mr Forbes?'

He stared back at her, his gaze almost hypnotic in its intensity. 'I'm sure we could come to an agreement that would suit both of us.' He finished his wine and stood up. 'Think about it. We'll talk again soon.' He walked to the door and let himself out.

Jessie sat alone, sipping the rest of her wine, stunned by the conversation, her mind in a whirl. She had just been handed an opportunity for a better life. Something that could lift her and Conor above their working-class roots without any worries about the future. No more concerns about meeting the bills. Conor would no longer have to work in the docks, which would be good for him as she knew his leg troubled him and that worried her. He could work in the hotel with her. Her mind was in turmoil. But then would her husband agree to taking up the offer? Would he be happy that she would be beholden to Larry Forbes – and what exactly did Mr Forbes really want out of such a business transaction? He hadn't said and, although today he had been charm itself, she remembered his ruthless streak when he wanted to take over the cafe. Did he want to take her over too? If she turned him down, would he renew her contract? If he didn't, she would have nothing!

She picked up the glasses and, taking them into the kitchen, washed and put them away. She needed time to think. She decided not to tell Conor at the moment, until she learnt more from her landlord. After all, he had said they'd talk again.

While Jessie was in turmoil, Larry Forbes was feeling very pleased with himself. He knew how ambitious Jessie was and how she would be pondering over the prospect of fulfilling her plans, which at this stage would have been nothing but a pipe dream, yet now was a possibility. He also realised she was a canny woman and she'd be wondering why he, of all people, would consider financing her. Well, he really wasn't too sure himself. He was a shrewd businessman and was convinced she'd be a success, but he was aware that, at last, she'd have to answer to him and that had given him immense satisfaction. All he needed now was to find a property that would be viable, then he thought Jessie McGonigall wouldn't be able to turn down his offer. Her ambition would be too much for her to refuse.

When Conor arrived home that night, Jessie could see he looked drawn and he was limping slightly. She didn't comment on it, but when she filled his bath, she put a handful of Epsom salts in the water to help alleviate his aches and pains. While he was soaking in the bath, she prepared their evening meal, thinking all the time that if she took up Forbes's offer, Conor would be spared this discomfort. But she kept her counsel and said nothing of the offer she'd received. As Conor climbed out of the tin bath in front of the fire, she couldn't help but think how marvellous it would be to have a proper bathroom and an inside toilet. That would be a luxury she'd really enjoy!

As they sat at the table, Conor was telling her about his day, but Jessie was only half-listening. Her mind was on how different their life could be and she was trying to plan how Conor could help her in the hotel if it came to fruition. He was a charmer and would be good with people, but he'd have to have a proper role. He'd need to feel he was working, doing a proper job, or he would feel less of a man and that would never do; he was too proud for that. He would definitely want to be making a contribution to the running of the business or he'd be hard to handle.

Suddenly, she was aware that Conor had stopped talking and she looked at him. 'What?' she asked.

'You've hardly heard a word I've said; you are a million miles away.'

'Sorry, darlin, it's been a long day. I'm just tired.'

He leant across the table and took her hand. 'I know – me too. If only I was in a position financially to take us out of here and to another life I would.'

She wanted to tell him that it was a possibility, but remained silent; after all, she had only had an offer of the finance, but not any other details. It was far too soon to make a decision.

She squeezed his hand. 'I know, but we're doing just fine. I'll get the pudding.'

That night in bed, she was beset by dreams. She was running a hotel, Conor was sweeping the carpet in a corridor with a stiff brush, looking very unhappy, and Larry Forbes was sitting at the bar, drinking. She woke suddenly in a bath of perspiration. Beside her, Conor was sleeping peacefully. She went downstairs and, taking a torch, went outside to use the toilet. It was dark and cold, and walking back a cat sped across her path, making her jump. She went inside and made a cup of tea, thinking, *I can change all this if I want to*. It was unsettling.

Chapter Sixteen

During the following two weeks, Jessie was on edge. Forbes hadn't contacted her and she was in a quandary. Would he offer her a new contract for the cafe or had he come up with something else? If he did, would she accept? And if she didn't, what then? The uncertainty kept her awake at night, she was short with Conor and she was becoming a nervous wreck.

While Jessie was on pins and full of uncertainties, Larry Forbes was searching for small hotels in various trade papers and estate agents, but as yet nothing he had seen was right. He left his name with various agents asking them to contact him should something suitable come onto their books. Time was running out and he didn't want Jessie to sign another contract which would tie her to the cafe. He wanted her to be free to take up an offer from him if he was successful in his search. He decided he'd go and see her at the end of work the next day.

* * *

When Larry Forbes entered the cafe just as the last customers were leaving and sat at an empty table, Jessie felt a sense of relief. Now she'd find out if she still had a job. She asked him if he wanted anything to drink, but he refused. He just sat and watched her with her final customers, chatting and joshing as she opened the door for them. She was a natural with people and he could see why she was so popular. Eventually, the place was empty and Nancy, too, had gone home.

Jessie removed her white apron and sat opposite Forbes. 'What can I do for you?'

He admired her demeanour. After all, she had no idea what was ahead of her, whether she had a new contract on offer or if he had other plans for her, but she appeared calm.

'As you know, you have two more weeks before the new contract is needed for you to carry on here.'

She just nodded.

'I've been searching for a small hotel.' He saw her eyebrows rise in surprise, but she didn't comment. 'Now, I don't want you to be tied down here just in case a viable hotel comes on the market, so I suggest when the contract runs out, we keep it on a monthly basis.'

Jessie mulled this over in her mind for a moment. 'And if a hotel does come onto the market?'

'Then we both sit down and come to an arrangement ... or not!' He sat back in the chair and waited for her response.

'Tell me, Mr Forbes, what kind of an arrangement had you in mind?'

'I would buy the hotel, supply a working budget to begin

with until it was up and running. You would draw a salary as befitting your position and, eventually, a percentage of the profits.'

'I see. Does that include my living arrangements? I will be living on the premises? At least, that's what I expect to do.'

'Of course. You'd have to be there to be on call at all times.'

'That's good. Now, how much of the running of the hotel would be in *your* hands, Mr Forbes?'

'The finance, obviously. Any structural changes needed.'

'What about the decor, the choosing of the staff?'

'The decor we could choose together; you have good taste and so do I. The staff would be your responsibility, apart from the chef. I know one or two whose food I've eaten and who would work for me for the right incentives. After all, a small hotel can still have a fine reputation in the dining room. This would bring people in to dine and drink at the bar and recommend the accommodation. This is not a bed and breakfast, after all, but a tasteful if small hotel. It would be like finding a pearl in a small oyster.'

At this, Jessie started to smile. 'I had no idea you could be so poetical.'

'As I've told you before, Mrs McGonigall, you don't know me at all. So what do you think? A monthly rental of the cafe until we have something more suitable to run?'

The more she listened to Forbes, the more she liked the idea. His terms were reasonable. She'd be salaried and share the profits when the business took off. She could move out of her council house, have a bathroom and indoor toilet! She tried not to look too excited.

'Yes, that sounds sensible. Let's do that and see what happens.'

Larry Forbes beamed at her across the table. He hadn't been sure of her reaction. Jessie McGonigall was an unknown force and unpredictable, but she had agreed and that was great. He rose from his chair and put out his hand. 'Will you shake my hand *this* time?'

Cocking her head to one side, remembering how she'd declined to do so in the past, she hid a smile and put out her hand. 'Why not?'

Jessie wasn't the only one with a secret. Conor had been told that Dave Jennings had been seen loitering around the docks. He'd not seen him himself, but one or two of the dockers who knew of the trouble between them had told him of their sightings.

'You watch your back, Conor,' one warned. 'He's a miserable bugger when he's been crossed and now you have his job, that wouldn't go down well, I'm sure.'

Conor thanked him and was watchful when he was at work. He'd not seen a van in the docks like the one Jennings drove at him, but whenever he heard any vehicle, he would turn quickly to see what was coming his way. He tried to behave as normal around his gang, but he was tense and sometimes it showed.

'Everything alright with you, Conor?' asked Bill Brown as they walked home together at the end of a shift.

Conor gave a puzzled look. 'Yes, fine. Why do you ask?'

'You've been a bit jumpy lately and that's not like you. I wondered, that's all.'

Putting an arm across the other man's shoulders, he laughed. 'No, Bill, I'm fine. Maybe a bit weary, nothing more,' and they continued on their way. But as Conor reached his front door, a movement at the end of the empty street caught his eye. He recognised the figure of Jennings just as he turned the corner! Running as fast as he could, he reached the corner and looked along the road, but apart from various pedestrians, and the horse and cart of the coalman, Jennings was not to be seen. He stood watching for a while before walking slowly back to his house.

What was that bugger after? he wondered. The fact that the man was near his home was unnerving. He could understand Jennings skulking around the docks. A confrontation there was understandable, but here. . . ? This was far more serious. This could put Jessie in danger, if the troubled man had some devious plan. He didn't think it wise to go back to Jennings' house again. Last time he'd caught him by surprise, but that only worked once. What *was* he to do? The one thing he mustn't do was to let Jessie know. He didn't want her worried; this was his problem, but how to solve it? He'd have to think about it.

Dave Jennings peered out from the doorway of a house where he'd taken refuge when he realised that Conor had seen him. All seemed clear now, so he walked quickly away. It had been foolish of him to even contemplate being around Conor McGonigall's home and he had no idea why he'd done so. He walked into The Glasgow pub, ordered a pint of bitter and sat down. Looking around, he searched for a face he knew, but there was none. He was a lonely man, he admitted. He'd never married; his job in the docks had been his life. He could cook, after a fashion, and if he needed sex, he paid for it. These days he had to go further afield for a woman after his run-in with the girls in The Ditches. But now, without his life in the docks, he was without purpose, except for paying back the man who now held the job that had been his life. But he had to be careful, especially after the beating he took from Conor. He'd had to have his nose reset and it had never looked the same since. Yet another reminder. *But one day, one fine day, I'll pay that young bastard back for the trouble he's caused me,* he vowed silently.

Chapter Seventeen

It was now the end of August and life for Jessie was without any worries. She was still running her cafe, now on a monthly basis as her benefactor was yet to find a hotel that was suitable. She wasn't particularly concerned. She was still in business and making a living, with the promise of a better life in the future. She could wait, she told herself.

As for Conor, after seeing Jennings disappearing from his street, things had quietened down. Conor had been vigilant when working, but there had been no sign of his adversary and he began to hope that the man had eventually lost his taste for vengeance.

It was the school holidays and Conor had suggested that he, Jessie and the next-door neighbours, Percy and Maisie, take the boys to Leap Beach for a picnic, and he would try and teach the children to swim. An idea that Conor had had after the incident at the pier, when the boys almost drowned.

It was a warm, sunny Sunday and they eventually arrived, laying rugs on the sand, slipping out of their clothes and donning swimsuits. The boys were pleased to paddle and nobody pushed them to do anything else, letting them get used to the water. Then they enjoyed a picnic the women had made, played ball on the beach, built sandcastles, until the two men said they'd go for a swim. Jessie took the boys to paddle at the water's edge, then walked them just a little deeper, but not enough to frighten them. They stood in the water up to their thighs, allowing them to still play with a beach ball she had taken.

Conor swam back and joined in. After a while, he took Jessie by the shoulders and the two of them floated together on their backs in the shallow water. The boys watched with interest. Jessie was kicking her feet and laughing, showing her enjoyment in the hope that the children would see she had no fear of the water.

Then they stood up and, going over to Jack and Tommy, casually asked if they wanted to try. At their hesitation, Conor spoke. 'You can each climb on our backs and have a ride, like a piggy back but in the water. Like this . . .' Jessie lay on his back, holding his shoulders as he floated. 'Only here in the shallows, not in deep water. You'll be perfectly safe and it will be such fun.' He waited. If the boys said no, then he'd leave it, but Jack, who was the more adventurous, said he would.

Tommy watched as his brother climbed on Conor's back. Conor swam up and down, keeping in shallow enough water that just allowed him to keep afloat. Tommy began to relax and started laughing.

Jessie looked at Tommy. 'We can't let them have all the fun, can we? Come onto my back and we can join in. What do you say?'

Not wanting to be outdone by his brother, he climbed onto Jessie's back, keeping tight hold of her. 'Right now, I'm going to lean forward into the water, you just hold on.' She slowly lowered herself into the sea and started to swim slowly, talking to Tommy all the time until she felt his little body relax.

After a while, she and Conor took the boys back to the beach where everyone poured praise upon them, saying how well they'd done. 'Another day we'll teach you to swim if you like,' Conor said casually.

The youngsters, thrilled with themselves, both agreed.

Conor smiled at Jessie and kissed her cheek. 'A job well done, darlin'. Best not to do any more today, but we will have these boys swimming by the time they go back to school, I swear it!'

Jessie looked at the happy expression on her husband's face, thinking how sad it was that he didn't have children of his own, although never once had he shown his disappointment. She was delighted that at least they had these two little ones to spoil.

Larry Forbes was excited. An estate agent had been in touch with him as he had a hotel on his books in Bernard Street that he thought would interest him. He made an appointment to see it the following morning.

The hotel was on four floors. It had a good entrance, a bar, dining room and ten rooms situated on the next two floors. The top of the house would be ideal for private living arrangements, especially with one of the walls knocked down to make a larger living room. A bathroom could be installed, and then there was a double bedroom. It all needed redecoration and refurbishment, but he could see it had great potential. But before he made any decision, Jessie McGonigall needed to see it. He rushed round to the cafe to tell her.

When Larry Forbes walked into the workman's cafe, Jessie was serving a customer, but she could see that he was excited about something. He could hardly wait for her to be free.

'I think I've found the premises for the hotel,' he said, grinning broadly. 'I need you to come and see it when you close.'

Her heart started to pound as she, too, became excited. As far as she was concerned it was still a pipe dream, but now . . . 'Where is it?'

'Bernard Street. It's been running as a hotel until recently, but has been neglected. It will need to be redecorated and refurbished, and one wall knocked down, but I really believe it's what we have been looking for. What time can you meet me there to take a look?'

'Three o'clock. I'll get Nancy to finish off and lock up for me.'

He gave her the address. 'I'll see you there,' he said and rushed out.

Jessie hadn't told Nancy about Forbes's plans. Indeed, she'd wondered if they would come to fruition, but, in any case, if they did, the girl would certainly be a member of her staff.

Towards the end of the day, she told Nancy she had an appointment without saying where and left her to close up. Then quickly washing her face and hands, she made her way to the address in Bernard Street and found Larry Forbes walking up and down outside waiting for her.

As she walked into the reception area, Jessie could hardly breathe with excitement. Although it was apparent that the place needed upgrading, she liked what she saw. Then walking over the rest of it, she knew this was exactly what she wanted and when Larry took her to the top of the house and explained what he wanted to do to make it her living quarters, she was speechless. She could immediately picture a new life for her and Conor.

'What do you think, Jessie? Will it do?'

She gave a quizzical look 'You can't have any doubts, surely?'

He was like a boy with a new toy. 'I knew you'd be able to see the potential. Let's take a look at the kitchen; we need to sort that out. Come on.'

Eventually, both exhausted, they sat at a table in the dining room.

'There's a lot of work needing to be done. I'd like to be ready to open for Christmas.'

'That's only four months!' Jessie exclaimed.

'I know. But if we get the kitchen and the next two floors decorated and refurbished, and the wall in your living quarters done, we can continue with any unfinished rooms after Christmas. After all, I can't imagine we'd be fully booked by then.'

'It's a lot to think about. It's also going to cost a great deal.' She looked at him.

'Now you're wondering if I have the money to do this, am I right?'

'Yes! Then when it opens, it will cost even more until it starts paying for itself. There will be the staff wages to cover, and mine. That is a huge investment. I don't want to give up my business to then find you can't meet the bills.'

He chuckled softly. 'You never beat about the bush, do you?'

'Oh, come along, Mr Forbes, you are a businessman, surely you can understand my concern?'

'Of course I do and, because of your business brain, I know we can succeed. For your information, I do have the financial resources to meet this commitment.'

'Fine, but as yet we haven't discussed my salary. I expect to be paid for my experience, the responsibility that will be mine as the manageress and I also expect it to include my living arrangements! After all, it will mean giving up my home to move in.'

Forbes stared at her without answering, thinking that for a woman, she was extraordinary. How many women in this day and age would be offered such a position of importance? Not many, but here she was demanding – yes, demanding – her rights. He couldn't help but admire her spirit. It was because of this that he knew she'd succeed. Why else would he be prepared to back the whole thing financially?

He took out a notebook from his pocket and a pen and wrote down a figure and handed it to her. She looked at it and, without changing her expression, asked, 'What will my percentage of the profits be when we start making money?'

'Twenty-five per cent.'

'Thirty would make me happy!'

'I'm not sure I'd be so happy.'

She leant back in her chair and smiled. 'The choice is yours, Mr Forbes. Thirty or nothing!'

He started to laugh. 'Jessie McGonigall, I've never met a woman like you; you should have been born a man!'

She didn't answer, but just sat, waiting.

'Very well. Thirty!'

'I'll need this all written into my contract, of course.'

Shaking his head, he said, 'Of course. Now, are we done negotiating? Can I now go and see the estate agent and say he has a buyer?'

'There is just one thing more. I will continue with the cafe until such time as the hotel is ready; after all, I can't afford to be out of work for so long. I don't have your finances behind me and that is non-negotiable.'

In exasperation, he said, 'Whatever you say. Now I suggest we get on.'

As Jessie walked home, she was thrilled with the result of her meeting. She could see the hotel in her mind's eye, all redecorated and open for business. Now she would have to tell Conor of their change of circumstances. She frowned. *How would he receive the news?* she wondered. Whatever he said, she wasn't going to let an opportunity like this pass her by. It was the chance of a lifetime. She was still somewhat concerned that Larry Forbes was her backer, especially as they had crossed swords so in the past, but the salary was good, she'd have decent living accommodation as part of her job and it meant a secure future. He was an acute businessman and could see the potential in the hotel. He needed someone to run it and had chosen her. Everything would be down in writing, so what was there to worry about? But deep in her subconscious, there was still a doubt; however, she decided to ignore it.

Chapter Eighteen

Jessie decided to wait for Conor to have his bath, his dinner and time to relax before talking about her offer from Larry Forbes. She was decidedly nervous about doing so, wondering what her husband's reaction would be. She'd not told him of the new monthly contract for the cafe, he'd just assumed the old one had been renewed.

After she'd cleared away the dirty dishes and washed up, she and Conor sat together on the settee, with a glass of Guinness each. Conor gave her the perfect opening.

'So, darlin', how was your day?'

Taking a deep breath, she began. 'Interesting. Mr Forbes wants me to run a small hotel for him in Bernard Street, instead of the cafe.'

He looked at her in astonishment. 'What?'

'He came into the cafe a while back and said I had a good business brain and was worth more than running a workman's cafe and that he'd wanted to buy a small hotel, and would I be interested in running it for him if he found one.'

'Was he being serious?'

Jessie's eyes flashed in anger. 'Don't you think I'm capable of doing such a thing?'

He tried to placate her. 'I think you are capable of many things, darlin', but a cafe is in a different category to a hotel. What do you know about such things?'

'There would be a chef in the kitchen, staff to clean the rooms, a couple of waitresses in the dining room. It's not the Great Western Hotel, Conor, it only has ten bedrooms. I don't feel that's beyond my capabilities to manage a small staff and look after the clients. Certainly, Larry Forbes doesn't and he's a knowledgeable businessman!'

He didn't answer, but sat frowning as he looked at her. 'I thought you hated the man and didn't trust him. Good heavens, Jessie, you've stomped around here often enough cursing him and now you want to go into business with him? What's changed your attitude? I find it a puzzle.'

'Yes, I know, but ever since he bought the lease and has become my boss, his attitude has changed. He realised how well I ran the cafe, he made money because I was a success and now he thinks I'm the one he needs to run this hotel.'

He could see the determination in her expression and asked, 'So what is he offering you to take this position?'

'A good salary, a flat to live in on the top floor. Oh, Conor, we could move out of here, we'd have a proper bathroom and a toilet!'

He chuckled softly. 'Are you sure the last two things are not what makes you want to accept such an offer?'

She sat up and glared at him. 'You are not taking this

seriously, Conor. This is a chance of a lifetime and I'm taking it!'

His smile faded. 'Even if I don't agree?'

She paused, then, 'Why would you want me to refuse?' She handed him the piece of paper that Forbes had given her with the salary he would pay her. 'This is what I would be earning, with the living accommodation thrown in.'

Conor looked at the sum. It was more than he used to earn as a stevedore.

'Wouldn't I let you down in your illustrious position when I walked in the hotel in my working clothes, covered in filth?'

She recognised the bitterness in his voice and knew she had a problem.

Settling back against him, she said quietly, 'I thought it would be an opportunity for you to leave the docks and work in the hotel. Let's face it, your leg gives you trouble after a heavy day. You could put all that behind you.'

He looked furious. 'Now just you wait a minute. This is *your* opportunity, not mine. I'm a docker, have been all my life. It's what makes me a happy man – it's who I am! Can you honestly see *me*, working for *you* in some position or other in a business that is totally foreign to me?'

She knew to argue further would be useless. She rose to her feet. 'I've said I'll take the job, Conor. Will you at least move into the flat with me?'

He shook his head. 'No, I'll keep the house on. I'm earning enough to do so and to live. This is your dream, Jessie. You deserve it and I wish you luck, and if it all falls through, at least you still have a home.'

'Conor! But what about our marriage? Don't you still love me?'

He stood up and took her into his arms. 'I adore you, and I always will. You know where to find me; I'll be here. You'll have some free time when we can be together. I'll even get dressed in me best suit, and come and have a drink at your bar, so I will. It means we won't be together all the time, that's all. I'm proud of you, Jessie, you deserve this break.'

'I'll still be working at the cafe until December and living at home,' she said with desperation. 'It's not as if I'm moving out tomorrow.'

'Then let's make the most of our time. Come to bed.'

She followed him upstairs, tears brimming in her eyes. This wasn't working out the way she planned at all. She knew that Conor was a man filled with pride. He needed to be in charge and now he wouldn't be, and for him that was untenable. But during the time she had left, sharing the house and his bed, she'd make very sure he realised how important he was to her and maybe, later he'd change his mind.

Their lovemaking that night had a feeling of desperation about it. Both fraught with their own anxieties but wanting to prove that their love and need for each other was still paramount.

Jessie, completely exhausted, soon fell asleep, but Conor lay still for a while. Then getting out of bed, he pulled on his trousers and went downstairs. He made a mug of tea, lit a cigarette and, taking a deep draw, tried to understand what changes now loomed in his life. Jessie, manageress of a hotel! Small or otherwise, he still couldn't take it in. They were simple, hard-working folk, fighting to make a living as were their friends. Now Jessie would be earning far more money than he ever could, would be moving into a higher social circle and he felt he had no part in it.

He didn't want to take this chance away from her and indeed he knew deep down she was determined to move on, but in time, would he be left behind? Could their marriage sustain the break? She was the only woman for him and had been from the day they met, but once Jessie became more and more involved with the hotel business and meeting people from a better class, would she still be happy with him and his way of life? Would it become an embarrassment to her that her husband worked in the docks? Then he dismissed the notion. Not his Jessie, she was fiercely independent and loyal – but it was a concern.

The following two months were busy. Jessie was still working in the cafe as usual, but after closing time she had meetings with Larry Forbes where they worked together, choosing the decor of the hotel, the furnishings, carpets and curtains. She had to agree that he had good taste and a nose for a bargain, finding offcuts for the making of the curtains, saving money, replacing some of the furnishings from those in auction sales and making deals as he replenished the bar fittings. The hotel was in chaos, but Jessie could already see the improvements. It was smart, tasteful and understated. Enough to invite a good class of clientele, but not too opulent to turn people away, thinking it as beyond their pocket.

She tried not to appear too enthusiastic in front of Conor, which was not easy as inside she was bursting with pride and enthusiasm. But already things had changed. She wasn't always there when her husband came home and he had to fill his own bath sometimes and warm some food she'd left in the larder from the day before. He didn't make any comment, but he was quieter than usual.

Daisy was making some new dresses for Jessie, who wanted to look the part when she took over the running of the hotel. They chose plain-coloured materials that looked smart and professional. The dresses were simply styled with round necks, long sleeves, fitting at the waist with fuller skirts that were ankle length, but with Jessie's slim figure and colourful tresses, she looked stunning. She shied away from black, thinking it looked too funereal, but chose dark brown, dark green and rust, which suited her colouring. After all, the waitresses would be wearing black with small white aprons. She wanted to state her position and wearing these colours would do so. Daisy had also made small jackets to be worn over the dresses for the evening with the smallest of trimmings to elevate the outfit: a contrasting flower made from soft material, which could be pinned on the lapel; or a collar made in velvet in a deeper shade than the dress. All very understated, but so very clever.

Thanks to Daisy's original customers, Maggie and Doris, her clientele now included the landlady of the Horse and Groom and one or two of her friends, which delighted Bill that it was no longer only prostitutes that were her clients. Being a man, he prided himself on the fact that he had let her continue her work, allowing it to grow. When he said this at times, Daisy just smiled to herself. She now had a steady income, which was a saving grace, especially if he was to be out of work.

Jessie had been wondering what was to happen to the cafe when she left to run the hotel and the idea of closing it didn't sit well with her, so she asked Larry Forbes to call in and see her at the end of her working day.

'What's on your mind?' he asked as they sat down together.

'The cafe is on my mind. I want to still run it. Nancy can take over the cooking – after all she's worked with me for so long she knows the menu inside out and is perfectly capable. I'll hire a girl to do the serving, then the men will still have somewhere to come and eat. I'll still make money and so will you, so why waste a good business?'

He sat listening to her idea. In truth, he hadn't made plans for the cafe; he'd been so busy setting up the hotel. He'd vaguely thought of selling on the lease as he would have no further use for the building: all his finances would be tied up with his new venture.

'Alright. I'll give it three months after you leave. If it's still making money, I'll keep it going, if not – then it closes.'

'Fair enough. I'll have a word with Nancy in the morning. Thank you.'

'How does your husband feel about moving into the hotel?'

The unexpected question left her speechless. There was no way she could lie, Forbes would know she was living there alone as he would be around for a while in the beginning until he was sure the hotel was running smoothly.

'Conor is keeping our house on and will be living there.'

Forbes frowned. 'Why?'

'It's what he prefers. Now if you don't mind, I have to get home.' She stood up and walked to the door, opened it and waited for him to leave.

Nothing more was said and they both departed.

But as he walked away, Larry Forbes began to wonder if Jessie's rise in the world of business was a problem for her husband. Would her marriage suffer because of it and if it did, what would she do? Only time would tell, but he knew that she was so enamoured with this opportunity that she'd fight for her right to better herself.

Chapter Nineteen

In a few days it would be December and the opening of the Grosvenor Hotel, as it was now called. With only hours to spare, the workmen had finished and removed all their paraphernalia. Jessie and Larry Forbes walked round every square inch of the place inspecting it, making sure it was perfect for opening.

Jessie had interviewed and hired the staff, except for the chef – Forbes had seen to that. The staff were now setting the tables in the dining room, giving the rooms a final dusting and tweak, and the florist had arrived with various arrangements for the reception and dining room. The barman was cleaning the glasses and checking the barrels in the cellar. On the second of the month there was to be a grand opening with drinks and canapés served. Forbes had informed the press, sent invitations to all the top businessmen in the area and their wives, and he'd hired a small ensemble to play softly in the reception area.

'Come along, Jessie. I think we deserve a drink and who better than us to be the first to use the bar?'

They sat on a couple of bar stools as the barman opened a bottle of champagne.

Holding up his glass, Forbes made a toast. 'Here's to the hotel and to us, may it all be a success!' He clinked her glass.

Jessie sipped her drink, then looked around. 'It does look amazing, doesn't it?'

'Yes, it does. I think between us we've chosen the right decor. Sitting here, I like the feel of the place. It's elegant, yet comfortable – but with a definite air of class. I've advertised it in the national newspapers too.'

'You have?' Jessie looked surprised.

'Why ever not? First of all, we are offering an alternative to the Great Western Hotel for those people taking passage who want to stay overnight before embarking the next day. It's close to the docks and some would prefer a smaller hotel – and here we are. Then there are the business people who come down from London. I certainly am not contemplating our clientele being just local, dear me, no. There's not enough profit in that! I've had cards printed and taken to various gentlemen's clubs in the city, I've left some with a few people I know to hand out to some of their influential friends, and I've advertised in a couple of magazines. Publicity is so important.'

She gazed at him in admiration. She had so much to learn.

'Are you happy with your staff?'

'So far. I'll see how they perform when we open, but I'm certain I've chosen well.'

Without her knowledge, Forbes had listened in to one or two of her interviews and had been impressed. She'd laid out exactly what she expected of them and had made it very clear if they didn't meet her standards they would go.

'I'm sure you have.'

'I've hired a slightly older woman as the receptionist. She's experienced, has worked in London, and has excellent references, which I've checked. She's smart in appearance, has an elegance about her and she has a cultured voice. I felt that was important.'

'Absolutely! It's the first contact the client has, so it's essential that the impression is favourable. Well done.'

'Tomorrow is my last day in the cafe. None of my customers know I'm leaving and, without their knowledge, Nancy has been cooking the meals for the past two weeks and no one has noticed the difference. I've increased Nancy's wages, which is only right, and have already hired a young girl to serve who's been fine, so nothing much will change apart from my not being there.'

'That was clever of you to let Nancy cook, but you'll find the men will be sad at your leaving. Be prepared because it will be emotional; I don't think you realise this. The cafe has been an important part of your life for a very long time. It will be like saying goodbye to a dear friend.'

'You never cease to surprise me,' Jessie said.

'Why, because I have a heart? I've told you often enough, you don't know me at all.' He got to his feet. 'Good luck tomorrow. Don't bother coming in here after, take the rest of the day to get your things together for moving in. I suggest you move as soon as possible so you can be settled.'

As she watched Forbes walk away, she suddenly had a sinking feeling. It wasn't just the opening making her nervous, it was moving out of her marital home without Conor! It just didn't feel right – but she had no choice.

The following morning, Jessie and Nancy sat down to plan for when Nancy finally took over. Nancy was au fait with the ordering and knew that if she had any worries, she was to ring Jessie at the hotel. She admitted she was nervous.

Jessie caught hold of her hand. 'No need for that! You are perfectly competent and you know it. You've been in charge these past two weeks really, doing the cooking, the preparation and some of the ordering. I'm on the end of a telephone not that far away. You'll be fine. I'm telling the men today and from tomorrow, it's yours to run!'

The two women had worked together for a very long time and had formed a great bond. Nancy looked at her friend. 'My God, Jessie! Who'd have thought it when years ago we worked for old George we'd be in this position. Me in charge here and you running a hotel.' She shook her head slowly. 'If only my dear old mum was alive to see the day.'

'Mine too. I was only nineteen when she went back to Ireland and I didn't see her again. That I bitterly regret.'

'Never mind, love. I bet they're up there looking down and having a good old gossip about their girls.'

Jessie chuckled. 'We'd better not let them down, then! Come on, let's get started.'

Later in the day when the dining room was full, Jessie stood by the cash desk and banged on it loudly. There was a surprised silence. 'Sorry to interrupt your meal, gents, but I've an announcement. This is my last day here.' There was a loud murmur from her diners. 'Now there's no need to get excited, the cafe remains open and Nancy will be in charge.'

'But you won't be cooking!' one man complained.

'That's right, Stan. You've been in every day. How was the food?'

'Great, but then you've been here.'

'Correct, I have, but I've not been cooking these past two weeks, Nancy has.'

'She's done it all?' asked one man suspiciously.

'Every bit and none of you noticed a difference, did you? Be honest!'

They all had to agree that this was the truth. 'Why are you leaving, Jessie?'

'I'm going to be the manageress of the new hotel, The Grosvenor, which opens in a few days' time.'

'Bloody hell, Jess, that's moving up the ladder, girl!'

She laughed loudly. 'I guess so, but I'll miss every one of you and I want to thank you all for your custom over the years. I ask you one favour: please keep coming. It's still the best workman's cafe in Southampton and I still own it, so don't put me out of business.'

One man stood up. 'Well, Jessie McGonigall, I've got to hand it to you, you deserve to go up in the world. We've seen how hard you've worked and, Nancy, we'll still come, won't we, lads?' There was a loud cheer at this and Jessie felt the tears fill her eyes. He picked up his mug of tea. 'A toast, to Jessie McGonigall!' The diners rose as one and echoed the toast.

Jessie couldn't stop the tears rolling down her cheeks. She was too full to speak. She put her hands to her lips, blew them a kiss and fled into the kitchen.

Today she was at home before Conor, which lately was unusual. She put the pans of water on the stove in preparation for his bath, put a pie in the oven to warm, peeled some potatoes and put them on to boil, and quickly made a pot of tea. Then she went upstairs to start packing her clothes. As she placed every garment into her suitcase she was filled with guilt. Was she letting her ambition come before her marriage? she asked herself. No, what she was doing was for both of them, for their future, for their own house – their old age. It didn't matter who earned what, their wages were for the two of them and if Conor found he couldn't work eventually because of his leg, which had been her constant concern, it wouldn't matter because financially they would be secure. She had a quick wash when she'd finished packing and went downstairs to await Conor's return.

Putting the key into his front door, Conor was feeling dejected. It had been a long day, he was tired and his leg was aching. The idea of boiling water, then dragging the tin bath into the living room was the last thing he wanted to do, but he had to remove the daily grime. He hated returning to an empty house and soon he'd be doing it every day.

He opened the door and stepped into the living room. To his surprise, Jessie was sitting by the fire. 'Hello, this is a nice change,' he said as he leant over and kissed her.

She poured him a cup of tea. 'Here, drink this and

relax, then I'll get your bath ready.' She saw how weary he looked. 'Busy day?'

'Yes, we had a cargo ship to load, but it's all done now.' He sipped his tea. 'And you? How was your day?'

Jessie had told him days before that she was handing the cafe over for Nancy to run; he'd been very non-committal.

'I handed over to Nancy today. I told the men at lunchtime.'

'How did that go?'

'A lot better when I explained she'd been doing the cooking for the past two weeks! But they were all very kind and said they'd still come every day, which was a relief.'

'When will you be moving out?'

'Don't say it like that, Conor, you make it sound as if I'm leaving you.'

He grimaced. 'Well you are, in a way.'

'No, I'm not! I have a new job, is all, and I need to be on the premises, but here is my home. Here with you.'

He let out a deep sigh. 'I know, it just seems strange that you won't be here when I get home or in my bed at night. You might get to like your new world better, mixing with the toffs. I'm just an ordinary bloke working in the docks. I can never compete with them.'

Jessie rose to her feet, eyes blazing. 'How dare you even suggest that I'd get carried away like that, forgetting who I am and where we came from? How bloody dare you!' He made to intervene, but she carried on. 'What happened to the wild Irishman I married? You know, the one who was full of himself, the one who couldn't give a shit for anyone else, who indeed thought he was a cut above *everybody*. Where the hell did he go?' She stood, hands on hips, glaring at him. 'Well don't just sit there, answer me!'

Conor sat looking at his wife. Suddenly, the sides of his mouth began to twitch and he started to laugh, which infuriated Jessie.

'What's so bloody funny, then?'

He leant forward and grabbed her, pulling her onto his knee. 'Jesus, darlin', when you blow, you really go. I love it when you're angry. Those green eyes flash, and you're like a bloody tiger, so you are and I love it. It's very sexy; it makes me feel like the hunter of old and I desperately want to conquer this raging female. Here, feel this.' He took her hand and placed it on his crotch.

She felt his hardness and, looking into his eyes, saw the desire, then she, too, started to laugh. 'You're not touching me, covered in filth from the docks!'

'Then after my bath I'll show you just how great a man I feel and you'll be glad of it!'

She got to her feet and grinned at him. 'Now there's the man I used to know. I'll get the bath ready.' She flicked her skirt at him and went to the kitchen.

Later, as she lay in Conor's arms she tried to explain how she felt. 'In this life we have to grab every opportunity, like you did after your accident when you had to join the call-on. That took courage. I'm only doing the same and I'm doing it for both of us. If we can save enough for our old age between us, we can have that house we've dreamt of one day, maybe take a trip home to Ireland. I don't want to stay in the hotel, I want to be with you, but it's the price we have to pay. That's all.' She paused. 'Will you come to the opening?'

'No, darlin', you'll be busy and I'll be standing around feeling out of place. It's your night; you've worked hard for it, so go and enjoy it!'

She turned his face to hers and, looking at him, she threatened, 'There's just one more thing: don't you dare go looking at another woman while I'm not around or I'll cut off your balls!'

He grinned broadly. 'I believe you would, too.'

'That's no idle threat, Conor McGonigall, it's a bloody promise!'

He pulled her to him. 'I might say the same about your boss, the smooth Larry Forbes. If he tries to get close to you, I'll castrate him, too!'

She looked at him in astonishment. 'You are out of your mind to even consider such a thing. Mr Forbes is only interested in making money. Besides, he isn't my type, you are.'

He became serious. 'Just be careful, darlin'. You are not only bright and competent, but you are a very desirable woman. He's a man, for God's sake! He'd be crazy not to want you, especially when you're spending so much time together. Just take care to keep your relationship on a business level, is all.'

She snuggled into him. 'You've no reason to worry, I can assure you, but I take your point. Now can we get some sleep, you've worn me out.'

He chuckled. 'That good, was it?'

'Looking for compliments again, are you?' she teased.

'You know what they say, any port in a storm!' As he went to grab her she cried out. 'Alright, you were bloody marvellous, now let me go, I'm tired.'

As he snuggled up to her Conor kissed the back of her neck. 'I love you, you crazy woman. Don't ever change or then we'll really have a problem.'

As they settled down, Jessie sighed. Tomorrow she would move out of her home into the hotel. A new beginning in many ways and she knew that there would be difficulties to begin with, until she found a routine that would satisfy her work ethic that wouldn't encroach on her marriage. She knew it wasn't going to be easy, but she was determined to make it work.

Chapter Twenty

The next morning after seeing Conor on his way, Jessie made the bed, washed and dressed, made up the fire and eventually, somewhat reluctantly, picked up her suitcase and walked to the hotel. Once there she took the lift to the top floor and into her flat. The sitting room was small but comfortably furnished with a two-seater settee, a couple of armchairs, a coffee table and against one wall a fold-down table with two chairs. The bedroom had a double bed, a wardrobe and chest of drawers with a triple mirror on the top. The bathroom held a bath and toilet with a small washbasin beside it. She stood looking at it with great satisfaction, then gleefully pulled the chain. As the water flushed in the lavatory bowl, she smiled to herself. Now *this* was living! She left her case in the bedroom and took the lift back to the ground floor and went to check on the dining room.

'Good morning, Mrs McGonigall,' said one of the waitresses. 'Is there anything I can do for you?'

'No, I'm just looking to see that everything has been done. Any problems?'

'No, madam, everything is fine.'

Jessie walked round checking and not finding any fault. She then went in search of the two chambermaids. Together they inspected every bedroom. One was without a hand towel beside the small washbasin and she asked where it was.

The two girls were very apologetic as they'd forgotten it.

She looked at them with an expression of displeasure. 'This will not do, ladies. For heaven's sake it's not as if you have any clients to worry you. Don't let it happen again; there are no second chances in my book!' She walked out of the room.

'Blimey!' said one. 'We'd best not cross her again or we'll be out on our ears.'

Jessie looked at the rest of the rooms, then made her way to the kitchen.

'Everything alright with you, Chef? Any problems?'

'No, thank you, Mrs McGonigall. Here are the menus for the first week.'

She read through them and handed them back. 'Excellent! If it tastes as good as it reads, we should soon have a full dining room. Have you everything that you need for the canapés on opening night?'

'Yes, everything is at hand.'

'Then I'll leave you to get on.' Finally, she went to the bar to check on James the barman. The huge mirror behind the bar was lined with shelves full of glasses and bottles of spirit. The beer pumps were brightly polished and the ashtrays clean. Small lights beneath the shelves made everything gleam.

'The bar looks lovely, James. Congratulations!'

He looked delighted. 'Thank you, Mrs McGonigall. I must say I'm looking forward to opening night.'

She smiled. 'So am I. It should be really exciting. If everyone who has been invited comes, we should be pretty full.'

Behind the reception desk was a small office that was hers. There was a filing cabinet, shelves ready to be filled and her desk was already stocked with pens, pencils and hotel notepaper; on the wall, a phone that had lines to the kitchen and the housekeeper in the linen room. This would be her working place. She sat in her chair and looked about her. *Well, Jessie McGonigall*, she thought, *welcome to your new world!* There was a knock on the open door and Larry Forbes walked in.

'Good morning, nice to see you already working.'

She gave a quizzical look 'What else would I be doing? I've checked everywhere and so far there are no problems.'

'Have you moved in yet?'

'Yes, this morning, so for now I'm on call. Can I do something for you? I want to go over these accounts.'

'I feel as if I'm dismissed,' he said sarcastically.

'That's right. I have too much to do to waste time just chatting.'

'Then I'll let you get on. We'll talk later.'

Shortly after, Frances Gates, the receptionist, knocked on the door. 'I thought you'd like to know that today I took our first bookings, Mrs McGonigall.'

'Really?' Jessie was surprised. 'For when?'

'A few for the evening of the opening. I think they are guests who have been invited and are travelling down from London and a couple more for later dates.'

Jessie beamed. 'How marvellous! Now we are really in business.'

Frances smiled. 'I know. It makes it all feel real, doesn't it?'

'Indeed. Make sure they have bedrooms at the front if you can. Once those rooms have gone, then those at the back can be let.'

Opening day arrived. The bar was open, but the dining room was closed to the public for today's private reception. To James the barman's delight he had quite a few customers who came in for a drink out of curiosity, some from the White Star Line offices. They all seemed to be very impressed. There were business cards on the counter and some of those were taken by one or two who said they would recommend the hotel to their clients wanting overnight accommodation before sailing. James quickly sent a message to Jessie telling her this and she went to the bar and introduced herself.

The men were charmed by her as they chatted. One offered her a drink, but she refused politely. 'That's very kind of you, but I never drink on duty.'

'I'll leave one behind the bar for you,' he said, 'then you can enjoy it at your leisure.'

'How very kind of you. A gin and tonic would go down very well.'

Larry Forbes walked into the bar and Jessie introduced

him. 'Gentlemen, this is Mr Forbes, the owner. Now, if you'll excuse me. It was so nice to meet you. I hope you'll come in again and maybe try our dining room, which opens tomorrow. James, show these gentlemen the menu.' She walked away, smiling.

A little later, Larry Forbes came into Jessie's office. 'That was very smooth of you earlier in the bar. The men have booked for lunch tomorrow.'

'I hoped they would. They could become regulars, being so close, then they can spread the word and hopefully bring in their clients too. We also have some bookings for the rooms.'

He looked pleased. 'If this evening goes well, we should be off to a good start.'

'I can assure you the staff and I will do our best.'

He stood looking at her without speaking.

'What?' asked Jessie.

'I was just thinking of you before, in the cafe running around with your white apron. Just look at you now – the picture of sophistication.'

She chuckled. 'A woman is many things, Mr Forbes. Whatever life dictates is what she becomes.'

'You are an extraordinary woman!'

Laughing, she said, 'I know!'

He just shook his head. 'I'm off to take a bath and get ready for this evening. I'll see you later.'

At seven o'clock, people started arriving. Jessie, in a stunning dark-green dress, its deep neckline inserted with coffee-coloured lace, greeted them alongside Larry Forbes, in the foyer as they arrived. The waitresses served champagne and canapés. The ensemble played softly in the background, while reporters took photographs.

It was a long but fruitful evening. Several guests were invited to inspect the bedrooms and later James was busy at the bar as some of the men filtered towards it, leaving their wives to chat. Future bookings were made for the dining room and the bedrooms.

Jessie spoke to some of the ladies and introduced herself, suggesting the hotel would be ideal for them to meet and have lunch together, which was greeted with enthusiasm.

'It's nice to find a small and exclusive hotel,' one said. 'It's quieter and I love the air of elegance here.'

'I'm delighted you think so, madam. If in the future I can be of help, please be free to ask.' She walked away, feeling satisfied.

Much later, when the hotel closed and the staff had cleared away, Jessie suggested to her boss that they gather the staff together and thank them for their work. 'You look after your workforce, Mr Forbes, and they'll stay loyal, I've always found.'

'An excellent idea. Get them into the foyer and I'll talk to them.' He walked to the bar and asked James to open three bottles of champagne, and bring them and some glasses to the foyer.

The staff were thrilled to be given a glass of bubbly as they gathered. For some it was the first time they'd tasted it and they giggled as the bubbles went up their nose. Forbes spoke.

'Ladies and gentlemen, I would like to thank you for the efforts you have made to bring the hotel together for tonight's opening. Our guests were most impressed with The Grosvenor and so they should be. It's classy, tasteful and well run. We have a reputation to build and then to uphold. Let's drink to its success. The Grosvenor!'

'The Grosvenor!' was uttered by all who were gathered. Forbes went round everybody and had a few words before they all went home, tired but content.

'You'll be alright with just the night porter on duty tonight?'

'Yes, thank you, Mr Forbes. If any of the residents ring down, he can see to them, and if there's a problem, I'm upstairs.'

'I thank you, too, Jessie, for your efforts. I can't imagine anyone else in your position. I knew I'd made the right choice. I'll see you in the morning. Goodnight.'

After giving the night porter his final instructions, Jessie took the lift to the top floor. Five of the rooms had been let for the night so there would be guests for breakfast in the morning. She undressed and climbed into bed. As she lay back on the pillow, she went over tonight's event, asking herself could anything have been done any better, but she eventually settled knowing that this was not so and in the morning she would be there to say goodbye to the guests, hoping they would return often.

While Jessie was working on the opening night, Conor had gone across the road to the Builders Arms for a quiet pint. He hoped the opening had gone well. Not that he really had any doubt about it, but knowing how much it meant to his wife, he was naturally concerned. He knew, also, that she wouldn't be coming home after to tell him how things went. Indeed, he didn't really know when he'd see her again. It was a strange feeling and one that was still unsettling. He looked up as the bar door opened and saw it was Bill Brown.

Getting to his feet, he walked over to the bar. 'Let me buy you a pint, Bill.' Then the two men sat down for a chat.

'Jessie's big night tonight,' remarked Bill. 'You didn't go?'

Shaking his head, Conor explained, 'She did ask me to, but she'd be busy greeting the guests and I felt I'd have been in the way, Best she do her job without having to worry about me.'

'You know your missus, Conor. Whatever she takes on will be a success. I've never met a woman like her!'

Conor laughed. 'I know exactly what you mean, so I do. There is only one Jessie McGonigall! She's one in a million and I'm very proud of her.'

The men played darts, sank another two pints and returned home, to sleep and get ready for the morning shift.

At the Grosvenor Hotel the following morning, the overnight guests settled down to have their breakfast in one of the smaller reception rooms, before leaving. Jessie went round the tables asking if everything was to their satisfaction and they were all delighted with the service, the food and the bedrooms. Several said they would book in again whenever they had to come to the town and would recommend it to their friends. They tipped the staff generously and went on their way. She breathed a sigh of relief as they left. Then she went to check on the main dining room to make sure it would be cleared and ready for the normal lunchtime clients. Some bookings had already been taken and she hoped to have others from the passing trade and the local offices.

As she, eventually, sat in her office, she thought about her husband. It had seemed very strange sleeping alone last night. She had longed to share her success with Conor, to tell him what had happened, to snuggle up to him, to feel his arms around her. It had felt strange without him, but this would be her life now, snatching time to be together, and she knew that was not the route to a happy marriage. Once she'd become organised, she would make sure they spent quality time together. He needed to know that he was still the most important thing in her life, but she had to work. It was for their future, the only real chance to save enough money to make her dream come true. She just hoped that he would understand.

Chapter Twenty-One

The local paper gave the opening of the hotel a double-page spread with a great write-up and several pictures. Dave Jennings sat in his local, reading the paper. He saw a picture of Jessie standing with her boss, greeting the guests and, knowing who she was, he scanned the pictures showing the people gathered, looking for Conor and was surprised not to see him. *Maybe he wasn't there*, he thought, then spitefully decided it was probably because it was too classy a do for a common stevedore to be present. It wouldn't do for the manageress's husband to lower the tone of the evening.

He continued reading. They certainly had all the VIPs from the town in attendance. The McGonigall family were moving up in the world – well Conor's wife was. He gave a sly smirk. Well McGonigall wouldn't like that. He knew the Irishman of old. He liked being in charge. Head of the workforce – head of the house. No doubt his wife was earning good money, probably more than Conor. That certainly would dent the man's pride.

Well, serves the bugger right! It was through him he was still working as a delivery man for the builder when he should be in the docks, where he belonged. Where he knew what he was doing. Where he earned respect for his position, not like now at everyone's beck and call. He was no more than a delivery boy and earning less money. He hated it and blamed Conor for his loss of face. How he would love to meet him now, just to be able to remark about his wife's success – leaving him behind.

He sat drinking for a further hour until he was more than a little drunk and even more belligerent. He eventually got to his feet and made for the door. Once outside, he walked to Union Street and the Builders Arms.

Conor and Bill were sat having a pint and a chat after a game of darts, when the door opened and Jennings entered somewhat unsteady on his feet. Both men looked up.

'Oh no!' Bill muttered. Conor didn't speak.

Jennings ordered a pint, took a drink and turned to the two men with a smirk.

'Saw your wife's picture in the paper,' he said. 'She's going up in the world, isn't she?'

Conor didn't answer.

'Yes, there she was surrounded by all the important people in the town, dressed to the nines, doing her stuff, mixing with the toffs like she belonged. I take my hat off to her. Before long she'll leave you behind if you're not careful!'

Conor continued to ignore him, but the air was full of menace and the other locals became silent and watched.

Jennings didn't like being ignored. He'd come in to try and upset his sworn enemy. He staggered over and stood in front of the two men. 'Lost your tongue, McGonigall? That's not like you. As I recall you were always *full* of it!'

'What do you want, Jennings? You've obviously come in here with a purpose, so get on with it, then get out!'

'I was just curious, that's all, wondering how you felt, no longer being the man of the house, your wife now earning more than you. You see, pretty soon she'll realise she can do better than a stevedore. Mixing with class as she is, she'll soon realise the difference. She's a beautiful woman, after all. Someone with money will come along and before you know it—'

Conor stood up and punched him on the jaw, sending him flying across the floor on his back. Leaning over Jennings, Conor quietly said, so no one else could hear, 'I gave you a beating once before. Now, I'm warning you, stay away from me or I'll have to sort you out, then you won't be fit enough to work anywhere!'

Bill and the landlord hauled Conor to his feet. Then someone threw a jug of water over his adversary, bringing him to his senses. The landlord pulled Jennings up off the floor, then after making sure he wasn't seriously hurt, pushed him outside into the street.

'You're barred! You come here again, I'll call the police. Now shove off and take yourself elsewhere.' He watched as the man staggered away.

When the landlord returned, Conor apologised to him. 'Sorry about that, but I had to stop him.'

'He's a nasty piece of work, Conor. I'd watch my back in future, if I were you.'

Conor returned to his seat. Bill looked at him and

frowned. 'Jennings will never forgive you for losing him his job and getting him blacklisted from the docks, you know that, don't you?'

'Aye, I do. One day, somewhere at some time, it will be settled once and for all.'

'That's what worries me, Conor! I don't want to see you end up behind bars.'

With a rueful smile, Conor said, 'That's not something I have in mind either. Come on, let's have a drink and forget about it.'

But as his friend stood at the bar waiting for their drinks, Bill was worried. He liked his neighbour, admired him even, but he also knew that Conor would only be pushed so far and, when raised, his Irish temper was fearsome.

It was three days after the opening that Jessie decided she could safely take the night off. The hotel was running smoothly, the staff now organised and working well. There were only three residents staying and the night porter could manage if he was required, so she decided to go home and spend some time with her husband. On the way home, she bought some fish and chips and put them in the oven to warm when she discovered the house was empty. Sitting with a cup of tea, she sat in front of the fire and relaxed. Home! How she'd missed it. Not during the day, she'd been too busy then, but it was at night when she retired to her rooms that she missed being here with Conor. Never had she felt so alone and if *she* felt that way, how was he coping? She looked at the clock; it was eight-thirty. Perhaps Conor had popped across the road to the Builders for a drink? Then she heard the key in the door and got to her feet. As Conor stepped inside, she rushed to him and threw her arms round his neck.

'Well, here's a desperate woman if ever I saw one,' he said.

She held his face in her hands and kissed him. 'Hello.'

'Would you mind telling me who you are? The face is familiar, but . . .'

She gazed at him, expecting to see a teasing smile and a twinkle in his eye, but there was neither.

'Conor?'

'Forgive me, but I'm so used to being alone that I'm taken by surprise, that's all.' He sniffed the air. 'Is that fish and chips I can smell?'

'Yes, I bought some on the way home. I'll dish them up now.'

Taking them out of the oven she unwrapped the paper, then portioned the food onto the plates, cut two slices of bread and spread it with butter. 'Sit and eat,' she said.

Removing his jacket, he picked up his knife and fork. 'There was a time when *you* used to cook for me, but that's been a while.'

Jessie felt utterly deflated. She'd been so looking forward to spending a night at home and now her husband was behaving like a spoilt child.

'Don't start, Conor! You know why I can't be here all the time. I've been looking forward to coming home. Don't spoil it, please.'

'Well, it took you long enough, that's for sure! It's been three days since you opened. You were obviously in no great rush!'

Her back stiffened and her nostrils flared. 'So that's how it's going to be, is it? You punishing me for not being here looking after your every need? Well, it doesn't wash with me, you ungrateful bastard! I'm working my legs off to give us a future, putting in long hours to organise the staff and the steady running of the hotel, but do I see a minute's show of interest in my work or a sign of gratitude? Do I hell! You knew we'd have to make sacrifices, the main one being I'd not be at home all the time. I'd *really* looked forward to tonight, spending time with my hard-working husband, thinking our time would be precious and enjoyable.' She got to her feet suddenly, sending her chair flying. 'Well, fuck you, Conor McGonigall!' She swept her plate off the table, sending it across the room and, picking up her coat, she stormed out of the house, slamming the door behind her.

Conor took another mouthful of food, but then he cast aside his knife and fork, and with a deep sigh, bowed his head and banged the table with his fist. *What a bloody great fool I am*, he thought, *letting my resentment get in the way*. He was proud of Jessie, but deep inside his masculine pride resented her rise in status – only because he couldn't match it. He knew to her it didn't matter one bit, but it did to him. He ran his fingers through his hair as he pondered on the situation. *Jessie was thrilled to be home and I end up behaving like an eejit. No wonder she blew her top.* He took out a cigarette and lit it. *God! But isn't she magnificent when she's angry.* He gave a rueful smile. *How the devil am I going to put this right?* he wondered.

* * *

While Conor was regretting his behaviour, Jessie was still furious. How dare he treat her that way? She was still filled with fury as she reached the hotel. The bar was still open and she walked in, sat on a stool at the end of the counter and asked James for a gin and tonic.

He placed the glass before her. 'Everything alright, Mrs McGonigall?'

Her mind cleared quickly, and she smiled. 'Yes, James, everything is fine.' She didn't believe in airing her troubles to all and sundry, especially not your staff. Soon, she finished her drink and left the bar, heading towards the lift.

'I thought you were off tonight, madam,' the night porter called.

'My plans changed so I'll be upstairs. Goodnight.' She entered the lift, pressed the button and entered her flat.

Undressing, she ran a bath and soaked in the hot water, letting her body relax. Conor could have moved in with her and enjoyed this luxury, she thought, but no. Not him! It would have meant a fall from grace in his mind, sharing accommodation she'd earned with her new position and not his. Well, let him carry on living alone because it would be a very long time before she again walked over the doorstep of the house they called home.

The following evening, Conor filled the tin bath and cleaned off the grime of the day, then changed into his good suit. He picked up a huge bunch of flowers he'd bought at the local florist's and made his way to the Grosvenor Hotel. He stood outside smoking a cigarette, trying to calm himself, not knowing what kind of reception he'd receive from his wife after her outburst. Jessie's temper was legendary when raised and he wondered if she'd calmed down by now. Throwing his butt end down, he stepped on it, putting it out, and walked into the foyer. He could see people at the bar and others walking into the dining room, but there was no sign of Jessie. He walked up to the reception desk.

'Good evening, sir,' said Frances Gates. 'Can I help you?'

'Is Mrs McGonigall available?'

'I'll find out for you. Who shall I say is asking for her?'

'Her husband.'

The receptionist's expression didn't change. 'I won't be a moment, sir,' she said and disappeared into the office behind the counter, pulling the door closed behind her.

'There's a gentleman at reception asking for you, madam.'

Jessie looked up from her books. 'Did he say who he was?'

'It's your husband, Mrs McGonigall.'

Jessie looked surprised and hesitated for a moment. 'You'd better bring him in here, Frances.'

Returning to the desk, Frances looked at Conor. 'Come this way, sir.' She lifted the flap at the end of the counter to let him through and led him to the office door, opened it and closed it behind him once he'd entered.

Jessie looked at her husband, noted his suit and the flowers, but didn't smile. 'You wanted to see me?' She looked coldly at him, waiting for his reply.

'I've come to apologise for my behaviour last night. You didn't deserve that and I'm really sorry.'

'No, I didn't deserve to be treated like that, you're right. You think an apology and a bunch of flowers is all it takes to put matters right?'

'Probably not, but it is a beginning, isn't it? What do you want me to do, get down on my knees and beg?'

She gave a derisory laugh. 'That'd be a first!'

He pointed to a chair beside her desk. 'May I sit down?'

She nodded. 'I suppose so.'

'Look, Jessie, nothing I can say will remove the scene last night, but I'm truly sorry. I let my pride get in the way. It's not that I'm not proud of your achievements, I am, and you deserve to get on. But this living separately is awful. I miss you being there. It's not the cooking for me, that's not it at all. I just feel we're no longer married; it's like we've parted company. I hate it!'

'You could have moved in here with me. I asked you to.'

'Yes, you did, but can you imagine how I would feel coming in here in my working clothes covered in dirt. That's not good for your image and I would feel I was letting you down.'

'You could always come in the back entrance.' She saw the anger in his eyes at her suggestion. 'But that wouldn't suit *your* image, would it?'

'If I'm honest, I couldn't do it!' He tried to explain. 'You have your position to live up to and so do I. In the docks, I'm looked up to because of my work and my ability. I worked hard for that, coming in the back way of the hotel in my working clothes would strip me of my dignity. Is that so wrong?'

She smiled softly, understanding his point of view and, knowing him as she did, she knew it would be impossible for him. 'I understand, Conor.'

He looked relieved. 'I'm happy that you do.'

'But you, too, must understand, it isn't easy for me to slip away from the hotel whenever I feel like it. Once we are up and running for a while, it will be easier; at the moment it's not. Do you think I don't miss you? When I get into bed at night, I feel so alone and I long for you to be beside me, but you chose to stay in the house. So, there you are, that's how it is.'

'Ah, Jessie darlin', what a situation. It's taking some getting used to, I can tell you, and I'm finding it real hard. I realise it isn't easy for you too.' He leant forward, took her hand and kissed it. 'I didn't mean to upset you, I'm sorry for that.'

'Best we put it behind us, then.'

He breathed a sigh of relief. 'Do you mind if I smoke?'

'No, carry on.' She pushed an ashtray over to him. 'Do you fancy a beer?'

'To be honest, I could murder one.'

Jessie went to the door. 'Frances, will you ask James for a pint of bitter and a gin and tonic please. I'll pay him later.' She came back and sat down.

'So, tell me, how are the neighbours and the two Williams boys? I've missed all the gossip being here.'

They sat chatting and drinking together in the privacy of the office, but Conor didn't tell her of his run-in with Jennings – that, she didn't need to know. Eventually, he rose from his chair. 'I'd best be off, then. Am I forgiven, Jessie?'

Jessie got up and walked over to him. Putting her arms around him, she said, 'Yes, you are, but just don't push your luck! I'll try and get home in a couple of days' time, I promise.'

He drew her into his arms and kissed her. 'Don't leave it too long or else everything will stop working and that would be a terrible sin!'

She opened the office door. 'That's most unlikely!'

He leant forward and whispered in her ear. 'I love you, you crazy woman. I swear too long away from me, I'm liable to come in here and drag you out by the hair. That's a promise, so it is!'

'Away with you now. I'll see you soon.'

When she was alone, Jessie went over their conversation. She understood Conor so well, but he had to learn to accept the situation or their marriage was in deep trouble. Her next problem would be Christmas, which was only three weeks away. Last year, their neighbours joined them. It was on Boxing Day she'd found poor old Iris cold in her chair. This year there was a Christmas dinner here at the hotel and the bookings were good. No way could she go home until the evening. How would Conor react to that?

The next morning, Jessie left the hotel, walked to Union Street and knocked on Daisy Brown's door. The look of surprise on her neighbour's face when she opened the door made Jessie laugh.

'Yes, it's me. Can I come in?'

'Of course, come on. I'll make a pot of tea. Oh, Jessie, it's so good to see you.'

'I've missed you too,' she answered as she sat down, 'but I have a problem and I'm wondering if you can do me a favour?'

'Of course, if it's possible, you know I will.'

Jessie explained the Christmas dilemma and her concerns, without telling her about the row she'd had with her husband.

'That's no problem,' Daisy exclaimed. 'I was going to ask you and Conor to spend this Christmas with us anyway. He can come and have dinner with us and you can come when you can get away. I'll keep a plate of food ready for you and we can warm it in the oven.' She pulled a face. 'God, I hope we don't find anyone dead again!'

The two women sat chatting for a while until Jessie had to go.

'Thanks, Daisy. If you don't mind, I'd like to tell Conor about the arrangements myself.'

'That's fine. I'll see you soon.' The two women hugged each other, and Jessie left.

She had planned how she was going to tell her husband and she was sure he'd be amenable.

Chapter Twenty-Two

It was two nights after Conor's visit and the hotel had settled for the night. The dining room was closed and there was just another hour for the bar to be open when Jessie put on her coat. She had a word with the night porter, then she left and made her way to Union Street. As she expected, the house was in darkness, so she let herself in quietly and crept up the stairs.

The bedroom door was ajar and she pushed it open. Conor was fast asleep, lying on his side, one arm across the empty pillow next to him. Jessie stood and looked at her husband. God how she loved this wild Irishman and how much she'd missed him.

Slowly, she undressed, then she lifted the sheet and climbed into bed, putting her head across his arm and moving her naked body close to his. She stroked his face, then she kissed him gently, moving her mouth over his. He stirred.

'Jessie, is that you?' he muttered, half-asleep.

She answered quietly in his ear. 'If you were expecting someone else then, Conor, you are in real trouble!'

He opened his eyes. She put one leg over his.

'Jessie! I thought I was dreaming.'

She took his hand and placed it on her breast. 'Is this real enough for you?'

He caressed her gently. 'I need convincing,' he said as he moved his hand to her thighs, then parted her legs. 'Oh my, welcome home, darlin'.'

Their lovemaking was slow and languid, neither wanting to rush the intimacy they'd had to do without. They explored each other's bodies, knowing of old where to give the other pleasure. It was a delicious coupling and eventually they lay together, satisfied and happy.

'Oh, sweet Jesus! I'd forgotten just how good that could be,' Conor said as he kissed his wife and held her close.

Jessie let out a sigh of contentment. 'I've missed it too. I've longed to be in your arms and loved. I promise to come home as often as I can. Soon it will be easier, you'll see.'

'Can you stay the night?' he asked.

'Yes, but I'll have to leave early in the morning.'

'Then let's get some sleep and then after a while, *I'll* wake *you*.'

Laughing, she said, 'You're insatiable!'

'No, darlin', just making up for lost time.' He pulled the sheet over them both and snuggled into her. 'Get some sleep, you're going to need it.'

It was six in the morning when Jessie returned to the hotel. She went to her rooms and took a quick bath, dressed, went to the kitchen and made some toast and coffee, which she took to her office. Pouring the coffee, she sat back in the chair, smiling softly as she thought about last night. How good it had been to be with Conor, the closeness, the sex. The sleeping next to him, able to feel his body close to hers. How she had missed it! Last night had healed the cross words they'd exchanged; once again they were a couple. Now she felt content.

There was a bounce in Conor's steps as he walked to the docks. He was a happy man after last night in the arms of his wife. No longer did he feel they were drifting apart. Jessie felt it too, he knew that. He also realised that she was doing her best and he was just feeling aggrieved – but no longer. Their marriage was as solid as ever and now he knew she'd come to him whenever she could and that made him happy.

His change of mood was soon noticed by the men working with him.

'You come into a fortune or what?' asked one.

'What do you mean?'

'Well, you're full of piss and vinegar this morning, what's changed?'

'The love of a good woman, that's what. You should try it, my friend, then you wouldn't be such a miserable old git!'

The others laughed. And so the day began.

It was a long day. The vessel that they were working on was shipping out at midnight and the cargo had to be loaded. The men worked on overtime to achieve this until, eventually, the job was finished.

'Well done, you men,' said Conor. 'You earned your overtime, now away to your families. I'll just finish up here. See you in the morning – and don't be late!'

Conor did a final check and when he was satisfied, climbed out of the hold, down the gangway and sat on a bollard to have a quiet cigarette. He gazed out over the docks, looking at the vessels tied up, waiting to sail eventually. It was quiet now apart from one or two members of the crew, making their way to the nearest pub for a few drinks with their mates before sailing.

The December night was cold, but the sky was clear and the moon shone on the water. Conor was at peace with the world. He loved his job, he had a wife he adored, never had a man been more fortunate he mused as he sat there, lost in his thoughts.

He thought back to the day he first walked into the workman's cafe where Jessie was, rushing around, joshing with her customers. How sparky she was as she took his first order. There had been something about her from the first minute he saw her. The way she tilted her head, tossed her hair, the green eyes that could twinkle with amusement and flash when angered. He loved her attitude, her determination. Look at her now! No longer serving great food that she'd cooked, dressed with a long white apron, but a sophisticated woman, manageress of a fine hotel. Mixing with the toffs as if she were born to do so. What a woman!

A sudden noise made him turn. Silhouetted against the sky was a figure, holding something aloft. He automatically ducked as the man was about to strike, but he was hit on the side of the head. The force of the blow sent him flying across the dock. Although dazed, he recognised the figure.

'Jennings!' Conor gasped.

Jennings lifted his arm to aim another blow, but Conor rolled out of the way, shook his head trying to clear his mind and got to his feet. His opponent was unbalanced, having missed his target, which allowed Conor to push him. The man staggered but regained his balance. He held a large spade ready to strike.

'I'm going to kill you, you bastard! You've ruined my life.'

Conor moved and the spade caught his shoulder, making him cry out with pain. But he aimed a punch at Jennings, who staggered a few feet away. The men struggled as Conor tried to hold on to the spade and take it away from the man intent on ending his life.

As they grappled, they were closer to the edge of the dock, but were unaware of the danger, engrossed in this desperate battle. Conor was now weakened by his injured shoulder and Jennings fought like a madman, fuelled with the thought that at last he was going to make this man pay.

Conor managed to twist the handle of the spade, making Jennings lose his hold, then Conor swung it at Jennings' head. The man staggered backwards but, as he did so, he grabbed the front of Conor's jacket and held on. The two of them toppled over the edge of the dock into the water, Conor bumping his head on the concrete as he fell.

Chapter Twenty-Three

The next morning in the docks, the men stood waiting for Conor to show. The fact that he was late was most unusual as normally he would be stood waiting for them.

Bill Brown was worried. Had he been taken ill? 'I'll go home and see if he's there,' he said.

'Take my bike,' suggested one, 'it'll be quicker.'

Bill set off, peddling furiously until he arrived at Conor's front door. He banged loudly on it, but there was no answer. He peered through the window, but the room was empty. He walked around the back but couldn't see anyone. He quickly went and asked his wife if she'd seen Conor, but she hadn't. He then went across the road to the pub and asked the landlord to ring the Grosvenor Hotel and ask for Jessie. When she came to the phone he took the receiver.

'Jessie, it's Bill. Conor hasn't shown up for work. Is he with you?'

Jessie's heart missed a beat. 'No, Bill. I stayed with him the night before last, but I've not seen him since. Please let me know when you find him.' He promised he would.

When he returned and saw that his friend was still missing, he called the office from a phone box and the man there said he'd send someone to take his place. Bill then went to the police on the gate and told them what had happened and how concerned he was. He explained that they'd worked late the previous night and had left Conor to finish checking up.

Conor was well known in the docks and the man on duty knew that this was, indeed, unusual.

'I'll report it,' he told Bill. 'I'll get some men to search the area in case he's had an accident. At night in the dark with so much machinery about it can be hazardous.'

The men were on a short shift that morning and when it was over, they joined the police searching the docks.

It was late in the afternoon when there was a cry from one of the policemen from the far end and the others ran along the dockside. There in the water, caught up in a couple of fenders, were two bodies. It took a while before they could be hauled out of the water onto solid ground. There was no doubt about their identity, despite them being bloated from their time in the water.

Conor's men were stunned. This was the last thing they expected. Bill Brown's face drained of colour as he gazed upon his old friend and tears filled his eyes. This was no way such a vibrant man should meet his end. He had no doubt that Jennings had been the cause of this tragedy and he cursed the man under his breath. But how was he going to tell Jessie?

* * *

In time, a van arrived to take the bodies to the morgue to be examined. The dockers and policemen stood around talking quietly. A police sergeant approached Bill.

'Have you any idea what could have happened here?'

Bill told him about the bad feeling between the two men and the reason behind it.

'You'd best come down to the station tomorrow and make a statement,' he said.

Bill said he would. 'But now I've got to go and give the bad news to Jessie, his wife, and I'm not sure how I'm going to do that.'

The sergeant looked at him. 'Ah yes, Jessie McGonigall. Well, she's a strong woman and she'll need to be now. Good luck, my friend. Do you want one of my men to come with you?'

'No, thank you. I think it best if I go alone. A uniformed policeman is the last thing she'll want to see. She and Conor are our neighbours so we know each other.'

'Then you are the best man for the job.' He patted Bill on the shoulder.

Bill made his way slowly to the hotel trying to find the words to break the news, but his heart was heavy and he couldn't think. Apart from which, *he* was still shocked from the discovery of his friend's demise. He felt the tears brim in his eyes as he walked and tried to pull himself together. He had to be strong for Jessie now; his own grieving could come later.

Taking a deep breath, he walked into the hotel and up to the reception desk. Jessie was behind it, talking to the receptionist. She took one look at Bill's face, opened the flap to the counter and ushered him into her office, closing the door. She tensed, her whole body rigid as she leant against the door and waited.

Bill took both of her hands in his. 'Jessie, love, I have some very bad news.'

She let out a cry of anguish and gripped his hands tighter. 'It's Conor, isn't it?'

'I'm afraid so. Conor is dead, Jessie.'

She collapsed in his arms, sobbing and crying out Conor's name.

Bill just held her tightly until she'd stopped the wracking sobs and was now crying quietly. He led her to a chair and sat her down, kneeling beside her until she was able to talk.

'What happened, Bill?'

'We don't yet know, love, but Conor's body was found in the water at the dockside with another man, Jennings.'

'I've heard about Jennings in the past. A nasty piece of work by all accounts. But why was he there?'

Bill then told her the whole story and of the animosity between them. 'We don't know what happened last night, Jessie. We can only guess that Jennings went looking for Conor and they had a fight, but that's only supposition at this point.'

'Where is Conor now?'

'His body was taken to the morgue where the coroner will examine him to try and find the cause of his death.'

'When can I see him?'

'They'll let you know. I'll come with you, if you like.'

She looked at him gratefully through tear-filled eyes. 'Thanks, Bill, I would like that.'

'Let me get you a brandy, love. You've had such a shock.'

'So have you; we'll both have one. Ask the receptionist, will you?'

Bill closed the door behind him and softly explained to Frances Gates what had happened, but asked her to keep it to herself for now, then he asked for the drinks.

'Of course, sir. I'm so very sorry, what dreadful news. I won't be long.'

When he returned to the office, Jessie was sat in her chair smoking and staring into space. 'Come and sit down, Bill. It was only two nights ago that I was at home with Conor. We spent the night together. We were so happy, Bill, at least I'll have that to remember.' Then the tears trickled slowly down her cheeks. She shook her head. 'I can't believe I won't see him, hold him ever again. I can't bear it!' Putting her hands to her face, she started sobbing.

Bill went over to her and held her, fighting back his own tears unsuccessfully.

There was a tap on the door, and Bill went and took the tray of drinks from the receptionist, with a nod of thanks. Then he handed one to Jessie.

'Here love, sip this.' As she took it he held his up. 'To Conor!'

'To Conor,' she whispered, 'the love of my life!' She sipped her drink. 'What am I going to do without him?'

Bill groped for the right words. 'You have to be brave, love. Conor was so proud of you, of your determination, your strength. You have to be strong for him now. Life has to go on, Jessie. You have to carry on, too. It won't be easy, you know that, but you don't have a choice.'

At that moment there was a tap on the door.

'Go and see who that is for me, Bill.'

Frances stood outside and beckoned him. He shut the door behind him. Standing there was Larry Forbes.

'I'm the owner and I've called to see Mrs McGonigall, but Mrs Gates has just explained what's happened.'

She looked at Bill. 'I'm sorry, sir, but I had to explain.'

'It's alright, I understand.' He looked at Forbes. 'You'd best come in, then, but as you can imagine, Mrs McGonigall is still in shock.'

'Of course. She needs to go home; this is no place for her at this moment.'

Bill opened the door and the two men entered. 'Jessie, Mr Forbes wants to see you.'

Forbes walked over to her. 'I am so sorry for your loss, Jessie. I can't begin to know how you feel, but I think you should go home and be with your friends. We can manage; after all, you've trained your staff well. Is there anything I can do?'

She looked at him and saw that he was being sincere. 'Thank you, but there isn't anything you can do. We have to wait for things to take their course, and at the moment I honestly can't hold two thoughts together!'

'Of course you can't. I suggest you go to your rooms, collect anything you need. I'm sure your friend here will help you, then go home. Call me when you know what's happening and I'm here if you need anything, anything at all.'

Jessie rose to her feet 'Thank you for your understanding. I'll let you know what's going on. Come on, Bill, you can help me pack a few things.'

He followed her to the lift and when they entered her

rooms, he looked around. 'My word, Jessie, this isn't like Union Street, is it?'

She smiled when she saw the expression of awe on his face. 'No, Bill. Here, take a look,' and she showed him the bathroom with the inside toilet and bath, flushing the toilet with a grin. 'This is living, Bill!'

Shaking his head, he said, 'If my Daisy could only see this! Wait until I tell her.'

Jessie pulled out a small suitcase and put some clothes and toiletries in it, shut it up and, turning to her friend, said, 'Let's go home.'

Picking up her case, he said, 'Fine, but first we'll go to mine and get something to eat.' He saw her about to argue. 'Now you listen to me, my girl. You need to keep up your strength for the days ahead. Daisy and me will look after you. You won't have to face anything alone. Understand?'

She hugged him. 'Thanks, Bill, I'll never forget your kindness.'

'Conor was my mate and I discovered it was him that got me the job on the gang. We look after each other.' He looked at her. 'Ready?'

'Ready.'

As they walked down Union Street, Jessie was relieved to see the street was empty; she couldn't have coped with any questions at this moment, knowing how quickly news spread. Bill opened the door and they stepped into the living room. He glanced at his wife, who just nodded to him, letting him know that she'd heard about Conor. She walked to Jessie and embraced her.

'Come and sit down by the fire, you're frozen. I've made some soup. We'll have a bowl soon to warm us up.' She sat beside Jessie. 'I can't tell you how sorry I am about Conor. But you don't have to pretend with us, love. You want a good cry, then have one.'

'I still can't believe it, Daisy. Two nights ago, I was curled up in bed with him at home.'

'I can't believe it either. Now, when you've thawed out, we'll sit at the table and eat some soup. It'll do us all good; we're all suffering from shock.'

After their meal, Bill took the keys to Jessie's place and lit the fire so the house would be warm when she went there later. While he was doing so, the two women curled up together on the small settee, Daisy with her arms around her friend, trying to bring her a modicum of comfort. Eventually, Jessie took her leave.

'Do you want one of us to come with you, Jessie?' asked Daisy.

'No, thanks, love, I need to do this alone.'

She hugged them both goodnight, walked next door and put her key into the lock. Taking a deep breath, she stepped into her living room. The fire was blazing away and the room was warm. Bill had brought her case in with him, closed the curtains and left the light on so it was cosy and welcoming. Jessie looked around the room. On the mantelpiece, among a few small ornaments, was a picture of her and Conor taken last summer on a Sunday when they'd taken the train to Bournemouth for the day. She stared at his smiling face and kissed the picture. Clasping it to her chest, she went into the kitchen. Hanging up behind the door was one of his working jackets. She took it down and buried her head into the material and breathed in the essence of the man.

There was the smell of the docks buried in the cloth. The dust, the dirt, the tang of oil, the scent of a man's sweat as he worked. Her man's sweat. She put it on and, walking back into the living room, sat in a chair by the fire. Conor's chair. She pulled the jacket around her, turning up the collar and, clasping the photo, sat staring into the flames of the fire.

Chapter Twenty-Four

Jessie woke with a start. The fire was almost out, the room had chilled and she'd been asleep for several hours. Slowly she got to her feet and threw a small log on the fire and when it caught, she added some lumps of coal. She placed the picture back on the mantelpiece and the kettle on the top of the stove to make some tea. The clock on the mantelpiece said four-thirty. She stretched her aching limbs, moved her head from side to side as her neck had a crick in it from sleeping awkwardly in the chair. Then she removed the jacket, hanging it back in its place, made a pot of tea, placed a shawl round her shoulders, sat down, lit a cigarette and wondered what the hell was she going to do now.

There would be a funeral to arrange once the coroner released the body. Her stomach tightened when she thought of that. The body was her husband, although she didn't believe he still inhabited it. No, now it was a carcass. Her Conor's spirit was free to roam wherever it had been sent.

There were hymns to choose. *'Fight the Good Fight' would have been appropriate*, she thought bitterly.

As she was trying to plan, she thought of Larry Forbes. How kind he was and his kindness was genuine, she could tell. 'Well, thank God I have a job; I won't have to worry about money,' she muttered to herself. Then she laughed. 'Christ, Jessie, you're talking to yourself now. Well maybe that's what you do when you're alone!'

Finishing her tea, she washed up the cup and teapot, then walked wearily upstairs to the bedroom. Here she undressed and, climbing into bed, gazed at the empty place beside her. Taking Conor's pillow, she buried her head in it for a moment, then; clutching it to her, fell asleep.

When Jessie woke later that morning, for a moment she was disorientated, then the realisation crept in. She lay still, looking at the ceiling. So this hadn't been a bad dream after all. Conor was dead! Throwing back the covers, she hurriedly dressed in warm clothes, then walked over to the window and looked out. It was cold and crisp. She could see folk going about their business. In one or two windows of the houses across the street were Christmas trees all decorated, ready for the holiday. Looking across at the pub, she thought of last Christmas Day when she, Conor, Daisy and Bill had been in the pub and old Ivy had staggered out drunk . . . then how later the next day, she'd discovered the old lady dead in her chair. Yesterday *she* became a widow! 'Merry bloody Christmas!' she cried and walked downstairs.

Picking up a poker, Jessie raked the ashes and disposed of them, then laid a fire. She blew into her hands to warm them it was so cold, before putting a lit match to the paper. While it was catching, she swilled her face in cold water to freshen up, filled the kettle and stood it on the top of the stove to boil once the fire had warmed it. At that moment there was a knock on the door.

'Morning, Jessie,' said Daisy, and she stepped inside with a fresh pot of tea and a jug of milk. 'I thought you could do with one of these,' she said as she went to the cupboard for two cups. 'Sit down, love. This'll warm us until the fire catches. 'How are you, or is that a stupid question?'

Jessie gazed at her friend. 'To be honest, Daisy, I've no idea. I didn't know where I was when I woke, then it hit me. I still can't believe it's happened, I don't want to believe it's happened, but I have to face up to it and I just don't know what to do.'

'There's nothing you can do, love, until the coroner releases the body. Then there will be the funeral. After that, the best thing you can do is work! Sitting around is not the answer. You need to keep busy, so, in the meantime, let's clean the house. You will have to sort Conor's clothes, for a start. I'll come and help you with it all, Jessie. We'll do it together. When we've had a cup of tea, we'll go to my place for a bite of breakfast and we'll start at the top of the house and work down.'

Jessie gazed at her friend and, with a slow smile, she said, 'What happened to that quiet little thing that moved in next door who wouldn't say boo to a goose?'

'She met Jessie McGonigall, who stood up for her and encouraged her to start her own business. I owe you, Jessie, and now I have the chance to return the favour. Drink up, we have lots to do!'

At lunchtime, the two of them sat down for a rest. The kettle had boiled and it was Jessie who made the tea. The two women sat drinking the welcome brew.

'I don't know about you, Daisy, but I'm knackered!'

'Me too, but that's healthy. We'll go home after this, have a sandwich and do downstairs. Then we'll sort out the clothes.' She knew this would be the hardest task of the day, but felt it would be best for her friend to do it and get it done and out of the way. And that's what they did.

After the downstairs had been scrubbed and cleaned to within an inch of its life, the women started on the clothes. It didn't take long. The underwear and working clothes were put in a bag to throw away. Conor's one good suit was folded with a few decent shirts and wrapped in brown paper to take to the Salvation Army, at Daisy's suggestion.

'Some poor chap would be delighted to have these to wear. It would be a pity to throw it all away. I'm sure Conor wouldn't mind – what do you think?'

Jessie agreed, remembering when they were short of money in the early days. But she insisted on keeping his working jacket hanging in the kitchen. Daisy didn't argue. But she took all the bags to her house for Bill to see to, so that Jessie wouldn't have to look at them knowing their contents.

* * *

During the following days while Jessie was waiting for the coroner's report, Daisy insisted they wrap up and go for a walk. Sometimes they went to a cinema, where they could watch the silent film and shut out their thoughts, or they went shopping for food. They bought some material for a dress to be made for a customer of Daisy's in the new year and some for a gown for Jessie. She had resisted this at first, but Daisy insisted.

'You have to return to work. There will be no widow's weeds there, Jessie. It's a business and you have to look the part. Besides, it's my gift to you for Christmas.'

Christmas was a week away and Jessie knew the hotel would be busy. She'd heard that the coroner's report wouldn't be until after the holiday and she decided to go back to work instead of waiting around with time on her hands. The next morning, she walked into the hotel with a small suitcase and walked up to the front desk.

Frances Gates looked at her in surprise. 'Mrs McGonigall, how good to see you. I am so very sorry for your loss.'

'Thank you, Frances, but I'm back to work until I know when I can arrange the funeral. So, what's the latest and are we booked up for Christmas?'

They moved into her office and went through the bookings, Jessie catching up on the days she had missed. When she had a moment, she rang Larry Forbes.

'Mr Forbes, it's Jessie McGonigall. Just to let you know I'm back at work.'

'I'm coming right over,' he said. She went to argue, but he'd hung up the telephone. Ten minutes later he walked into the hotel and to her office.

Jessie looked up as her boss walked in. 'Good morning.'

'Good morning to you. I didn't expect you back so soon. Not that it isn't good to see you here. How are things?'

'I can't do anything until after Christmas, it appears, so I might as well work rather than sit around feeling sorry for myself.'

He gave an enigmatic smile. 'No, that's not your style. Well, no doubt you've caught up with what's going on. The dining room is fully booked for our Christmas special. Have you seen the menu?'

'I have and it's excellent. The chef has worked hard to produce it. I haven't yet had time to go to the kitchen and see him. I see that most of the rooms are booked.' She looked up and grinned broadly. 'I'm so pleased for you, Mr Forbes. After all, this was a *mighty* investment on your part.'

He looked pleased. 'Mrs McGonigall, would you give me the greatest pleasure and dine with me here at lunchtime to celebrate?'

She was completely taken aback at his suggestion. 'But I've still got some catching up to do.'

'Not really. Everything has been running like clockwork. I've been here off and on most days. I can assure you, having lunch won't cause any disruptions to the business. Besides, it will do you good to relax. I won't take no for an answer. I'll book a table for one o'clock and I'll be back then.'

Before she could answer, he'd left.

* * *

The waiter took them to a table near the window and handed them the menu. The staff were all nervously on their toes with the boss and manageress dining together, which caused both the diners to smile.

'We should do this more often,' Larry said. 'It is good for the staff. It scares them to death!' He chuckled softly.

'That's so cruel of you,' she chided. Then looked up in surprise as the waiter brought over a bottle of champagne and an ice bucket.

'Well this *is* a celebration, Mrs McGonigall,' Forbes said, laughing after seeing the expression on her face.

The meal was superb and, during their time together, Larry Forbes talked business and about the hotel. 'If it's a success, and I fully expect it to be so, Jessie, I'm thinking of opening another small one. What do you think about that?'

'I think it's far too soon to contemplate such a thing,' she said without hesitation. 'You have an investment in this one to recover first. Then, maybe, but certainly not for a while. This one must become established first, surely?'

He looked at her with admiration. 'You are a fine businesswoman and, of course, you're right, but it is an idea for the future, don't you think?'

'Are you thinking of building an empire, Mr Forbes?' she asked wryly.

He started laughing. 'Would that be such a terrible thing, Mrs McGonigall?'

Shrugging, she retorted, 'Not if it paid!'

They finished the champagne and their meal, then they had a pot of coffee and a liqueur, at his insistence.

'I came to work,' Jessie argued. 'At this rate I'll not be in any state to do so.'

He studied her for a moment, then quietly said, 'After what you've been through, it won't do you any harm. You have some difficult days ahead, Jessie. I know you are a strong woman and I do admire that, but you're only human. You need to be kind to yourself, take it slowly. I don't want to lose my manageress.'

She was at a loss for words for a moment and emotion suddenly whelmed up inside her. She was fine as long as no one was kind to her – *that* she found hard to take. She swallowed and, taking a deep breath, said, 'Thank you. I'll be fine, you'll see. Tonight, I'm moving back into the hotel. I don't want to be in the house for the time being.'

'That's perfectly understandable. Do what is right for you.' He folded his napkin and placed it on the table. 'Thank you for joining me for lunch. I enjoyed your company. When you need to take time off for the funeral, just let me know. I'm at the end of a telephone if you need me. Just call.'

They left the dining room together. Jessie returned to her office as Forbes left for his.

She sent for another pot of coffee and sat thinking about the lunch and her companion. She really couldn't make him out. There had been times when she'd hated this man, but ever since she'd worked for him, she'd seen a different side to him. As he'd often said, she didn't know him at all. Well, that certainly seemed to be so. But he was a shrewd businessman and she admired that. He'd given her an opportunity to better herself, for which she'd be forever grateful. The saddest thing in her life was that Conor was no longer around to reap the benefit with her, so she'd have to go it alone. Well, if that was the case she'd damn well do it – and succeed!

Chapter Twenty-Five

It was Christmas Eve. Jessie stepped out of the lift, ready for the evening's business; she was dressed for the occasion in a long emerald green gown, with a high neck. The bodice swathed across her, with just a few gold sequins, which caught the light. Her hair was dressed in a chignon on the crown of her head with a tortoiseshell comb and a few tendrils of her vibrant red hair round her face.

With a feeling of pride, she looked around the foyer. In one corner stood a tall Christmas tree, tastefully decorated. There were winter garlands draped along the front of the reception desk. Ivy twisted round the two pillars with colourful baubles intertwined. There was no mistaking that it was Christmas. She made her way to the dining room where a dinner dance was to be held that night. A small platform had been placed at one end to house a small five-piece band and in the centre of the room a space for dancers. The tables were laid with pristine white cloths and napkins folded artistically. Christmas crackers adorned each place setting and in the centre of each table a small, low flower arrangement, enough to dress the table, but not big enough to intrude.

The head waiter came over to her. 'Good evening, Mrs McGonigall, can I be of help?'

'No, Henry, just taking a look and I must say the room looks wonderful.'

He looked delighted. A compliment from the manageress was always appreciated, because she was quick to point out any discrepancies, if she found any.

'Are the extra agency staff up to your standards?' She smiled as she asked because her head waiter was like her, a perfectionist.

'Oh yes! I gave them a good schooling yesterday and this morning. They'll do.'

'Then I'll leave you to it. Have a good night.'

She then made her way to the kitchen to see the chef. Everything was up to scratch there, too. She complimented him on his menu, which pleased him, and then, just as she was about to go to her office, Larry Forbes arrived, wearing evening dress.

'Jessie! May I say how elegant you look. That gown is exquisite. You look beautiful, Mrs McGonigall!'

She felt her cheeks flush. 'And you, Mr Forbes, are, as usual, well turned out!'

'Everything ready for tonight? Although I don't know why I ask as you run a tight ship, as my grandfather would say.'

'Yes, everything is fine.'

'Good, then you and I can go to the bar and have a quiet

drink before everything starts. Come along.' He took her arm and led her away.

'Good evening, madam, sir,' said James.

'What can I get you?' Forbes looked at Jessie.

'I would love a gin and tonic with ice and lemon please.'

'Make that two,' Forbes said. 'I must say the hotel looks very festive. The decorations are very tasteful, not cheap and cheerful. Your choice, I suppose?'

'Yes. Classy not brassy was what I wanted and I am pleased with the result. The staff were so helpful giving up some of their free time to lend a hand.'

'You have earned their respect, that's why. Believe me, I know about staff!'

'I've been meaning to ask you,' she said, 'what happened to Henry Marshall, the young man you sent to the cafe to take the money just in case I cheated you?'

Forbes gazed at her with a look of uncertainty at her tone. 'He's fine, working well, a less pompous young man after his time at the cafe.' He paused. 'I had to be sure, Jessie; after all, I'm a businessman.'

'Of course you are, and a successful one, but also ruthless, when necessary. Without knowing it, Mr Forbes, you've taught me a lot.' She smiled at him, leaving him wondering if he'd misheard the rebuke she'd thrown his way.

Jessie picked up her glass. 'If you'll excuse me, I'll take this to my office and have it when we close. I don't like to drink when I'm on duty as a rule, but that one sip was very welcome. I'll see you later.'

Forbes sipped his drink, wondering why Jessie was so different tonight. But, of course, talking about business, he'd forgotten for a moment about her personal situation. She was grieving for her husband after his unexpected death; mentally she'd be coping with that while trying to work. How difficult that must be for her.

The bar started to fill up and Forbes greeted the customers, playing the host and owner, charming everyone as was his way when the situation called for it.

Jessie was doing exactly the same as the guests entered the hotel. Those going to the bar were offered tasty canapés while they drank, which impressed them. The diners were led to their tables as dinner was to be served at eight o'clock. And so it began.

It wasn't until she knew that the dessert course was served that Jessie entered the dining room. She went round every table asking the clients if they were enjoying the food. All of them agreed that it was excellent. Knowing that most people would be eating turkey or goose on Christmas Day, the chef had offered two courses as an alternative. Roast beef or salmon, with apple charlotte or lemon soufflé for dessert, followed by a cheeseboard. All of which only enticed more to make a booking.

The five-piece band had been playing quietly in the background, but when the coffee was served, they started playing dance music. Jessie was delighted to see several people take to the floor, and by the third number the floor was a little crowded. Yet after a fine meal and plenty of wine, the diners didn't seem to mind. Jessie had had the licence extended until midnight and as the bandleader announced the final waltz, she let out a sigh of relief, went into the kitchen to thank the chef and his staff for their hard work, and to tell them how successful it had been. She stood behind the reception desk as the guests left, and only then did she go to her office and drink her gin and tonic.

Larry Forbes tapped on her door and walked in. He sat in a chair opposite her desk.

'Well, that went even better than I expected. One or two men have spoken about holding business lunches here in the future, which is excellent. Would you like me to send to the kitchen for some coffee?'

'No, thank you, I would appreciate it if you didn't,' she said, staring at him with a steely glint in her eyes. 'The staff are on their knees, ready to go home. They've done enough for tonight!'

'Very well, Mrs McGonigall! You made your point very clearly.'

She rose from her chair. 'I too am tired, Mr Forbes, so I'm afraid I am leaving. My bed calls. The bar is open for two hours tomorrow but after that the hotel is closed for the day. Happy Christmas!'

As he walked with her out of the office, he asked, 'What will you be doing, might I ask?'

'I'm spending it with my neighbours, like last year.' She hesitated. 'Well, not quite like last year.'

He didn't know what to say, hearing the sudden emotion in her voice.

'I'll see you on Boxing Day, Jessie, and thank you for all your hard work.'

She just nodded and walked to the lift, got in it and closed the door.

Larry Forbes stood for a moment. Jessie would find tomorrow difficult, but he hoped her friends would be able to lift her spirits. He bade goodnight to the night porter and left the building.

Jessie undressed, ran a bath, poured some salts in the water and stepped in. Lowering herself into the water, she lay with her head against the back, tears running down her face.

The following morning, Jessie was soon up and ready for work. She went into the kitchen and cooked eggs and bacon, toast and coffee for her and the night porter. They sat together in the kitchen and ate.

'This was most kind of you, Mrs McGonigall, but I could have done this and saved you the trouble.'

She smiled at him as she poured the coffee. 'I know, Tony, but I needed to be occupied; after all, I made my reputation as a good cook. I wanted to prove I hadn't lost my touch.'

'I can testify that you haven't,' he said as he tucked into his food.

'But you can wash up!' she said, laughing.

Eventually, Jessie collected her suitcase packed with gifts and a change of clothes, put on her coat and hat and walked towards Union Street, her friends and her house. She'd sleep there tonight. But her first stop was at Daisy's front door, where she tapped on it and waited.

Her friend greeted her warmly with a hug and a kiss, then ushered her to a chair by the fire. 'I'll make a nice cup of tea,' said Daisy.

'Just grab a couple of glasses instead, love, I've got something much better!' Jessie held up a bottle of whisky. 'One of my satisfied customers sent it in to me for Christmas. It's just what we need on such a cold day.'

The two friends sat chatting, discussing food for Christmas, Jack and Tommy, the two children next door, Daisy's sewing and her clients – everything but Conor, until Daisy took Jessie by the hand, looked at her intently and asked, 'And how are you, Jessie? Really, I mean.'

'Numb! If I'm honest, just numb. At the hotel, I'm kept busy, which is my saving grace, but at night, alone in my room . . . I'll just be glad when the coroner says we can have the funeral, then I'll have some sort of closure. At the moment everything feels unfinished, does that make any sense?'

'Of course, it does. Now, then . . . is there anything you need next door? I've put some bread and butter in the larder and a couple of eggs. I thought you'd probably enjoy breakfast in the quiet tomorrow, before the day began and you could wake when you liked. Bill lit the fire earlier, so the place should be warm.'

'Where is he?'

He popped next door with a couple of gifts for the kids, but he'll be back soon.' She hesitated. 'Once everything is cooking we will be going across the road to the pub when it opens, like always. Do you want to come with us, Jessie?'

She knew this was a probability; after all, it was a Christmas Day ritual and she didn't want to ruin anyone's enjoyment. 'Yes, of course I'll come. Give me a call when you're ready.' Picking up her suitcase, she left her friend and went next door.

The curtains were open and the fire was burning in the grate, but there was a musty scent in the air that lingers when a property is empty. It's almost like a breath of despair from the house at being left unattended and unloved.

Despite the cold, Jessie opened a window to let some fresh air in, then she went into the kitchen and did the same. Out of her bag she took a couple of cake boxes filled with petit fours and home-made biscuits, with gingerbread men for the children, a large pork pie made by the chef, for Daisy to help put on Boxing Day, and a bottle of white wine for the Christmas dinner. Then she unpacked two large kites she'd wrapped for the boys. Picking them up and the cake box, Jessie slipped out of her house and on to her other neighbour.

Percy Williams opened the door and, inside the room, Jessie could see wrapping paper and gifts, in the midst of which were Jack and Tommy, looking flushed with excitement.

'Auntie Jessie!' they called at seeing her. 'Merry Christmas!'

'Merry Christmas to you, too. What did Father Christmas bring you?' They both spoke at once showing her their presents, until she said, 'Well, this is from me,' and handed hers to them. The children tore off the paper and let out cries of joy when they saw the kites.

'Dad, can we go and fly them now?'

It was Jessie who answered. 'Now listen to me, you two. Christmas Day is busy for parents, there's so much to do, so you be patient because Mum and Dad need time to enjoy part of it too. There's plenty of time for kite flying another day. In any case, there isn't much wind about today.'

* * *

Just after noon, Jessie, Daisy and Bill went across the road to the Builders Arms as they had done in past years on Christmas Day. They were all very aware of the missing person, who had yet to be mentioned. Bill and Daisy were reluctant to upset Jessie and so were unsure of what to say.

This was soon solved by the customers in the bar who immediately came over to Jessie with their condolences, but what made it acceptable and eventually enjoyable was the first man who said, 'That Conor, he got me into real trouble with my missus one year. He took me out and got me so drunk, I forgot her birthday!' That was all it took. After that there were so many memories of the man who had earned so much admiration and affection from those he knew. It was indeed a kind of healing for Jessie and the heavy sense of loss she'd been carrying seemed lighter at the warmth of their words.

Some of the men had worked with him in the docks and praised his ability as a stevedore and the way he handled his men, all agreeing Conor was a tough boss, but fair.

Another chirped up with his own story. 'I was in the cafe, Jessie love, the day that Conor walked in. I remember you telling him the food was simple as was the menu and if he wanted a posh place go elsewhere, or words to that effect.'

Jessie roared with laughter. 'So I did. Ah, but he had a way with him even then.'

'I saw the way you flirted with him, Jessie McGonigall!' As she went to argue, he pointed his finger at her. 'Now don't you dare deny it! I was there. I saw the way you tossed your head at him.'

Jessie smiled softly. 'I did, didn't I?' She looked at her accuser and grinned. 'I tell you, it never failed, ever!' She tossed her head and her hair, which today was worn loose about her shoulders, swished like flames of fire in the wind.

'I'd fall for that Jessie, that I would,' called another and everybody laughed.

The rest of the day went well and when, eventually, Jessie climbed into bed, she sighed happily. She'd been dreading today, the first Christmas without Conor, but instead it had been fun. People had such good memories of him, as she did. They were to be treasured, stored away for those days that were hard to handle. She settled down for the night and, as usual, she clasped his pillow to her and slept.

Chapter Twenty-Six

Christmas was over and at last Conor's body had been released for burial, so Jessie could make arrangements for the funeral. Daisy accompanied her friend to the funeral directors. It was a soulless feeling, choosing a coffin, hymns for the service and talking to the vicar of St Mary's Church about a man he'd never met.

'How can you talk about a man you didn't know?' Jessie demanded. She was feeling aggrieved at this fact.

'I do it all the time, Mrs McGonigall. It's part of my job.'

'But my husband was a special person.'

'I'm sure he was. Perhaps you could write a few things about him for me to read before the funeral. I want to do him justice.'

She nodded. 'I'd like to do that. Thank you.'

Jessie had returned to work on Boxing Day afternoon, but when she was at last free to book Conor's funeral, she informed Larry Forbes, who had called into the hotel.

'You'll be pleased about that, I'm sure. Take whatever time you need. Are you having a wake?'

She looked up at him and grinned. 'Are you kidding? Conor was Irish, as am I. A funeral is to be enjoyed. It's a celebration of a person's life, so it is. It's not a place for tears.'

He looked bemused. 'How marvellous! Oh, I've been to too many funerals that were dire and full of gloom. Where are you holding his?'

'In our local pub, of course! Where else? Where everybody knew Conor, where we used to go for a drink and a game of darts. It's been our local ever since we married.'

'How many are you expecting to attend?'

'I've no idea, but there will be plenty of food. All the wives contribute.'

'But you won't have the time to do that, Jessie. Get the chef to make whatever is your share – and a little extra with my compliments.'

She was completely taken aback by the generous offer. 'Well, thank you, Mr Forbes, I appreciate that.'

'Get one of the kitchen staff to deliver it to the pub. You'll have your hands too full to be concerned about it.' Before she could thank him, he walked to the door of her office.

'I hope it all goes well, Jessie.' Turning on his heel, he left.

It was a crisp, cold January day when Conor McGonigall was laid to rest. His coffin, carried in a horse-drawn hearse, stood outside his house in Union Street. Jessie had slept there the previous night, and had eaten with Daisy and Bill after she'd checked that all was fine at the pub for the following day. Now it was time.

Dressed in black and widow's weeds, Jessie stepped out of her house. She walked behind the hearse and stood there, pulling up her fur collar against the cold. She was joined by Daisy and Bill, then Maisie and Percy Williams came out of their house, joined by two solemn-looking boys. Behind them a few of the locals took their place. The procession started. At every turn it was joined by others. Dockers who'd worked with Conor. Four docks police in full uniform joined in. As it continued there were customers from the cafe. Nancy had closed for the day and she too was there. The numbers grew.

Daisy took hold of Jessie's hand and quietly said, 'Look behind you, you won't believe your eyes.'

Jessie looked over her shoulder and all she could see was a mass of people following the hearse. She couldn't see where it ended. She stared at her friend in disbelief.

Daisy squeezed her hand. 'It's for Conor, love.'

The church was full, with people standing at the back. Jessie sat in the family pew, and asked Daisy and Bill to sit with her. The vicar had said one or two people had asked to speak during the service and she'd agreed. The first hymn began.

Jessie went through the service in a haze, really. She followed the service subliminally; spoke the twenty-third psalm automatically. The vicar took his place in the pulpit.

'We are gathered here today to pay our respects to Conor

McGonigall. I didn't know the man, but I've read about him from the notes his wife, Jessie, gave to me. From this I learnt that he was a good man, a loving husband and a friend to those he liked. But I've only to look around at this crowded congregation to see that he was a man to be admired, too. It takes a special person to earn this much respect from his peers. But I'll let those who knew him speak for him.'

To Jessie's surprise, John Irving, Conor's old boss, walked to the lectern to speak and Jessie wondered what he was going to say.

'Conor McGonigall was a fine man. He had worked in the docks for many years working his way up to stevedore. He was good at his job, strict but fair and, above all, he was reliable. His men knew that, with him, they were safe working in the hold of these ships, that Conor was a perfectionist and never ever took chances with the lives of his men. Apart from which, he was full of Irish charm. He was liked and admired by his peers. I am proud to say he was one of my men. He was a real man and he will be missed!'

Jessie felt the tears fill her eyes. This indeed was a compliment to her late husband.

Then Bill stood up and walked past her and Daisy to take his place. He was not as assured as his employer, but it was obvious to all he wanted to say a few words.

'Conor was my neighbour and my mate,' he began. 'Times were hard when I first came to Southampton from the north. I joined the queue in the dreaded call-on every morning, trying to be chosen, and we all know how difficult that is. But eventually I was chosen to belong to a gang and had a permanent job as long as there was work.

I only discovered some time after that this was through Conor. He never mentioned it so neither did I, knowing he wouldn't be pleased that I knew. But that was the manner of the man. I feel privileged to have been called his friend.' He stepped down, wiping his eyes, overcome by his speech.

The final hymn was sung and the service brought to the end. The vicar told the congregation that, after the burial, they would be welcome at the Builders Arms. Jessie left the pew and stood by the door to speak to the mourners as they left the church. It took a while as there were so many. Then they made their way to the cemetery.

'Ashes to ashes, dust to dust,' intoned the vicar. Daisy and Bill stood either side of Jessie, holding her by the arm until she stepped forward and picked up a handful of soil and dropped it on the coffin. Silent tears ran down her cheeks and she felt rooted to the spot until Daisy joined her, threw her soil on the coffin and led Jessie firmly away.

As she left with Daisy and Bill, the vicar told her there was a car to take her and her friends to the pub, compliments of Mr Forbes. They all climbed inside, as well as the Williams family, to be driven to Union Street in style.

When they arrived, they were surprised to see trestle tables laid outside and the landlord waiting to greet her. She climbed out of the car and looked around.

Charlie Watson, the landlord, said, 'Mr Forbes attended the funeral, but when he saw how big the congregation was he realised that we wouldn't be able to accommodate everyone inside,' he explained. 'So he left and sent over some tables, more food and a couple of waiters! The food is laid out; ready to bring out when they arrive.'

At that moment the waiters were bringing plates of sandwiches, pork pies and sausage rolls, with plates and paper napkins. Shortly after, as people started to arrive, Jessie saw the wisdom of his idea.

The beer flowed, the pianist played, songs were sung and Conor was remembered long into the night. There were a few tears, but it was a joyous occasion. A real Irish wake.

When eventually the mourners had gone home, many of them somewhat unsteadily, Bill, Daisy and the Williams family congregated at the Browns' house and drank a welcome cup of tea. The two boys came over to Jessie.

'We are so sorry about Uncle Conor dying, Auntie Jessie,' young Jack said. 'We remember how he rescued us when we went to the pier on our own and nearly drowned.'

'And how he taught us to swim in the summer,' added Tommy.

She smiled at the recollection. 'He didn't want you to be scared of the water and wanted you to be able to swim so you'd be safe in the future.'

'We loved him, Auntie Jessie, and we love you too.' Both the boys hugged her. 'We'll look after you,' they said as they clung to her.

It was all she could do to stop crying, but she managed to stammer her thanks. Their mother came over and rescued her, then took the boys off home to bed.

Daisy and Bill, kicked off their shoes and drank some of Jessie's whisky with their tea. As Bill sipped his drink he turned to Jessie.

'Conor will be bloody furious that he missed such a good party,' he said.

She chuckled. 'So he would. I'm amazed that so many people came. It was incredible.'

'You didn't notice, of course, but they seemed to come out of every corner and didn't stop. I've never seen the like,' said Daisy. 'But now he's at rest and you have to take a deep breath and get on with your life. That's what he would expect of you, love.' She held Jessie's hand. 'You can't let him down, you know that.'

Jessie nodded. 'I know.'

She eventually took her leave and let herself into the house. She picked up the photo of Conor from the mantelpiece and kissed it. 'That was a hell of a party, darlin'. There'll be a few thick heads tomorrow, I can tell you.' She sat down in a chair, still looking at the picture.

'Oh, Conor! I still expect you to come walking through the door, even now.' Shaking her head, she had to accept that this would never happen. She had good memories of their life together; however, she never could linger on the way that he died. That was far too painful. She shut that away in a box at the back of her mind until the day she could cope with it. But not right now.

Chapter Twenty-Seven

Three months later

It was now April and Jessie had been working long hours in the hotel. It was her way of coping with her grief. At night she was so tired, she'd crawl into her bed after soaking in a bath and fall asleep through sheer exhaustion.

Larry Forbes watched her closely, aware that this was her way, but concerned that she would go too far. Early one evening he walked into her office with a pot of coffee and sat down. He poured two cups and handed one to her.

'You are finished for the night!'

She looked at him in surprise. 'I have—'

He didn't let her finish. 'Jessie, it's time to slow down or you will make yourself ill and be no use to anyone. I need you to be on top of your form. Enough is enough!' He sipped his coffee. 'I realise this is your way of shutting out the loss of your husband and we all handle grief in our own way, but you need to slow down, work reasonable hours. When was the last time you left the hotel?'

Jessie just shrugged.

'Right, go and get your coat, we're going for a walk. It's a reasonable night so let's get some fresh air. I'll wait in the foyer!'

From his tone she knew that argument would be useless, so she finished her coffee, rose from her chair and left the office. As the lift took her up to her rooms, she had to agree that her boss was right. She hadn't been out for over a week, and she had the sense to know she was driving herself too far. She just didn't seem able to stop. No, that wasn't it at all. She was too *frightened* to stop, because then she'd have to face the fact that Conor was dead. She let out a deep sigh. It was time to come out of hiding.

Larry Forbes offered her his arm and they walked along the road towards the high street. People were milling around, looking at the shops, enjoying the early spring weather after the cold winter. Daffodils were blooming in the parks. Trees were beginning to bud. Nature was renewing itself and, as Jessie walked, she realised that was what she needed to do. She had never been a person to run away from a problem or trouble, quite the opposite. For the first time in her life, though, she'd done just that. Conor wasn't a problem, her facing being without him was. What had Daisy said that day? 'You can't let him down.' She straightened her back as she walked, took a deep breath and made a promise to herself. *Conor will be proud of me.*

Her companion had been silent during their walk, sensing that she needed time to unwind, but as they approached Scullards restaurant he turned to her.

'Have you eaten today?'

'I sent for a sandwich at lunchtime.'

He shook his head and propelled her through the door and into the dining room.

The head waiter hurried over. 'Mr Forbes, how nice to see you. Good evening, madam. A table for two, is it?'

The waiter took their coats and left them with a menu.

Jessie felt herself relax for the first time in an age. Looking around the room, she said, 'This is nice, could do with a few changes in the decor.'

Larry started to laugh. 'Will you stop. Just sit back and enjoy the food. The chef is good, I promise you.'

'Better than ours?' she asked, trying to hide a smile.

He looked at her and said, 'That's the first time I've seen you smile for a long time. Let me order some wine and we can celebrate the fact.'

'Oh dear, has it been that bad?'

He nodded. 'You've smiled at the clients, of course, but that's being professional. I would expect no less from you.'

The waiter came with the wine list and returned with a bottle of champagne.

When Jessie saw this, she looked at her boss with raised eyebrows.

'It's the best pick-me-up I know, so drink up. Doctor's orders!'

The change of scenery and the champagne did indeed lift Jessie's spirits as did the excellent food, and she once again began to feel like a human being. She looked across the table and, picking up her glass, held it up.

'Thank you,' she said.

'For the champagne?'

'No, for dragging me out of the deep pit I was in.'

'You'd have made it on your own eventually, Jessie. I just couldn't wait, that's all.'

They talked about many things. Her homeland, her parents. Conor and his life. The business, but on a light level – and of the news. The threat of war. Churchill as Lord of the Admiralty, causing mayhem in the House of Commons.

'Do you think there's any truth behind it?' Jessie asked.

'I've no idea.'

'What would happen to the hotel if there was a war? Would we still be in business?'

'I would hope so – we are a port, after all – but let's hope it doesn't come to anything.'

At the end of the meal, they walked slowly back to the hotel. Forbes stopped at the entrance where he turned and stared at her.

'Right. Tomorrow I want to see the old Jessie McGonigall on duty. I don't want to have the trouble of finding her replacement!'

Seeing the steely look in his eye and the timbre of his voice, she knew this was no idle threat. She smiled to herself. That ruthless streak was still there, then. It was somehow comforting, in a strange way.

'I wouldn't dream of putting you to so much trouble. In any case, I didn't put in all this hard work for some bloody stranger to walk in and take over!'

He started laughing. 'Now that sounds like the stroppy manageress I hired. I'm happy to know that you're back on board. Goodnight, Jessie.'

She watched him strut away; knowing he'd made his point. Shaking her head, she thought, *He really hasn't changed*. She walked into the hotel, checked with the receptionist that all was well and went to her rooms.

Once there, she took off her coat and put it away, kicked off her shoes and sat down. Going over the conversation she'd had with Larry Forbes she was disturbed about the uncertainty of a war. Should such a thing happen, would the hotel still be in business? She still had her interest in the cafe. Workers and dockers would always need feeding, so she would have some income. But it was a worry. It would be a pity, as the hotel was thriving, but Forbes's hopes of opening another wouldn't be viable, that was for sure. She undressed and climbed into bed without having any solution. Time alone would tell.

It didn't take long before Jessie's concerns began to take shape. Two months later, on 28th June, Archduke Franz Ferdinand and his wife were shot in Sarajevo and the country was in uproar. Both Jessie and Larry Forbes were fearful as to how this would affect their business.

'So far we're fine,' he said. 'The bookings are still healthy, but there is no way of knowing how this will affect the country – and then us.'

July was busy and the August Bank Holiday, but on 4th August, Britain declared war on Germany and the atmosphere changed. Lord Kitchener's posters were all around the town, calling for volunteers. 'Your Country Needs You', it proclaimed.

It wasn't long before the troops came to Southampton, marching to the docks and the waiting ships, taking them across the Channel to face the enemy. Some of their staff volunteered; carried away with the thought that it would all be over by Christmas and things would get back to normal if they did their bit.

Trade dropped off. Business luncheons were cancelled. Clients were afraid to spend too much company money, uncertain of how the war would affect them. There were still those who were able to continue with their lives. The men with private money, who were not affected financially, but the business was suffering and takings were falling rapidly.

Seeing the troops marching through the town, there was no doubt that the war had truly started.

A month later, Larry Forbes came to the hotel for a meeting with Jessie. He looked strained and she wondered what news he had to impart.

He sat opposite her and without preamble he told her.

'I've sold the building,' he said.

'You what?' Jessie was so shocked, she thought she'd misheard him.

'I've sold up. As you know, I invested a great deal of money in this venture and if I don't want to lose most of it, I have to sell the property. I'm sorry, Jessie. You of all people don't deserve this, but I have no choice.'

'Is it still being run as a hotel?' she asked hopefully.

'No, not exactly. The Admiralty want to buy it and use it as offices and a place to house some of their staff. They are prepared to pay a good price and I can't afford to turn it down. I will give you a good severance pay. It's the least I can do.'

She was stunned. 'How long have we got until they take over?'

'One month. They've bought it lock, stock and barrel. They didn't want to have the trouble of furnishing it.'

'What will you do once it's gone?'

With a grimace he said, 'I have other business interests. I never believed in putting all my eggs in one basket, and soon, not having to concern myself with the financial running of the hotel at a loss, I will be able to sleep at night.'

'What about the staff we have left? What about them? They will have lost their living.'

'I know, and I feel badly about that, but had we continued, they would eventually have been unemployed anyway. I'll give them some extra in their pay packet to tide them over. I'm not a monster. I do understand their predicament, but I'm a businessman, Jessie. You know that!'

'How could I ever forget?' she said with some sarcasm. 'What about the lease on the cafe? You're not selling that too, I hope?'

'No, I will keep it for a while, anyway – unless you want to buy it off me?'

'You are full of surprises, Mr Forbes!'

'Well, Jessie, you made that cafe into a thriving business, it seems only right to give you the opportunity. After all, it's still making money. I am really not interested in the cafe, but I wouldn't close that down on you too, unless I had to.'

'I'll think about it and get back to you. But now, when are you going to tell the staff?'

'I'll come in early tomorrow morning. Have them gather in the foyer at eight o'clock, will you?' Getting up from his chair, he said, 'I'm genuinely sorry about this, Jessie. As you know, I had plans for another hotel, and after that, who knew how far we could have gone together.'

She heard the disappointment in his voice and felt a surge of sympathy. 'We all had plans, but sadly life isn't always kind.'

'As you know only too well,' he replied. 'But you and I are survivors, Jessie! We'll come out on top, eventually. I'll see you in the morning.'

When she was alone, Jessie sat and tried to take it all in. The hotel would close and her staff would be unemployed, which worried her. Then she started to laugh. 'From rags to riches and back to rags again!' she said aloud, thinking of her own position. Back to the cafe, then. But she began to consider her possibilities. If she did have the lease . . .

The following morning the staff were assembled. As they waited there was much murmuring among them, wondering what was going on, then they became silent as Larry Forbes arrived and stood on the bottom of the staircase to speak to them.

'I'll come straight to the point,' he began. 'As you must be aware, ever since war was declared, we have been losing business and I've had to make a serious decision. The hotel has been sold.'

The staff all started talking at once.

'Ladies and gentlemen, please, let me finish. In a month's time the Admiralty will be taking over the building for their own use. I realise this will cause you some hardship and there will be a bonus in your final pay packet, which I hope will help to tide you over until you can find work. If you do so before we close, that's fine, I'll understand. I would like to take this opportunity to thank you for your loyal service. You helped to give the Grosvenor Hotel the fine reputation that it has. If I could have found a way to keep it open, I would have done so. I sold it with a heavy heart, I assure you. Thank you for listening. You can all return to your stations now.'

There was a definite air of gloom as the staff took their leave and ambled away. Forbes walked over to Jessie. 'That's one of the hardest things I've had to do for a very long time.'

'Let's go into my office,' she suggested.

Larry Forbes sank into a chair and let out a deep sigh, then he lit a cigarette. He rubbed his forehead wearily. 'Oh, Jessie, this is such a bloody shame. We both had such plans, and look around you, this place could have been an absolute gold mine.'

'It's not your fault! When you bought this place and furnished it, it was a great undertaking, and then it was certainly the right one. Your perception of what it could be was solid. You didn't fail! It's only circumstances that scuppered you.'

'Scuppered! That is exactly the word to describe the situation. Hopefully if the war *is* over by Christmas, as everybody seems to think, then who knows, we still could make it.'

With a chuckle, Jessie said, 'Well I have to admire your optimism. It breaks my heart to see the troops marching through the town to the docks, thinking they'll be home soon.'

He gazed at her. 'There is one thing I was right about and that was you for my manageress. You've done such a splendid job, it's such a pity that you couldn't have continued in your elevated position and have gone even higher. You have such great potential.'

'Oh, I haven't given up the ghost yet, Mr Forbes, I just haven't yet worked it out, that's all.'

'You are quite a woman, Jessie McGonigall!'

'So I am, just you wait and see!' She grinned broadly at him.

'I must be off. I'll pop in tomorrow. You look after yourself.' He left the office and the hotel.

Jessie put on her coat and headed for the cafe to tell Nancy what had happened and to do some quiet thinking. She had to have a future to plan. But what? As yet she didn't know, but she had to find an answer soon.

Chapter Twenty-Eight

Jessie was greeted warmly by some of her old customers as she entered the cafe.

'You slumming, then, Jessie?' asked one.

'Lovely to see you, girl,' said another.

She smiled at them all. 'Coming here is never slumming in my book, gentlemen, and it's lovely to see you all too!' She walked into the kitchen where Nancy was preparing another order.

'Hello, love,' she said, 'I won't be a minute.'

Jessie said hello to the girl Nancy had hired as a helper and gratefully accepted her offer of a cup of tea. When Nancy returned, she took her over to a corner of the kitchen.

'The hotel has been sold to the Admiralty and closes in a month,' she told her.

Nancy looked shocked at the news. 'Bloody hell, Jessie, that's come like a shot out of the blue. Did you have any idea?'

Shaking her head, Jessie said, 'No, but trade has dropped off and we've been running at a loss – but no. I'm as shocked as you are.'

'What will you do?'

'Come back here, of course. I don't have a choice.'

Her friend was full of sympathy. 'Oh, Jessie! That's a bit of a comedown after being manageress of a posh hotel.'

'Not really. A job's a job, and yes, I see what you mean, but I have to make a living. Larry Forbes has offered to sell me the lease if I want it.'

'Do you want it?'

Jessie was hesitant. 'I'm not sure at the moment. I've got to sit and do some serious thinking about the future, but I just wanted you to know what's happening.' She finished her tea. 'I must get back.' She kissed her friend on the cheek and left.

Once back in her office, she shut the door to give her some privacy. Despite the severance pay Forbes had promised, she'd been used to earning a good salary and she didn't relish the thought of being out of pocket. She wracked her brains looking for a solution to increase her finances, but she couldn't think of a thing.

The month seemed to fly by. There was a shortage of coal. Street lights were dimmed to save on electricity. It made the streets gloomy and depressing.

Eventually, the day of closure arrived. Larry Forbes was on hand to give out the wages and bonus himself, so he could personally say goodbye to his staff. It was a sad day for all that had remained. A few had found other employment, but the majority of them lined up outside the office for their final wage packet. Christmas wouldn't be celebrated in the same manner this year by many.

When eventually they were alone, Forbes turned to Jessie. 'The new owners have purchased the contents of the bar for their use, but I think they won't mind if we two have a final drink together. I don't hand the keys over until this afternoon. Come on!'

He went behind the bar and poured them both double measures of gin and some tonic water, then led her over to a table. He held up his glass.

'Here's to the future, Jessie. I hope it's a good one!'

She clinked glasses. 'I'll drink to that.'

'What are your plans?' he asked.

'I'm moving my stuff back to the house,' she said, adding with a grimace. 'I will miss the bathroom. I'm going to go back to working with Nancy in the cafe for the time being.'

'Have you thought about buying the lease?'

'I'm still thinking about that, I'll let you know in due course.'

'There's no hurry,' he assured her. 'Things are going to change in the country now we're at war and no one is yet certain how. Some will make money from it, others will suffer. Lives will be lost, families destroyed. It's a sad time.'

'But people say it will be over by Christmas,' she argued.

Forbes shook his head. 'Sadly, I doubt that, but I pray I'm wrong.'

They finished their drinks and Jessie washed the glasses and put them away.

'I'll just go upstairs and get my case,' she said, 'then you can lock up.'

There wasn't much to pack as she'd taken a lot of her things home in the previous days. She looked around her rooms and took one last lingering look into the bathroom. Gazing longingly at the bath and toilet before closing the door and taking the lift down to the foyer.

Larry Forbes locked the door to the hotel behind them. Neither of them spoke. It was so final. The end of an adventure, to their dreams and the success they'd worked hard for. It was a sad moment.

He gripped her hand in both of his. 'I'll be in touch, Jessie.' His voice was choked with emotion. Jessie couldn't answer, she just nodded and, turning, walked away.

Entering her house in Union Street, she put down her case and set about lighting the stove. She filled a kettle and placed it on top of the stove to boil when the fire had taken a hold. Then she washed her hands and sat in a chair watching the flames as the fire began to burn.

I'm back where I started, she thought. No luxurious bath, no indoor toilet any more. No more decent salary! During her time at the hotel, she'd saved her money; after all, she'd been fed and housed, and her savings had originally been towards a home of her own for her and Conor. Now there was no Conor either. Just her. She did, however, still have the income from the cafe. Thank God for that! She assumed – or hoped would perhaps be a better

248

word – that business would remain healthy. The dockers would still be employed with ships coming in to move troops over to France and would continue to be needed as long as the war continued.

In September, the prime minister, Herbert Asquith, had called for another 500,000 men to sign up for the army, and Queen Mary had asked the nation's women to knit socks for the army. On the British front in Flanders, troops were fighting a battle for Ypres. In Britain, the papers were read with mounting fear for those who had family members serving abroad.

Jessie was now concerned that there would possibly be food shortages that could impede her business. If so, she and Nancy would just have to be inventive with a menu. Home-made soups were always an acceptable starter, but men liked a hearty main course. If meat was short, that could make things difficult. She could keep chickens in the backyard of the cafe, but men would soon get fed up with that too often. Fortunately, she had a good relationship with the local butcher in The Ditches, but he, too, could be restricted. She was wracking her brains trying to foresee the difficulties ahead so she had an answer for when they arrived, but it was all guesswork.

Jessie decided that while she waited for the fire to catch properly, she'd pop along to the butcher who was just down the road and have a chat with him to see if he'd heard anything.

Fred Warner greeted her warmly. 'Jessie, love, how nice to see you. I'm so sorry to hear about young Conor and now I heard the hotel is closed. Not having a lot of luck, are you, girl?'

She shrugged. 'Sure, 'tis true, but life has to go on. I'll be back at the cafe and I was wondering if there'll be food shortages in the future and if you'll be affected?'

'Don't know, Jessie. It's likely, but I'll always look after you as best as I can. You know that.'

'That I do, Fred, and I thank you. It breaks my heart that we are at war. So many lives will be lost, family life changed, and for what?'

'Power-hungry buggers, that's what!' His face flushed in anger.

'While I'm here, I'll take half a pound of stewing steak, please, and four slices of lamb's liver. I've nothing in the house.'

A customer was waiting to be served so Jessie thanked Fred and took her leave, then bought some fruit and vegetables from the greengrocer before returning home.

As she unpacked her shopping, she mused that she felt like a housewife again, but then she realised she would only be cooking for herself. It was like a knife being plunged into her heart. It was unexpected moments like this that took her by surprise and seemed to hurt the most.

She busied herself, peeling the vegetables, preparing the stew, filling a stone water bottle to put in her bed in case the sheets were a little damp from not having been slept in. Then she made a cup of tea and sat down. Tomorrow she'd return to the cafe and start all over again.

Chapter Twenty-Nine

It was a bright but cold morning when Jessie arrived at the cafe. Nancy and Dorothy, her helper, had already started prepping the food for the day. They looked up as Jessie walked into the kitchen and put on a clean white apron.

'Morning, ladies!' she said. 'What's on the lunch menu today, and what can I do?'

'Bangers and mash with onion gravy for one and meat pie for the other, both served with mixed vegetables,' Nancy told her. 'If you were to make the pastry for the pies, that would be a help. Your pastry was always better than mine.'

'And dessert?' Jessie asked.

'Treacle pudding and custard. You know it's the men's favourite and that hasn't changed.' Nancy laughed. 'Oh, Jessie, it's like old times to be in the kitchen together, although through unhappy circumstances, of course.'

Jessie grinned at her. 'I know, but it feels good just the same.'

* * *

When a little later the customers for breakfast arrived, Jessie walked into the dining room to take the orders and was greeted warmly by those who knew her.

'Welcome home, love,' said one. 'The place hasn't been the same without you, not complaining, you understand. Nancy has looked after us real good, but it's nice to see your smiling face back again.'

'Sorry about the hotel closing, Jessie, but their loss is our gain!' another chipped in.

A customer new to her walked in and sat down. With a grin he said, 'Morning! New waitress, eh? Good-looking too – you married, love?'

Her regulars waited for her response.

'Good morning, I'm Jessie McGonigall, the owner. Thank you for the compliment, but as for being married' – she looked him up and down – 'you wouldn't stand a chance! Now what can I get you to eat?'

The other customers burst out laughing and started to tease the newcomer.

'Well, I didn't know, did I?' he retorted, face flushed with embarrassment.

In the kitchen the girls chuckled, having overheard the conversation.

'Oh, I have missed you, Jessie,' said Nancy, grinning broadly. 'You light up the place. You always did!'

The day went well and, as usual, they were kept busy. After they closed, Jessie and Nancy sat quietly and chatted over a cup of tea. Jessie sat back in her chair and sighed.

'Today was lovely. The customers were great and we

were busy as usual, but I keep wracking my brains trying to think how we could make more money. I don't mean putting the prices up, but doing something else as well as the cafe.'

'But where – and what?' Nancy looked puzzled.

'That's just it, I can't think of a thing, but there must be something. I have some money saved so that wouldn't be a problem, if only I could come up with a plan.'

It wasn't long before Jessie's problem was solved. She was watching as the troops continued marching towards the docks, company after company. The seagoing exodus continued all day long and into the night. The last sailing, a hospital ship, was at two o'clock in the morning. She'd only discovered this when she'd overheard a conversation between two dockers. Then she had an idea. They would stay open until the evening!

'We can work in shifts,' she told Nancy and Dorothy. 'You two can do one and I'll hire another girl to help me run the next shift. The dockers will need feeding to keep them going and, who knows, we may get a few of the crew as well from the tugs. I'll go and have a word with the butcher to increase our order. It's no good opening and running out of food. We could make sandwiches, too, for those who don't have the time for a meal. And we'll open on Sundays as well.'

So it began. Nancy and Dorothy worked from seven in the morning until one o'clock and then, Jessie with Mary, an older woman whose husband had joined up, took over. They worked from one o'clock until seven o'clock in the evening.

The dockers who also worked shifts were delighted with

the new arrangement and the cafe was kept busy. The trade in sandwiches was also welcome, especially by the crews from the tugs, who were constantly on the go, taking each vessel out of the docks into Southampton water, before removing their ropes so the ships could sail across the Channel under their own steam.

Although they were busy, the girls were saddened by the steady stream of troops continuously marching by these past months, knowing that some wouldn't return to their families, but the amount of horses being shipped as well took them by surprise.

Nancy was very upset upon seeing them. 'Those poor animals!' she cried. 'They'll be terrified at the sound of gunfire. It's not right!'

'But they're needed, Nancy. It's a form of transportation for the soldiers and the officers. I was told that some had taken their own horse with them,' Jessie explained.

This didn't stop Nancy's outrage, so everyone made sure not to mention it in front of her. They had enough to cope with, catering for their customers.

Two weeks later, Larry Forbes paid Jessie a visit early one evening. He made his way to the kitchen. Both the women were busy serving a full dining room.

'Business is good I can see,' he said as Jessie returned to the kitchen. 'I heard you were now open in the evening. That was a smart move. Why am I not surprised?'

'Well, I can't afford to sit on my backside!' she retorted. She looked at him and grinned. 'I've had to order another oven, how about that?'

Shaking his head, he said, 'You are unstoppable!'

'Well you did say that some people make money when there's a war on, and at least I'm doing it for a good reason, keeping the workers fed! How are you? I've not seen you since the hotel closed.'

'Oh, I'm ticking over nicely, thanks. You know me.'

'I wouldn't expect anything else. Now, I'm rushed off my feet so if you want to be useful, there are a couple of men who want to buy some sandwiches – would you serve them for me? They're waiting at the till. The prices are clearly marked.'

He was so surprised that, without saying a word, he did as he was asked.

On her way back to the kitchen, Jessie stopped beside him. Her eyes full of mischief. 'This really is hilarious. You once sent one of your men to run the till in case I cheated on you, now *you're* taking the money!' She walked into the kitchen, laughing. Then popping her head round the kitchen door, she said, 'Oh, by the way, I'll buy the lease off you . . . if the price is right!'

The next two months passed and the women were feeling the strain, working seven days a week. Mary didn't mind so much with her husband away fighting. It gave her something to do. Nancy's husband, however, was complaining about her working on a Sunday.

'It's my only day off and you're in that bloody cafe half the day. I hardly see you, and when I do you're too tired to do anything! The only day you had off was Christmas Day! Besides, it's wrong, you working on Sunday. The Lord made it a day of rest.'

'Well, he wasn't at war, was he? Those poor dockers are having to work even longer hours. Haven't you seen the troops marching? They're fighting for the country, and they don't have a break on a Sunday! Besides, I don't see you complain at the extra money I earn.'

He didn't continue with the argument, but he was not a happy man.

Jessie was tired as she had all the paperwork and the bills to sort when she was at home as well as keeping the house clean. But she was making money, which meant after the war, if she was lucky, she'd be able to buy the house of her dreams. She'd bought the lease off Larry Forbes after haggling fiercely about the price. But now she no longer had to pay him rent, the property was hers until the lease ran out, many years hence.

The following Saturday night had been very busy and she'd stayed on, letting Mary go home. It was almost nine o'clock when she let herself into her house. She raked the fire and put another log and some coal on it, made herself a cup of tea and, kicking off her shoes, sat in an armchair near the stove. Before long she'd nodded off, to be awakened by a furious banging on her door. Pulling herself together, she opened it.

'What the bloody hell—' She didn't finish when she saw a policeman standing there.

'Mrs McGonigall, owner of the workman's cafe?'

'Yes. What's wrong?'

'I'm afraid there's been a fire at your business. The firemen are there now; I've just come to let you know.'

She didn't remember moving so quickly in her life. Grabbing her coat, she pulled the door to, not even bothering to lock it and started to run.

She could see the smoke before she turned into the road. Then she saw what was left of the cafe, through the flames that had now reached the empty floor above. She was so shocked, she stopped and stared. A crowd had gathered and were standing well clear as ordered by the police. She pushed her way to the front.

'Don't come any closer, madam,' a policeman said, standing in front of the crowd, making sure they were a safe distance away.

'That's my cafe!' she snapped.

He looked at her. 'I'm sorry, madam, but there isn't much of a cafe there any longer. The lower floor has been badly damaged, and the firemen are trying to contain the top floor and the surrounding buildings, before it spreads.'

All she could do was stand and watch.

Chapter Thirty

Jessie stood watching her future burn, her senses and her body numb. She had no idea of the passing time as she watched the ceiling collapse onto the lower ground floor. She jumped as someone caught hold of her arm and turned to see it was Larry Forbes.

'What the bloody hell happened here? I rushed round as soon as I heard.'

Shaking her head, she said, 'I've no idea. I worked late tonight after Mary left, just tidying up and getting things ready for the morning. I checked everything as usual before I locked up. I can't understand how it caught fire.'

He took a flask out of his pocket. 'Here, sip this, you're freezing cold.' He took off his scarf and put it round her neck.

'How long have you been here?'

'I've no idea, what time is it?'

Looking at his watch, he said, 'It's well after

midnight.' He put an arm around her shoulders. 'You'll catch a cold standing here.'

She was grateful for the warmth.

Much later, the fire was under control. The firemen were still hosing down the rubble to make sure it didn't catch again. The crowd had long dispersed, leaving Larry and Jessie standing alone.

The fire chief came over to them. 'I believe you're the owner,' he said, looking at Jessie.

'Yes, I am. Have you any idea what started the fire? When I left this evening, everything was fine. I checked thoroughly; I always do.'

'It's too early to tell yet. We may know more tomorrow. We'll be in touch. I suggest you go home and get warm.'

'Can I take a closer look?' she asked.

The fire chief hesitated, but seeing the look of anguish on her face, walked her closer, keeping at a safe distance.

She could see the devastation. The tables and chairs were now charred remains; the counter was warped and burnt. Through the open door to the kitchen she could see that it, too, had been decimated by the fire. There was not a thing that could be rescued.

Larry took her arm. 'Come away, Jessie. There's nothing you can do. I'll take you home. We could both do with a hot cup of tea.'

Jessie made the tea once they were in the house. She did it automatically, saying nothing, her mind in turmoil.

Her business was no longer – just a burnt mess. Her livelihood: gone.

Larry sat drinking his tea, deep in thought. Looking up, he asked, 'Did you insure the cafe, Jessie?'

She shook her head. 'I meant to, but we were so busy, I didn't get round to it.' She looked suddenly angry. 'How could I have been so stupid? Me, who you say has such a good business head!'

He was lost for words, knowing that once the lease changed hands, the existing insurance was invalid. But this, certainly, was not the time for a reprimand.

'Oh, Jessie!' was all he could utter.

A while later, Larry took his leave. 'I'll be at the cafe in the morning to see it in daylight. We'll be able to see what has happened more clearly. Try and get some sleep, Jessie.'

She looked up. 'Thanks for being there. I did appreciate it.'

A few hours later, Jessie stood outside the cafe as Nancy and Dorothy arrived. They looked shocked, not having heard the news.

'Bloody hell. What's happened, Jessie?' Nancy asked.

'I wish I knew. A policeman called at the house last night to tell me the place was on fire. I've no idea how it started.'

Some of the dockers stopped by on the way to work and stood looking at what was left of the building. There was a barricade in front of the entrance saying it was unsafe to enter for the time being. Fortunately, the firemen had saved the buildings either side and the thick walls still stood separating the buildings one from another. The premises either side had been closed for the night, so no one had been inside, but as the staff from there arrived to start their day, they too were shocked at what they saw.

Jessie looked at her girls. 'I'm sorry, ladies, but that means you, too, are out of a job.'

Nancy tucked her arm through Jessie's. 'What will you do?'

'I have no idea. Unfortunately, I'm not insured. I hadn't got round to doing it. How stupid is that!' She shook her head. 'I still can't quite believe it's happened.' She stared at the remains as if hypnotised by the sight.

'Well it's no good standing here,' declared Nancy. 'Come on, we'll go to my place and get some breakfast, then we'll put our heads together and think of something.'

Jessie allowed her friend to lead her away.

When Larry Forbes arrived, the firemen were on the site, searching through the debris, trying to locate the source of the fire. Eventually, after several hours, they came to the conclusion that the wiring of one of the ovens had been faulty. Forbes remembered that Jessie had told him she'd bought a new one recently and wondered if it was that one. He'd call round to see her this evening and give her an update on the news.

Later, as they sat in the living room, he told her what the firemen had said. 'They haven't found anything else and have come to the conclusion that it had to be the faulty wiring.'

Shaking her head, she said, 'It seemed to be working alright, but I suppose that could happen at any time.' She gave a deep sigh. 'First, I lose Conor, now the cafe. What next, I wonder?'

'Hey! What happened to that wild Irish woman I knew? The Jessie McGonigall I know would never give in like that!'

She shrugged. 'Jessie McGonigall isn't superhuman! Even I have a limit.'

'Of course you do, and I do remember that you've not long lost your husband, which was such a shock, but don't go back into that deep pit again. Come along, Jessie, let's see that indomitable fighting spirit I so admire.'

She gave him a quizzical look. 'Now don't get carried away, Mr Forbes. Such compliments from you? It's almost more than I can take.' But she smiled as she said it.

'That's more like it, and don't you think by now you could call me Larry?'

She studied him with narrowed eyes. 'I'm not sure that would be such a good idea. It sounds just a little too cosy.'

He started to chuckle. 'Fine, if that's how you feel. Have you any idea about your next move?'

'Not at the moment. To be honest, I'm still reeling from the shock. I just need some time to get myself together.'

He got up to leave. 'Well, you know where I am if you need me. Just take care of yourself. Take some time to breathe, to recover. Are you alright for money?'

She looked surprised. 'I'm fine, thank you, but I'm not your responsibility, you know.'

He walked towards the door and opened it. 'That's not quite the way I see it, Jessie.' Then he left.

* * *

During the following two weeks, Jessie did, indeed, take time to breathe. Not by choice, but the reaction to Conor's death and the fire suddenly robbed her of her energy. She was so tired all the time and all she wanted to do was sleep. Daisy made sure she ate, by bringing food into her and keeping the fire burning. She made a pan of soup, which she kept on the stove to keep warm for whenever Jessie felt the need for something that didn't require any effort. She filled the tin bath and washed Jessie's back while her friend soaked in the hot water, helping her lose the stress in her body, talking to her all the time. Then, when she felt she was ready, she suggested to Maisie that she bring the two boys into see Jessie, knowing how much she loved their company. This was her saving grace and she agreed to look after them for the afternoon.

Jack and Tommy brought their schoolbooks into show her, proudly pointing out the gold stars they'd earned, telling her how they were learning to play football.

'I'm going to be a footballer when I grow up,' Tommy proudly declared.

She looked at Jack. 'What are you going to be?'

'I'm going to be a stevedore, like Uncle Conor, and work in the docks. I'm going to load the big ships like he did.'

This took her by surprise. 'It's very hard work, you know, Jack.'

'I know, but running a cafe like you did was hard work too.' He snuggled up to her. 'You used to help us make cakes.'

'I did.'

'When can we do it again?' he pleaded.

She looked at the boy staring up at her and heard the longing in his voice.

'What about now?'

They were both ecstatic at the suggestion and soon they had tea cloths covering their clothes as Jessie collected the ingredients on the table and gave them jobs to do.

Later, when Daisy came to see how they were, she was delighted at the sight of them, covered in flour, cooking together and as Jessie looked up at her and smiled, she knew her friend was back on the road to recovery.

Chapter Thirty-One

1915 started badly. The price of coal increased, there were queues for food, which was in short supply, and Jessie began to search the wanted adverts in the local paper. She did have her savings, but she didn't want to have to dip into those more than was necessary, so she had to find a job of some sort. With so many men away fighting the war, there were jobs to be had, but Jessie was finding it difficult to decide. The one thing she was good at was cooking and she had run a hotel, but only for a short time, so she wasn't really qualified for any position near the top in one that was already established. She couldn't see herself working in a shop, didn't fancy being a conductor on a tram. A barmaid? Maybe. She didn't have enough finance to find a location for a new cafe and have it set up with cookers, crockery, tables and chairs, which would have been ideal. Having saved so diligently, she was determined to hang on to the money she did have as long as possible. It was a worry.

* * *

Several days later, Larry Forbes called on her again, to see if she'd made any plans.

Shaking her head, she said, 'No. I can't seem to find anything I'm trained for or that I want to do. I'm not qualified to do the jobs that appeal to me and at this moment I'm at a loss, to be honest.'

'You could come and work for me.'

She looked at him in surprise. 'Doing what?'

'Running my office.' He sat back and waited for her response.

Frowning, she asked, 'Don't you have a secretary to do that?'

'I do have a secretary, but she deals with my correspondence and my appointments. I need someone to run the office side. I have several business interests and I want someone to keep a list of staff, check the wage bills and receipts, their welfare. Keep abreast of the filing system. You did all this in the hotel, very efficiently as I recall. A clerk is doing it for the moment, but I need someone of your calibre to take over and actually *run* my office.'

Tilting her head, she studied him. Why was he doing this? Was he making a job just for her? Or was there an ulterior motive behind his offer? She still didn't trust him completely.

'Do you have something on your mind, Jessie? You're looking at me with deep suspicion written all over your face.'

'How did this vacancy happen just at this moment?'

'It didn't just happen, it was already there. I just hadn't got around to finding someone, what with the hotel and all its problems. I had a million other things on my mind. Now it seems an ideal moment – and you need a job. It saves me

266

advertising, interviewing. You would be ideal. The hours are nine until five, half-day on a Saturday.' He chuckled softly. 'Think about it! Far less hours than you've been working. You'll have time to enjoy life as well.'

It sounded ideal, but Jessie was still hesitant.

Larry rose to leave. 'Think about it and if you decide to accept, I'll see you at my office at nine o'clock on Monday morning. If you're not there, I'll advertise for someone.'

As he was leaving, Daisy arrived. They said hello to each other and he walked away.

'That was a surprise,' Daisy said. 'Is everything alright?'

Jessie told her what had just taken place.

'But that's terrific! At least you'll be working for someone you know.' She saw the lack of excitement on the face of her friend. 'What's the matter?'

'To be honest, I don't know. The offer came out of the blue and it just seemed too much of a coincidence, that's all.'

Sitting down, Daisy stared at her. 'Are you mad? You know the man, have worked for him, got along alright and now you have a job! For heaven's sake!'

'Well, I suppose I could give it a try. I could always leave if I didn't like it. I'll think about it.'

Larry Forbes sat in his office deep in thought. He did need someone to run the office, that hadn't been a lie and he had been about to advertise for someone – until the fire. Although Jessie had said he wasn't responsible for her welfare, he felt that in a way he was. He'd taken her away from the cafe, to which she'd been able to return when he'd had to close the hotel, and now that, too, was gone. He felt indebted to her and this was his way of giving her a helping hand. Apart from which he admired her spirit. In many ways, they had a lot in common and at the hotel they'd made a great team. Had the war not spoilt their chances, who knew what they could have achieved together? But she was fiercely independent. Would she accept his offer?

Jessie was up early on Monday morning. She had a bowl of porridge for breakfast and then, putting on her coat and hat, made her way to the high street. Larry Forbes's office was just beyond the bank. She stopped and read the gold plate outside. *Larry Forbes. Company Director.*

Nothing else. No information about his business interests. She'd often wondered about that. How did he make his money? Well, perhaps now she'd find out! Taking a deep breath, she pushed open the heavy glass door.

Seated at a small desk was a receptionist. 'Good morning, madam. Can I help you?'

'I'm here to see Mr Forbes. He is expecting me. Mrs Jessie McGonigall.'

The girl rose from her chair and walked to a closed door, knocked on it and entered, closing it behind her. Moments later she opened the door and invited Jessie in.

Larry Forbes, smartly dressed as always, smiled at Jessie as he stood up from behind his desk to greet her. 'You did come. I wasn't sure you would. Sit down and I'll tell you about your position.'

During the next hour, Forbes gave her all the details of what her post would entail. She'd have the clerk who'd been running the office before as an assistant to help her with the transition and to remain as an assistant once she was settled and up to date, and she'd have her own office.

He then got to his feet. 'Your office is through here,' he said and led her to a door inside his office. There were two desks, one for her and the other for her assistant.

'Having your office so close to mine will be an advantage for when I need a file or want to check on something,' he explained. 'Get yourself settled and I'll send in Helen to help you in a while. Good luck, Jessie.'

Left alone, Jessie removed her coat and hat, hung them up behind the door, then she sat at the desk. Behind her was a window that shed its light, making the office bright and airy. There were paper, pens, pencils and all the other paraphernalia required.

There was a knock on the door.

'Come in!'

A young woman entered. 'Good morning, Mrs McGonigall, I'm Helen Mitchell. I'm to be your assistant and I'm here to show you how Mr Forbes likes the office to run.'

Jessie looked at the girl and liked what she saw. There was no animosity in her voice, having her position taken from her. She was neatly attired in a blouse and skirt, hair carefully dressed.

'Thank you, Helen. I have a lot to learn and I'll be more than grateful for your help. Shall we get started?'

That first morning was extremely busy, with Helen showing Jessie what was required and Jessie taking copious notes as she worked. By lunchtime, she was exhausted, her mind in a whirl, but her inbred sense of organisation came to her rescue. She knew that it would take a few weeks before she would feel in control and blessed Larry Forbes for having the good sense to let Helen be her assistant.

At lunchtime, he came into the office and sent Helen for her lunch break.

'How are you getting on?' he asked.

'My head's bursting with detail,' she cried, 'and it will take some time before I'm in control, but Helen is so helpful. Without her I'd be lost.'

'That's why she's here. Now, you need a break. Opposite here is a pub that sells sandwiches, so I suggest we go there to recharge our batteries. Now don't argue. I know you, you'd stay here and work. Well that isn't a good idea. Your brain needs a rest. Come along!'

He took her coat from behind the door and held it out for her.

They sat at a quiet table in one corner of the pub with sandwiches and a half of bitter to wash it down. Jessie savoured the freedom of leaving the office as she relaxed and enjoyed her lunch. She had discovered that Forbes did indeed have a finger in several pies, but as yet hadn't been able to study them, only where the files to the businesses were to be found, the names of the staff in each company and their level of pay. No doubt this afternoon, she'd learn even more.

The hour for lunch was promptly kept and they returned to their respective offices, and so, Jessie continued to feel her way into her new job. At five o'clock, she said goodbye to Helen, collected her pile of notes and left the office. Her employer had already vacated his.

When she walked into her house, she slumped down in a chair, took off her shoes and let out a deep breath. What a day that had been! Her brain was full of details that made her head spin. She closed her eyes for a moment to try to unwind. What she really needed was to sit in a bath, to relax. Oh, how she longed for the bathroom she'd had at the hotel where all she needed to do was turn on a tap! Reluctantly, she got up and laid a fire, filled some pans with water to warm when the fire took hold and after hauling in the tin bath in readiness, she sat down and waited.

Her thoughts strayed to Conor. How she longed for him. To hear his voice, feel his arms around her. Just to know he'd be there. But the house seemed empty without him, as she did sometimes, when she allowed herself to think. The manner of his death still haunted her. Did he suffer? Was he conscious when he hit the water? She knew he'd been injured from the coroner's report. Tears slowly trickled down her cheeks as she began to cry.

Eventually, Jessie filled the bath and undressed, then pouring some Epsom salts in the water to help relieve her aching bones, she stepped into the bath and lay there, letting her body relax.

She must be positive, she chided herself. Larry Forbes had offered her a job. She was earning money. The hours were reasonable. She was in a much better position than those poor men that had marched through the town, now having to fight the enemy. Some wouldn't ever return to their families. She understood how that felt.

The water in the bath had cooled and she climbed out, dried herself and put on some warm clothes, then started emptying the bath, carrying bowls of water to the kitchen sink, until the bath was light enough to drag to the kitchen and tip out what remained of the water into the yard outside.

She cooked some sausages and boiled potatoes to mash, made a gravy and sat at the table to eat her dinner, reading through her notes as she ate. Tomorrow would again be a busy day and she needed her sleep. She'd not be late to bed this night.

Chapter Thirty-Two

It was now two months since Jessie had accepted the new position and at last she felt she knew what she was doing. She now realised why Larry Forbes was a wealthy man. He was involved in so many businesses and he ran a very tight ship. She began to appreciate his ability to see an opportunity and run with it. His only failure as far as she could see was the hotel, but that had been a loss only through unforeseen circumstances. The war had played havoc in the business world, yet even so, he'd also benefited. He'd bought a factory, which was now making uniforms and doing well.

Jessie was kept busy, filing away each monthly return and checking on the wages account from each business. In fact, she'd quickly uncovered a discrepancy in one, which had led to a sacking, but she'd saved Forbes from being cheated even further. Naturally, he was delighted.

'I don't blame Helen for missing this,' he said. 'That bugger was so very clever in covering his tracks. I'm really disappointed in Harry Briggs. He's worked for me for some time, but it seems he'd started gambling and got into debt. Anyway, I'm taking him to court. It'll be some time before he will be employed again. Embezzlement usually carries a custodial sentence. I'm taking you out to dinner as a reward.'

'I was only doing my job!' Jessie argued.

He looked at her and frowned. 'Is that your way of refusing my invitation, Mrs McGonigall?'

She became flustered. 'No, of course not.'

'Then how about tomorrow? I'll pick you up at seven o'clock,' he said as he left the office.

Helen looked across the room at Jessie and smiled. 'You don't look particularly happy at being invited out for a meal,' she remarked.

'It was just such a surprise, that's all,' said Jessie as she returned to her work, but in her mind she was asking herself why she was so reticent about accepting the invitation. To her, Larry Forbes was still an unknown force. She hadn't forgotten the early days when they battled over the workman's cafe. He could be ruthless, this she knew for a fact, and yet she'd enjoyed working for him at the hotel. There they'd made a great team. He'd also been of great comfort when the cafe burnt down and now she was working for him again. He unsettled her – that was it! She'd always been able to cope with whatever life had thrown at her. She was a good judge of character as a rule, but he was still as much a mystery to her now as the first day they met. Being uncertain was not at all usual for her and she didn't like it. In fact, it worried her. She didn't like uncertainties.

* * *

It was a cool April evening and Jessie wore a gown that Daisy had made for her in a chestnut-coloured silk. Over this she wore a dark-brown velvet coat to keep her warm. She dressed her hair carefully, twisting it on top of her head and pushed her favourite tortoiseshell comb in it. Standing in front of a full-length mirror she studied her reflection, turning one way and another.

'Well, if I say so meself, Jessie McGonigall, you look bloody marvellous, so you do!'

At that moment there was a knock on the door. Jessie felt a flutter of anticipation and nerves as she opened it.

Larry, dressed immaculately, smiled as he gazed at her. 'You look quite beautiful, Jessie. Shall we go?'

They caught a tram to Watts Park and walked through to the Polygon Hotel, where Larry took her into the cocktail bar for an aperitif before dining. They sat at a table and settled down.

'Oh, I can't tell you how much I'm looking forward to tonight,' he said. 'I've not been out socialising lately, and I'm sure you haven't either.'

'Oh, and what makes you so sure of that?'

'You needn't be so defensive, Jessie, I know you. You lead a quiet life. Yes, you have lovely neighbours, but to go out on the town isn't part of your social life and hasn't been since Conor died. Tell me I'm wrong.'

Shrugging, she said, 'No, that's true, right enough. It's been sixteen months since I lost him, and my life changed in many ways.' She gave a wan smile. 'That's how it is.'

'It need not be. You are still a young woman and

beautiful. You still have a full life in front of you, a lot to offer. You shouldn't spend the rest of your life alone.'

At that moment a bellboy came over and told Larry their table was ready.

The dining room in The Polygon was classy and a little palatial, with its chandeliers and lighting. The head waiter led them to a table and, after taking Jessie's coat, held the seat for her. A bottle of champagne was in an ice bucket beside the table. Another waiter came over and poured two glasses.

Larry picked up his glass and held it up. 'Thank you, Jessie, for a job well done.'

She clicked hers with his. 'That's what you pay me for,' she said and grinned broadly at her companion.

'I do hope you don't mind, but I've taken the liberty of pre-ordering.'

'No, I don't mind at all.'

They had smoked salmon to start with and the waiter carried over a chateaubriand, carving it at the table. The steak looked succulent and the aroma smelt delicious. It was served with assorted vegetables and chipped potatoes, plus a bottle of red wine, which the waiter poured after Larry had tasted it and nodded his approval.

'I hope my choice is to your liking, Jessie?'

'It's absolutely lovely. This steak is so tender. Thank you.' She gazed at the man opposite her and began to wonder about *his* social life.

'A penny for your thoughts!'

She looked startled. 'What do you mean?'

He gave a soft smile. 'Well, something was going through your mind as you looked at me.'

She started laughing. 'Oh dear, was it that obvious?'

'So . . .'

'I was just wondering about *your* social life. Do you have one?'

He found this most amusing. 'Of course I do! You can't be in business and not have one. There are business meetings, business lunches etc.'

'No, that's not what I mean. I mean a personal social life.'

With twinkling eyes, he looked at her. 'Do I have a woman in my life, is that what you're wondering?'

She tilted her head as she returned his gaze. 'Yes! That's about it. Well do you?'

'Not any more. There was someone once, but that was a long time ago.'

Thinking of her own position, she asked, 'Don't you ever get lonely?'

He studied her for a moment and, eventually, said, 'Yes, I do. Very.'

The waiter came over to remove their plates. Then he served the dessert. A delicious peach Melba served in a cut-glass dish.

'I hope you like this,' Larry remarked. 'It was made to honour Nellie Melba, the opera singer, and is a favourite of mine. I imagine the peaches were grown under glass somewhere.'

Jessie hadn't eaten one before and really enjoyed it, taking each mouthful delicately and eating it slowly to enjoy every last morsel.

'It's really lovely,' she declared.

'You are such a pleasure to dine with, Jessie. So many women pick at their food, which I find such an irritation, but not you. The chef cooks for people like you. Someone who fully appreciates what's placed before them.'

'Ah well, Mr Forbes, you must remember I come from Irish stock who went through a famine! After that, families taught their children to appreciate whatever food they found on their plates!'

'Oh, for goodness' sake, Jessie, it's time to stop this "Mr Forbes", except in the office. After all, we've been through enough together for you to feel able to call me Larry, surely!'

Seeing the indignation of his face, she started laughing. 'Alright! Good heavens, you don't have to have a fit about it . . . Larry!'

He looked bewildered. 'You are the most cantankerous woman I've ever met!'

'You're not the first person to tell me that, nor the last, I expect.'

'I suppose you could say it's part of your charm, Jessie McGonigall! But sometimes . . .'

She just grinned at him and sipped her champagne.

After drinking coffee and a liqueur they walked back through the park, Larry tucking Jessie's arm in his. There was a crescent moon in a clear sky. It was quiet and peaceful and after such a meal, Jessie was feeling thoughtful.

'Isn't it the saddest thing? Here we are, walking through the park, all quiet and peaceful, and across the Channel men are fighting and dying. It doesn't seem right.'

'There will always be power-hungry men, Jessie. You find it in all walks of life. I've seen it in business, then you see it in nations. Some men have only the good of their country at heart, for others, it isn't enough. But come, young lady, let's not become melancholy after such a nice evening.'

They caught a tram back to the high street and walked through The Ditches to Union Street. Larry waited for Jessie to unlock her door.

'Thank you for a lovely evening, Larry,' she said. 'I'll see you in the office tomorrow.'

He caught her by the shoulders and kissed her forehead. 'And don't be late,' he said as he walked away.

Jessie let herself into the living room, removed her coat and sat down. She'd really enjoyed the evening. The food was superb, The Polygon was comfortable and Larry was good company, but she didn't know him any better. He was still a man of mystery. He'd said he was lonely and that *had* surprised her. He always appeared to be so self-sufficient. She wondered who the woman was who had once been a part of his life. What had happened there? she puzzled.

Getting to her feet, she made for her bedroom. Work tomorrow. 'Don't be late!' he'd said and he'd kissed her on her forehead. That had been a surprise! But when she considered this, she decided she hadn't minded at all.

Chapter Thirty-Three

The times of war were biting bitterly and food was getting short. Queues gathered outside all the food shops and prices rose. Germans were sinking ships carrying food supplies and then the *Lusitania* was another victim of a German submarine. To add to the horrors, Zeppelins had raided various towns, their bombs destroying houses and taking civilian lives.

Jessie and her neighbours, like everyone else, became experts at making food with very little meat. Many grew vegetables and kept chickens, as did her neighbours next door, but they had to kill a chicken when the boys were in bed asleep as they looked upon the birds as pets.

However, work in the office continued. Some of Larry Forbes's business interests were hit by the war, others were not. The factory making uniforms was kept busy and his finances were still healthy.

The case against Harry Briggs came to court and, eventually, he was let out on bail to return two weeks later for sentencing. Larry had mixed feelings about it.

'I'm sorry for the man getting himself into financial trouble through gambling, but he betrayed my trust. That I cannot forgive.'

'Does he have a family?' asked Jessie.

'Yes, he does, which makes matters even worse.'

'How will they manage?'

He hesitated, then said, 'I've found the wife a job in the factory, so at least she'll be earning and able to feed her children, but I've warned her, not one penny is to be given to him or she'll be out of work!'

'What did she say to that?'

He chuckled. 'I can't repeat what she said, but I can assure you her husband hasn't a chance. He isn't her favourite person at this moment. He'll probably welcome prison to get some peace!'

It had been a long day and Jessie was feeling weary as she walked home. She turned the corner of Union Street and heard hurried footsteps behind her. She looked round thinking it might be one of her neighbours, but she was confronted by a stranger. A man with his flat cap pulled down over his eyes and his collar turned up. He looked angry and Jessie felt a frisson of fear as she looked at him.

The man grabbed her by her coat and, putting his face against hers, he spoke.

'You bitch! You cost me my job!'

Jessie, used to standing up to awkward men during her days in the cafe, glared at him.

'What are you talking about? I don't even know you!'

'I'm Harry Briggs. You got me fired!'

She immediately recognised the name and pushed him away. 'I didn't get you fired, you managed that all by yourself by stealing from your boss. I just happened to be the one who found you out!'

'S'pose you think you're clever, don't you?'

'No! But I think you were stupid! You had a good job, a position of trust, but you stole money from your employer, all through gambling. You didn't consider your position, your employer – or your family!'

The mention of his family enraged him and he caught her by the throat. 'My wife hates me. She's earning, but won't give me a penny. I have to sleep on the sofa; the kids sleep with her in our bed.'

'That's no fault of mine,' Jessie said with some difficulty as the hold on her throat was constricting her breathing.

He leered at her. 'No conjugal rights. That ain't right. I reckon you owe me, lady.'

He began to fumble with her clothes, letting go of her throat. Jessie quickly kneed him in the groin and, when he bent double in pain, she gave him a blow on the jaw with a terrific left hook that any man would have been proud of. As he writhed on the ground she leant over him.

'Now you'll also stand trial for assault because I'm reporting you to the police. You come anywhere near me again, you'll pay dearly!' She stalked off and crossed the road to the pub, rubbing her sore knuckles, leaving the man on the ground.

Once inside the Builders Arms she phoned the police and reported the assault, but by the time they arrived, Harry Briggs had limped away.

The pub landlord insisted she sit down and gave her a shot of brandy. Now the confrontation was over, the aftermath began to sink in. She'd been so angry with the man, she'd not given a moment's notice to the danger she'd been in, but now she was shaken.

A police officer came into the pub and asked her to go to the station in the morning and give a statement. He picked up her hand and saw the bruised knuckles.

'Did you hit your assailant?'

'Bloody right I did! He tried to lift up my skirt. No man gets away with that!'

With a broad grin the policeman said, 'Looking at those bruises, Mrs McGonigall, he got the worst of it.' He paused. 'Just make sure you lock your doors and windows when you go home. Best be on the safe side, in case we can't find the man.'

Jessie's heart sank. She hadn't considered she may still be in danger, but it was a possibility she accepted, remembering the rage of Briggs as he grabbed hold of her. Well, she'd be prepared. If he came to her home, she'd be ready! She had a *shillelagh*, a wooden cudgel she'd brought over with her from Ireland. She playfully used to tease Conor that she'd use it on him if he misbehaved. Well, if Harry Briggs came calling, he'd understand a bit more about her Irish heritage!

After a disturbed night's sleep, Jessie arrived at the office the following morning. Larry Forbes greeted her, but was surprised when Jessie said she'd have to go to the local police station later.

'Whatever for?' Then he saw the tense expression on her face. 'Sit down and tell me what's been going on.'

She told him what had happened and he was furious.

'Have the police picked him up?'

'They hadn't last night, as far as I know. They told me to lock my doors and windows, to be safe.'

'Did he hurt you, Jessie?'

'Not physically. But I'm afraid he can't say the same.'

Forbes looked at her and saw her trying to hide a smile. 'What did you do to him?'

'I kneed him in the groin, then I punched him on the jaw.'

He put a hand across his mouth to try and stop laughing. 'Oh, Jessie McGonigall, what a woman you are! However . . . no way are you sleeping in your house until this man is caught. I'm coming with you to the police station. Helen can run the office while we're gone. Come along!'

Jessie, to her surprise, was pleased Larry had taken it upon himself to accompany her. He was so very efficient and on their arrival he took over, questioning the constable on duty, asking if Briggs had been caught and frowning when told he was still at large. He waited for Jessie as she was taken into an interview room.

The sergeant questioned her, asking her to tell him exactly what had happened, then gave her a pen and paper to write out her statement.

When she emerged, Larry took her by the arm. 'Right, now we go to your place and you pack a bag with a few things you'll need because you are definitely not staying alone in your house!'

As he propelled her along she asked, 'And where do you suggest I go?'

'To my place, of course! I've a spare bedroom you can have, then at least I'll know you're safe.'

She was too surprised to argue and, from the tone of his voice, she doubted that he would listen anyway.

Jessie hurriedly packed a few clothes, her nightdress and toiletries and walked downstairs. Larry picked up her case and said, 'I've looked around and everything is safely locked, so let's go.'

They didn't make conversation on their walk back to the office and when they arrived, he put her case in a cupboard and, looking at her, said, 'Fine. Now let's get back to normal. I'll see you at lunchtime.'

Jessie found it hard to concentrate for a while. She'd been swept along by her boss and was wondering how she was going to feel staying with him. Would she see a different side to this enigma of a man? But for a while it had been comforting to have someone take over the situation that had befallen her. It had been some time since that had happened and it left her feeling somewhat confused.

At lunchtime, Larry appeared at Jessie's office door, sending Helen for her lunch break and suggesting that Jessie go with him to the local for a beer and a sandwich, as they had done before.

Once settled, he relaxed and, turning to her, asked,

'How are you now? Do you feel any better having given your statement? That couldn't have been easy, having to go through that again.'

'It wasn't so bad. Thanks for coming with me.'

'What else could I do? I couldn't let you go on your own.'

'I've told you, you're not responsible for me!'

He gazed at her. 'Yes, you have, but somehow I do feel responsible and I don't mind at all, so why should it trouble you?'

'I wish I knew!' she retorted.

'Your trouble, Jessie, is that you are far too independent. You have spent your life fighting to survive. Relax a little, make room for your friends and people who care about you.'

'You make me sound unfriendly and I'm not at all.'

'No, you're not, but since Conor's death, you've built a wall around you to stop anyone getting too close. It's time to take down those barriers.'

'Now you're a psychologist?'

Grinning broadly, he answered, 'Not at all, just a friend.'

That evening at the close of the working day, Larry collected Jessie and her suitcase, then caught a tram to The Avenue, a wide long road at the edge of town, surrounded by trees and well-built houses. It almost felt like moving into the countryside.

Jessie was filled with curiosity as Larry stopped outside a large house and led her up the path to a solid carved front door, which he opened, then stood back to allow her to enter.

There was a large hallway with tiled flooring, a winding staircase and several doors leading off it. In one corner was a tall stand with a plant in it. It looked strangely old-fashioned, which surprised her.

Larry took her into his living room. It was welcoming, cosy and beautifully furnished. There was a large fireplace, with an ornate mirror over a mantelpiece. Either side of the fire facing each other were two comfortable sofas, a side table at the back of one of them with several bottles of spirits and cut glasses. Ornate rugs covered the floor. Around the room were one or two comfortable upholstered chairs and a French door, draped in dark green velvet. In the middle of the room a small but splendid chandelier hung from the ceiling, with standard lights placed in the corners, which would give a comforting light on a dark night.

He put a light to the already-laid fire and then walked over to the bottles. Picking up a glass he asked, 'Whisky and soda?'

'That would be lovely,' she said.

'Sit down, Jessie,' he said, pointing to one of the sofas. 'The fire will soon catch.' He poured their drinks and handed one to her, then sat opposite. 'Cheers!'

'Cheers!' she answered. 'You have a beautiful home, Larry.'

He looked pleased. 'Thank you. I bought it some time ago. It's peaceful here. Nice to get away from the bustle of the town and business. I have a housekeeper who comes in daily. She's left some food in the oven for us. She's a wonderful cook, so we should eat well tonight.'

Thinking of her own home with the outside toilet and tin bath, Jessie couldn't help the comparison. She'd tasted the better side of living when she'd worked for Forbes in the hotel, but for him, this was his style, his life. But he'd worked hard for his money, so she didn't begrudge him the comfort that brought.

Shortly after, Larry took her into a small dining room, where the table was already laid, and settled her. 'I'll just go into the kitchen and get our meal.'

He returned shortly with a tray of food, which he placed on the sideboard. He took a pie and placed it on a mat in the centre of the table, then another dish with vegetables, followed by yet another of smoothly mashed potatoes. Finally, he put a jug of gravy on the table.

Jessie watched as he served the food onto the plates. This was a side to him she'd never seen and it amused her to see him so domesticated.

'Tuck in,' he said. 'I don't know about you, Jessie, but I'm starving!'

The delicious aroma wafted across the table and Jessie realised she, too, was hungry. She took a morsel of food and ate it. 'This is delicious and the pastry is so light. Your housekeeper is indeed a good cook!'

'Coming from you, that is really a compliment. I remember you had a great reputation as a cook when you ran the cafe.'

'That seems like another life,' she said.

'Well it was. But time marches on. We just have to make the best of it.'

After dinner, Jessie helped to clear the dishes and insisted on washing up. While she did so, Larry made some coffee and they took it into the living room. The fire threw out its comforting warmth and Jessie felt herself relax. How nice it must be, she thought, to come home to such a comfortable place at the end of the working day. But then she realised that Larry would come back to an empty house. Yes, there would be a meal prepared, but he would sit alone to eat it. Now she realised why he said he was lonely. She could understand that, because she felt the same when she walked into her empty home.

When they finished their coffee, her host took her upstairs to the spare bedroom. It had twin beds, a wardrobe, side tables and a dressing table with a triple mirror. On the bed were clean towels.

'The bathroom is across the hall,' he told her. 'I'll give you a call in the morning, so try and get a good night's sleep.'

'Thanks for this,' Jessie said.

He just smiled and left the room.

Jessie washed and changed, then climbing into bed, thought how very strange life could be. Here she was sleeping in a bed belonging to a man she used to dislike intensely those few years ago, but he had been her salvation several times over. Weird, very weird!

Chapter Thirty-Four

The following morning, Jessie was awakened by a tapping on her door. 'Come in!' she called. Larry entered with a cup of tea, which he placed on the bedside table, opened the curtains and, turning to her, said, 'Breakfast in half an hour!'

The smell of bacon wafted in the air as Jessie came down the stairs and headed for the kitchen. Larry was at the stove cooking. The kitchen table was laid, the kettle boiling.

'There's the teapot. Pour the water into it, will you, while I cook the eggs.'

There was toast and marmalade to accompany the breakfast. As she tucked into the food, she looked at him. 'You really are full of surprises!'

He raised his eyebrows. 'How so?'

'I never ever saw you as domesticated.'

'I live alone, Jessie. You don't think I'm going hungry, surely?'

'To be honest, I've never pictured you at home.'

'I'm never quite sure what kind of picture you do have of me, but it's far from the man I am, that I'm sure of.'

They finished their breakfast without further conversation, aware of the passing time and the need to get to the office.

Three days passed and Briggs was still in hiding and so Jessie continued to go home each evening with her boss. They began to relax in each other's company and the evenings became enjoyable.

On the fourth day, Jessie spent the day with Nancy. They shopped, had lunch and went to the cinema. Jessie had planned to take a later tram to the house in The Avenue and Larry said he'd wait until she arrived to eat.

It was dark when eventually the girls went their separate ways. Jessie made her way towards Canal Walk, taking a shortcut to the nearest tram stop. It was quiet, the shops in The Ditches were now all closed. It was too early for the brasses to congregate for the evening's business and it was deserted. Jessie wasn't worried; she'd lived in the area for so many years and was familiar with the comings and goings of the place.

She stopped to peer into the window of the pawnshop, its contents dimly lit from a street light, when she was suddenly grabbed from behind and hit over the head.

Slowly opening her eyes, Jessie was dazed, her head ached. She was on hard ground. The place was in darkness apart from a shaft of light coming from a small window. She then realised her hands were tied. From what little light there was, she was able to see she was in a small room. But where and why? Who had hit her? She tried to concentrate. It could only be one person who would wish to harm her and that was Harry Briggs! She felt the blood chill in her veins. Where was he? Why had he left her here . . . and what was he going to do when he returned?

She managed to get to her feet, but feeling dizzy, put her head down until she felt more stable. Feeling round the walls, she found a wooden door. Feeling all over it, she looked for some weakness, but it appeared to be solidly built and locked. She turned and walked a few paces and stumbled over something. Feeling around, she found it to be a small stool and placed it back on its legs, then sat down. She was in deep trouble, she now realised. No one would know where she was – only that she was missing. Where was this place? She had no idea. It had to be part of a building, but which one and where? Getting to her feet, Jessie started calling for help, but there was just silence. No sound outside to help her. She tried to undo the bonds that were round her wrists, but was unable to move them. Tears of frustration trickled down her cheeks. She was thirsty and hungry . . . and angry! The only chance she would have was when Briggs returned. He'd have to open the door, and so she'd have to be ready for him to have any chance at all.

Larry Forbes kept looking at his watch. Jessie was very late. Surely her meeting couldn't have taken this long? Another hour passed and he left the house. He made his way to Nancy's home and knocked on the door.

When she answered it, she was surprised to see him there, but even more surprised when he told her Jessie hadn't returned.

'But I left her three hours ago!'

'Which way did she go, do you know?'

'She walked towards The Ditches.' She frowned. 'Do you think something's happened to her, Mr Forbes?'

He nodded. 'I'm afraid so. I'm going to report this to the police now.' He hurried away.

An hour later the police had a search party out looking for Jessie. They went to Briggs's house, but his wife said he hadn't been home for two days. They searched every inch of The Ditches and found one of Jessie's gloves.

Empty buildings in the area were thoroughly searched to no avail. Door-to-door searches were made, but no one had heard or seen anything of Jessie McGonigall or Harry Briggs.

At the end of the day, Larry Forbes walked up and down his living room, wracking his brains as to where Briggs could have taken Jessie. He must have found her in The Ditches, but knowing Jessie's fighting spirit, Briggs must have attacked her, maybe knocked her unconscious. That was the only way he could have managed to remove her. No one heard any screams or cries, so she must have been helpless. The thought terrified him. Was she badly hurt? Tomorrow when it was light he'd resume his search. What else could he do?

Jessie woke at daybreak. She'd slept huddled up on the floor and was stiff. Her mouth was dry and she was covered in dust. Now she could see her surroundings. Struggling to her feet, she looked around. The room was in a basement, this she could tell from the small window above. She could make out some buildings opposite, but they looked derelict. She couldn't recognise where she might be, nothing looked familiar. Her head still ached. She managed to get her tied hands to her head where she felt a bump, which was tender to the touch. She stretched her aching bones.

'You'll bloody well pay for this, Briggs! Just you wait until you come through that door. I'm ready for you, you bastard!' She stormed around the room venting her anger, then she sat upon the stool. She was bursting to go to the toilet, but there was no receptacle she could use. Through sheer desperation, she went into a corner and hoisted her skirt, then lowered her drawers and relieved herself. That indignity was the final straw.

She walked to the window and started calling as loud as she could until her throat ached, but there was no sound from outside. As the hours passed, no one came into the street. Jessie tried to overcome the rising feeling of panic that was beginning to overtake her reasoning. She must be strong! Briggs would have to come eventually. She would just have to be patient. She sat on the floor, propped up against a wall, and waited.

It was midday before she heard footsteps outside. She quickly got to her feet and, picking up the stool, she held it over her head to use it when her adversary entered the room. The steps stopped. She held her breath.

Suddenly, a small grille in the door, which she hadn't

noticed, opened and part of Briggs's grinning face could be seen.

'Did you sleep well, Mrs McGonigall? Not so cosy as that lovely house in The Avenue, I'm afraid.'

'You bastard! Let me out of here.'

'Do you think I'm stupid? But, of course, I forgot, you told me I was. Not any more. I'm the one in charge now.'

She tried another tactic. 'Look, Briggs, you are already in enough trouble with the police. This will only make matters worse. Be sensible and stop this, now.'

He became angry. 'I'm going to prison anyway, so what does it matter? At least this way I'll have paid back Mr Forbes and you, and that'll give me enough satisfaction as I spend the extra years. My life is ruined anyway, so what difference will it make?'

'I'm thirsty. Can I have some water to drink? It's the least you can do.'

'No chance! I'm not coming back. I'm leaving you to rot. You can sit and think how clever you were to find me out. Not so clever now, though. No one's going to find *you*, Mrs . . .'

She could hear him walking away, laughing loudly. She called after him continuously, but, eventually, there was nothing but silence. Jessie sank to her knees.

Larry Forbes had been searching the streets around the area where Jessie had last been. He reasoned that Briggs couldn't have gone far with her if he'd had to carry her, which was likely if she was unconscious. The police hadn't found anything either and Briggs was still missing.

There were headlines in the local paper with a picture of Jessie. CAFE OWNER MISSING. Then another picture of Harry Briggs: HAVE YOU SEEN THIS MAN? asking people to look in sheds and empty buildings, to keep an eye out for both.

The dockers who'd been Jessie's customers were enraged and upset that such a thing could happen to the woman they admired so much, but still further searches were fruitless.

Another night passed.

Jessie opened her eyes. She was laid on her side, her tied hands over her stomach. Her mouth was dry and she felt weak. Slowly, she tried to sit up. Every bone seemed to ache. Rolling over onto her knees, she struggled to stand, but as she got to her feet, she was so dizzy; she staggered against the wall, which stopped her falling. She looked around the bare walls and towards the door, but she was confused. How long had she been here?

Looking across at the window, she gazed at the buildings across the road. Why didn't anyone come? She opened her mouth to call, but her voice was but a croak. She slid down the wall and sat on the floor. Was this where she was to die? Briggs wasn't coming back, she remembered him saying so. Tears brimmed her eyes. This wasn't supposed to happen. She was supposed to live to a ripe old age, battling for survival probably as she'd seemed to have done for so long.

She thought about her parents. Her poor father, who had been so ill before he was taken. Her distraught mother who'd then returned to Ireland. If only she'd been able to see her just one more time before she had passed away.

Then there was Conor. Lovely Conor. Her wild Irishman whom she'd adored. He, too, had left her. How cruel life was. Her past life filled her thoughts as she faced what could be her final hours.

But then it hadn't all been bad, she reasoned. She'd run the cafe and, eventually, to her surprise, had become the manageress of a hotel, working for Larry Forbes. She thought of her days there. That had been nice. She smiled as she remembered the bathroom. Such a luxury. Then she thought of the house in The Avenue, which had been her salvation for a few days. Where was Larry? She called his name. Why couldn't he find her? He was so bloody efficient . . . where the hell was he? Then she passed out.

Larry Forbes was in the office, poring over a street map of Southampton. Ticking off the places he'd searched. Then he suddenly remembered the small one-storey building he'd bought years ago that had been used for storage, but was no longer in use. It was in a cul-de-sac and he'd forgotten it. He searched for the keys, grabbed his coat and left the office.

Forbes turned into the cul-de-sac. It was deserted. The buildings long empty and neglected. He opened the front door. There were two rooms, but they were empty. He let out a deep sigh. It had been his one last hope. He locked the door and began to walk away. He glanced down at the small window just below the pavement and walked on. He was desperate. Where the hell was Jessie? His one worry was that she was injured somewhere, or worse. Suddenly, he stopped and turned. That small window was part of the building, but he didn't recall a cellar. He entered the building again. He searched the two rooms, and then he saw a door so covered in dust that it was hardly visible. There was a key in the lock. He opened the door and stepped inside.

Chapter Thirty-Five

Larry immediately saw the figure of Jessie in a bundle on the ground. 'Oh my God. Jessie!' he called as he knelt beside her. He now realised that she was unconscious. For one dreadful moment he'd thought she was dead. He gathered her into his arms when he realised she was breathing, but looking at her, he knew he needed to get help quickly. Taking off his coat, he covered her, then he ran from the building, heading for a small office block he knew of nearby and, rushing in, demanded to use their telephone for an emergency. They happily obliged after seeing the state he was in. Then he ran back to the building.

Sitting on the floor, he held Jessie, talking softly to her all the time. 'You're safe now, Jessie, I've got you. The ambulance is coming. You hang on. Don't you dare leave me, do you hear? I'm responsible for you whether you like it or not and I'm telling you to stay with me! You're the most difficult woman I've ever met, but this time you are to do as you're told!'

* * *

Later, Jessie lay in the hospital bed, unaware of her surroundings. She was having the strangest dream. She could hear the quiet buzz of voices, but couldn't make out what they were saying. She thought she heard Larry speak. Then it all faded away.

Larry Forbes sat by the bed holding her hand. 'Come along, Jessie, don't just lie there. Give me some sign you're alright or I think I'll go crazy!' He gazed at the pale face on the pillow. This usually vibrant woman, now so still.

The doctor had spoken to him. 'Mrs McGonigall was so very dehydrated, but we've managed to get some fluids into her system, now we have to wait.'

Gazing at the patient, Larry remembered the early days, when he first encountered Jessie McGonigall. How she'd cleverly thwarted his plans to take over the cafe and how eventually he'd won, by buying the lease. That had given him so much pleasure to have bettered this feisty woman who'd stood up to him. Despite the fact she'd been a thorn in his side, he'd always admired her fighting spirit. How strange it had been that, eventually, they had worked together in the hotel. They had made a great team and, had the war not intervened, who knows what might have happened?

'You really are an extraordinary woman, Jessie,' he said. 'You should have been born a man because you are unlike any woman I've ever met!'

She stirred and he held his breath, but she didn't wake.

He became angry. 'If I find that bastard, Briggs, I'll do that man an injury, I swear I will, for doing this to you!' He felt her squeeze his hand. Could she possibly hear what he was saying? he wondered. The mind was a strange thing.

'You get better, Jessie, and I promise you, you'll never have to worry about another thing as long as you live.'

Eventually, exhaustion caught up with the man and he lay his head on the bed, still clasping Jessie's hand and fell asleep.

An hour later, the patient stirred and opened her eyes. She was totally confused as she looked around. She tried to move her hand, but couldn't, then she saw Larry's head, resting on the bed, clasping her hand beside him. Where on earth was she and what was he doing there?

The nurse, keeping a watchful eye on her, saw she was awake and walked into the room. 'Hello, Mrs McGonigall. I'm so pleased to see you are back with us.' She placed a hand on Larry's shoulder to wake him.

'Where am I?' she asked with some difficulty as her voice was still a little hoarse.

Larry, awake at last and delighted to see she was conscious, answered. 'You are in hospital, Jessie. Just relax. I'm here, don't you worry about a thing.'

The nurse held her wrist and took her pulse. 'That's better,' she said. 'I'll just let the doctor know you are awake.'

Slowly, Jessie began to remember. She looked at Larry. 'Briggs!' she said, eyes wide as she began to recall what had happened.

Larry caught both her hands in his. 'Don't you worry about him, Jessie. You're safe now and I'm going to take care of you.'

Her eyes began to fill with tears. 'I thought I was going to die, that no one would find me.'

Larry let go of her hands and climbed on the bed beside her. He took her into his arms to comfort her. 'I would have searched the ends of the earth to find you, surely you knew that?'

'But you took so long!' She began to sob.

He let her cry and just held her until the wracking sobs ceased and she began to recover.

'There! Feel better?'

'No, I feel so weak. I'm so thirsty and I can't speak properly.'

Getting off the bed, Larry poured her a glass of water from a jug on the bedside cupboard.

She drank it slowly. 'Where is that wicked bastard?'

'Briggs? I don't know. I've been here with you since I found you. But he won't remain free for long. The Southampton police force are looking for him.'

The doctor arrived. 'Ah, Mrs McGonigall, it's good to see you have a bit of colour back in your cheeks. How are you feeling?'

'A bit disorientated, to be honest, but I do feel hungry. I don't remember when last I ate.'

'Well, that's a healthy sign. I'll make sure you have something light in a while. Scrambled eggs alright?'

She smiled her thanks. 'With some bread and butter, would be lovely.'

The doctor looked at Larry. 'She's truly an indomitable woman!'

'Oh, Doctor, you have no idea!'

Gazing at his patient, the doctor said, 'Just rest and don't talk too much, give your voice a rest. You need to recover your strength.'

When they were alone, Larry took her hand once more. 'I think I died a dozen deaths looking for you. I've aged ten years – I know that!'

Jessie studied the face of the man beside her. He looked weary, concerned and worn, so unlike the person she was familiar with.

She gently squeezed his hand. 'Thank you for finding me. I knew if anyone could, it would be you.'

'Don't you dare put me through anything like this again, you hear?'

She just smiled and nodded, then lay her head against the pillow and closed her eyes.

Larry got up quietly and moved to an armchair. Knowing that Jessie was safe and recovering, he, too, fell asleep.

Three days later, Jessie was allowed to leave the hospital. Larry hired a taxi to take her back to his house. Still feeling weak, Jessie didn't say a word, but just let him take charge. When she walked into the hallway, she relaxed. Here she felt safe and comfortable. The housekeeper had lit a fire and Larry took her coat and made her comfortable on the sofa, tucking a rug around her knees.

'There! Now all you need to do is get better.'

'Thank you. It's so nice to get out of the hospital. They were all very kind and caring, but you know, it's not the same.' She turned up her nose. 'I'll never get used to the smell of ether!'

With a chuckle, he said, 'Well you won't smell that here, I promise.' He sat beside her. 'It's so good to have you home, Jessie, and I've some good news. Harry Briggs is now in custody. They found him hiding out on the common.'

Her eyes flashed with anger. 'Given half the chance I'd kill that bugger for what he did to me!'

'You'd have to join a queue. First in line would be me, then your neighbours, followed by a line of dockers, your old customers who have been outraged by what's happened to you.'

She slowly smiled. 'Really?'

'Really. You have no idea how popular you are, Jessie, how many people care about you.' He stood up. 'I'm going into the kitchen to fetch you some food. You can sit here and eat it off a tray. My housekeeper has made a fish pie and I can assure you it will be a delight. Now, you relax until I return.'

Jessie remained at the house in The Avenue for a further two weeks as Larry refused to let her go back to Union Street. 'You need looking after. Here I know you will be eating, keeping warm and recovering in comfort.'

She hadn't argued. It had been nice not to have to worry about the fire, preparing a meal and having to use the tin bath. Here she once again enjoyed the luxury of a bathroom, but as she began to regain her strength, she became restless. When Larry came home that Friday evening she decided they needed to talk.

'Larry, I will be forever in your debt for finding me, then looking after me so well, but it's time to get back to reality.

I'm feeling better and need to go back home and the office on Monday morning.'

He didn't look happy about her decision, but seeing the determined look on her face, didn't argue. 'Very well, if you insist. After lunch tomorrow, I'll take you home and light the fire to warm the house. After all, I don't want you catching a chill after all of my care and attention.'

She saw he was smiling as he spoke. 'I'll be very careful, I promise.'

The following morning after they'd had breakfast, Larry took her back to Union Street where he firstly laid a fire and lit it, filled the coal scuttle, then unpacked some groceries he'd brought with him. Then when the kettle had eventually boiled he made them a pot of tea.

While he was doing all this, Jessie was upstairs unpacking her clothes. The house was cold and unwelcoming, and she felt a stranger in her own home. Already she was missing the comfort of the house in The Avenue, but it was more than that. There had been companionship. No, it was much deeper. She'd been cosseted, cared for. Larry Forbes had been her saviour in more ways than one. But she *had* to carry on with a normal life. Briggs wasn't going to stop her doing that!

As the two of them sat drinking the tea, Larry sighed. 'I'm going to miss you, you know.'

Frowning, she said, 'But you'll see me in the office.'

'I didn't mean that, I meant I'll miss you at home. It's been so nice to have someone to talk to, eat with. I'll miss that.'

She sat considering his remark. 'I'll miss it too, and I won't ever forget your kindness and hospitality.'

'Is that how you interpret it, Jessie? Kindness and hospitality. Is that all?'

He was looking at her intently, but the note of disappointment in his voice hit a chord inside her. 'No, it was far more than that. I didn't mean to make it sound so cold. I'm sorry.'

He continued to stare at her as if trying to get through to her innermost thoughts, but he remained silent. Finishing his tea, he rose to his feet, took the cups and saucers into the kitchen and returned. 'I'll be on my way, then. I'll see you in the office on Monday.' Then he walked out of the door.

His abrupt departure took her by surprise. Had she hurt his feelings? She went over their conversation in her mind. How uncaring she must have sounded after all that he'd done. No wonder he was upset. Her thoughts were disturbed by a loud knocking on the door.

'Auntie Jessie!' Her neighbours' two boys stood there, broad grins on their faces.

'We saw that man bring you home. We've missed you!' They both flung themselves at her, hugging her tightly. 'Mum said we could come and say hello.'

'Oh, I've missed you two rascals as well. Come on in and tell me what you've been doing.'

Soon after, Maisie joined them, and Jessie settled to hear all the gossip.

When she was alone at last, she realised how lucky she was to have such friends and she suddenly understood

Larry's loneliness. Did he have friends other than business associates, close to him? She wasn't at all sure – and if he didn't, how sad was that!

She made a fresh pot of tea and sat in front of the fire, still feeling guilty about her lack of warmth and gratitude to Larry earlier. How could she have been so thoughtless? This man had searched for her, found her, sat by her bed in the hospital, taken her to his house firstly as a refuge from Briggs and then had cared for her – and she had just dismissed it all. Well on Monday, she would see him in the office and try and make amends. But would that be enough?

Chapter Thirty-Six

When Jessie entered the office in the morning, she was greeted warmly by Helen, her assistant. After a brief conversation, Jessie asked where Mr Forbes was as he hadn't been at his desk. Helen said he was in a meeting.

It was just as Jessie was about to leave the office at the end of the day that Larry arrived. Helen had just left and Jessie was putting on her coat when she heard movement in the outer office. Opening the door, she saw Larry standing behind his desk, sorting through some papers. He looked up.

'Hello, Jessie. Had a busy day?'

'Yes, just catching up and there were some letters to answer, new information to be filed.' She was about to continue when he picked up the papers and walked towards the door.

'Good. I'll see you in the morning.' And he was gone.

She was astonished and totally deflated. Knowing she'd

done him such a disservice with her remarks on Saturday, she'd been desperate to put things right, but now, she'd been coldly dismissed. She felt as if she'd been slapped!

Locking up the office, she walked slowly home, wondering how on earth she could make amends. Larry Forbes was as stubborn as she was. Once someone had disappointed you, it was difficult to forgive.

While Jessie was trying to find a way to get through to him, Larry Forbes had arrived home. He removed his coat, put his papers on a table in the living room and poured himself a large whisky and soda. Sitting in a sofa beside the fire, he sipped his drink. 'Women!' he said to the empty room. 'Bloody women! Who can ever understand them? Certainly not me.' He just couldn't fathom Jessie McGonigall. This woman whom he'd searched for, who had been so happy to be found, to have been taken care of. Who had, for once, dropped her air of independence and allowed him . . . to care *for* her. She'd thrown it all back in his face. 'Kindness and hospitality! Was that all it really was to her?' He continued to question himself aloud. 'No. I don't believe it. Under all that blustering, she was vulnerable.' He'd seen it for himself. He poured another drink. He thought of how she reacted when she came round in the hospital and told him she thought she was going to die, chastising him for taking so long to find her – but she'd also said she knew he'd be the one to do so. He gazed across at the other sofa where she'd sat when she had stayed. He hated that it was now empty.

* * *

Jessie climbed into her bed, in sheets warmed with a stone hot-water bottle and snuggled under her blankets. Never had she felt more alone apart from the time that Conor had died. Tomorrow she'd go downstairs to a solitary breakfast, unlike before when Larry would cook for them and they'd sit together in the kitchen and eat their meal together. Well, it had been her decision to return home, get back to reality, but already she was regretting it. However, she was determined to talk to Larry in the morning. Come what may.

Jessie arrived early in the office after sending a messenger boy to Helen's house, giving her the morning off so she wouldn't be disturbed. She sat at Larry's desk and waited for him after making a cup of tea in the staff room.

Larry walked into his office and looked with surprise at the figure sitting at his desk.

'Good morning, Mrs McGonigall. Have you taken over my company?' But there was a twinkle of amusement in his eyes as he asked the question.

'Only for half an hour, Mr Forbes. Kindly take a chair!' She motioned to the one on the opposite side of the desk.

He removed his overcoat and sat down. 'This had better be good,' he said.

'I need first to apologise for the thoughtless remark I made to you about your kindness and hospitality. It belittled what you had done for me and was unforgivable. You took me into your home when Briggs was on the loose; you rescued me when I thought I was going to die and you stayed with me in hospital and cared for me afterwards.

Yes, you *were* kind and you *were* hospitable, but, Larry, you were so much more.' She felt emotional and struggled to maintain her equilibrium, but she continued.

'You were a rock. I had no fight left in me when you found me and you took over. I felt safe and secure and for once I didn't have to find my own way out of trouble. You did it for me and I want to thank you. I only hope you can forgive me,' she hesitated, 'for my thoughtlessness – oh, whatever the hell it was that made me so stupid!' She sat back in the chair, gazing across at Larry, searching for his reaction.

He sat for a moment, shaking his head. 'Jessie McGonigall, you are the most infuriating woman I've ever met!'

Grinning, she asked, 'Does that mean I'm forgiven?'

His eyes narrowed as he considered her question. 'For what you said, yes, and I accept your apology. But we just can't carry on as we are.'

'Whatever do you mean?'

'In the hospital, when you were unconscious, I promised that if you recovered I would take care of you, that you would never have to worry again. That promise still stands.'

'I think you'd better explain,' said Jessie, now completely puzzled.

'It means that you vacate your house and move into mine. There you'll be comfortable, taken care of without a worry about the future.'

'I'm not a piece of merchandise, you know! You can't own me. I'm not to be moved about at will.'

Seeing her outrage, Larry started to laugh, which annoyed Jessie even more.

'This is no laughing matter, Larry!'

'No, indeed it isn't, but if you would climb down from your high horse for a moment, I'll explain.' He waited, but as Jessie remained silent he continued. 'Answer me this. Have you enjoyed staying at my house?'

'But of course, why wouldn't I?'

'Did you feel at home there?'

'Yes, completely.'

'Be honest with me, Jessie. How did you feel when you returned to your house in Union Street?'

This took her by surprise. She remembered how she felt a stranger when she walked through the door. How devoid of comfort it was after her previous accommodation and how lonely she felt after Larry had gone. But how could she tell him her innermost thoughts?

Seeing her hesitation and knowing her reluctance to show her vulnerability, he spoke for her. 'You hated it! You didn't feel at home, you weren't comfortable. There was no joy in you, Jessie. You were not at all thrilled to be back there, I *saw* that, so don't tell me I'm wrong.'

Taking a deep breath, she answered. 'No, you're right. That's exactly how I felt.'

His tone softened. 'I miss you not sharing my home. Let's face it, Jessie, we are two lonely people, we get along . . . most of the time' – he grinned at her – 'when you come out of hiding from behind that barrier. It isn't a sin, you know, to let someone else hold the reins, to make decisions . . . to take care of you.' He sat back and with a smile said, 'To be honest, I quite enjoyed it!'

She was at a loss for words. 'So, what are you suggesting?'

'Stay with me as you did before. It's that simple. You can still work and run my office, but you'll have a comfortable home, nice food cooked for you and you'll no longer be lonely, neither will I.'

It was a very tempting offer, but Jessie had some reservations. 'Won't people talk? I mean, working for you is one thing, but living in the same house permanently, well, think about it, the gossip it will cause.'

'There's a very simple solution to that.'

'Really? And what is that, may I ask?'

'Marry me.'

She was shocked. 'What?'

'I said, marry me. Oh, for God's sake, Jessie! Why do you think I searched high and low looking for you? Why do you think I stayed with you in the hospital? Despite being the most difficult woman I've ever met . . . I'm in love with you!'

'You are? Oh my God!' She looked at him in astonishment.

He just sat looking at her, waiting for her to recover. 'Does that "Oh my God!" mean "What a terrible idea" – or is it just surprise? I *really* need to know.'

'No, no, it's not a terrible idea, it's just unexpected. I hadn't realised, that's all.'

'Do you think you could give it some thought? You don't have to give me an answer now about marrying me, but I would like to take you out of that miserable house in Union Street and back to mine. Sod the gossips! Then maybe you'll find an answer. What do you say?'

Having recovered somewhat, Jessie gazed across the

desk and remembered how happy she'd been to see Larry at her bedside when she came to in the hospital, how tender he'd been and how much she'd liked it. With a wicked twinkle in her eye, she answered, 'Well, I do need to find out if we could get along together. It would be like a trial run.'

He started to chuckle. 'You are such a wicked woman! A trial run it is! When we close the office, I'll take you to your house and you can pack some clothes, then we'll go home . . . together.' He rose to his feet and walked round the desk. 'My chair, I think.'

Jessie vacated it immediately.

'There is just one more thing.' He took her into his arms and kissed her.

Feeling his arms around her and his mouth on hers, Jessie felt her legs weaken as she found herself returning his kiss. He, eventually, released her gently.

'Not at all bad for a trial run, Mrs McGonigall!'

Chapter Thirty-Seven

Jessie was packing her clothes into a couple of cases, while Larry waited for her downstairs. She looked out of the window. Across the road was the Builders Arms, hers and Conor's local. The other familiar two-up two-down houses. Her neighbours next door, including the house where she found old Iris passed away in her chair on Christmas Day. She was leaving her memories behind, and yet she didn't feel any guilt or remorse. She now had a chance to move on and she'd be a fool not to take it. She would know soon enough if it was to be permanent. It was one thing to share Larry's home as a refuge and after the hospital to recover. This time the reason was even more serious. It could be her future.

Sitting on a chair, she recalled how Larry sat by her bed in the hospital and held her hand and how when she was upset he climbed onto the bed, held her and told her he would have searched the ends of the earth to find her. How blind she had been not to recognise his feelings for her. But how did she feel about him? She was shaken when he'd kissed her and even more so at her response. The last man to do so had been Conor and that had seemed a lifetime ago. Conor had been the love of her life. She could never feel the same again for anyone, but she did like Larry, found him fascinating, but also a puzzle. These next few weeks were going to be interesting! She picked up her bags and, with a struggle, went downstairs.

'Why on earth didn't you call me, Jessie? I'd have come up for your luggage,' Larry protested.

'I managed, thank you.'

'Of course you did, why would you ask for help? It's against your religion!'

Jessie ignored the sarcasm, but she did stop to make a point. 'Oh, by the way, there is one thing before we go.'

'Oh really, and what is that?'

'I'll be sleeping alone in the same room as before. There is no test run in the bedroom, in case you had any plans!'

'Oh my, how you do ruin a man's dreams.' But he was grinning broadly as he spoke. 'Come along, *Saint Jessie*, let's go home.'

They soon settled into a routine: Larry cooked the breakfast, they worked during the day, and dined together in the evenings. They would sit and chat after, or Larry would go into his study to work, leaving Jessie to her own devices. She would read the papers, keep up with the latest wartime news. The Allies fighting the Turks in Gallipoli, the taking of ground in some places and the loss in others, the terrible number of casualties. She wondered how many of the troops marching through the town had survived. It was a dreadful time, yet those at home continued their own war against survival with the shortage of food. Jessie was lost in admiration for the meals Mrs Jenkins, the housekeeper, produced and had told her so.

The woman was friendly enough, but a little reticent and Jessie imagined it was because she was here living in the same house as Larry. She, a widow, although the housekeeper would know they didn't share the same bedroom. But she didn't let it bother her. The woman was not the type to gossip. It wouldn't pay her to be if she wanted to maintain her position.

One morning before they left for the office, Larry told her they would be going out to a dinner that night, held by the Ministry of Defence at the Dolphin Hotel. He was invited as the owner of the factory making uniforms for the army.

'You want me to come with you?'

'Of course. Who else would I take as my partner? So, get out your glad rags, Jessie. There will be dancing, so let's go and have some fun!'

During the day, Jessie tried to hide her excitement. It had been a very long time since she'd been out to a posh do. At the hotel as the manageress, she'd organised many, but had never been in a position to attend one as a customer. She was also curious to see how Larry would introduce her.

Since she'd moved in with him, he'd been friendly. They had many a laugh together and apart from kissing her on her forehead as he bade her goodnight, he'd not kissed her properly again. As she dressed for the evening, Jessie admitted to herself that she was a little disappointed. Then she laughed. 'You bad girl, Jessie,' she muttered. Preening herself before the mirror, she wondered if this evening Larry would still keep his distance, knowing how attractive she looked. 'Now who is the one playing games?' she asked herself and with one final twirl, she left her room.

Larry was waiting at the bottom of the stairs for her, looking resplendent in full evening dress. Jessie stopped halfway and looked at him. He was, indeed, a handsome man. He held out his hand to her.

'You look simply wonderful, Jessie. I'll be the envy of all the men.'

'So you will be, Mr Forbes. I'm pleased you realise how very lucky you are!'

'I hope that *I* live up to *your* expectations?'

She looked him up and down. 'You'll do very nicely,' she said, her eyes full of mischief.

'Are you flirting with me by any chance?'

With a toss of her head, she grinned at him. 'Shall we go?'

A taxi took them to the hotel and as they stepped out, Jessie looked at the other guests and realised that they were probably the youngest couple there. There were some men wearing officers' uniforms with a lot of brass on the epaulettes and she remembered that, of course, this was to do with the war effort.

Two uniformed army officers and their ladies stood together to welcome the guests. They recognised Larry and greeted him warmly. 'This is Mrs Jessie McGonigall, a good friend of mine,' he said. She shook hands with the people, and then walked into the dining room, checking the list to see where they were to sit.

There was a top table for the top brass, but around the dance floor, smaller tables were set, which seated four couples at each. Jessie was relieved because this made it less formal. At their table, the men were in evening dress, not uniforms, which was a bit of a relief as it made it seem more friendly. Introductions were made and the conversation flowed easily enough as the dinner was served.

In these difficult times, the menu was sufficient. Soup to start with, roast chicken as a main course and chocolate mousse for dessert, and there was wine with each course.

At the end of the meal, an army colonel gave a speech, thanking those who were helping the war effort, stressing just how important their input was to the troops fighting the enemy. It was a rousing speech, short and to the point. He ended by saying, 'Now, ladies and gentlemen, enjoy the dancing, you've earned it!'

The band started to play a waltz. Larry stood up, held out his hand to Jessie and said, 'You heard what the colonel said! We must obey orders.'

He led her onto the dance floor and took her firmly into

his arms. He was an excellent dancer and they travelled across the floor together with ease. Jessie followed his lead, enjoying every moment. When the music stopped, he still held her, waiting for the next tune to begin. It was a slow foxtrot and he pulled her even closer.

'The last time you were in my arms was in a hospital bed,' he said. 'I'm so very pleased that this time it's in more comfortable surroundings.'

'This time I'm not crying all over you,' she retorted.

'Oh, Jessie, you can cry over me anytime you want to; in fact, I'd be very upset if you did that with any other man.'

She looked up into his eyes and saw that tenderness in his expression that she'd seen in the hospital and realised just how much he cared for her. It brought a lump to her throat and she began to realise that she really did have feelings for this man.

'There is no reason for you to be upset. I don't think I could cry over anyone else.'

'Oh, Jessie McGonigall, be very careful what you say. I may get the wrong idea!'

The music stopped and they walked back to the table.

The rest of the evening was enjoyable. The men changed partners so that everyone danced with each other. Conversation was light, no talk of war, no details about each other. It was most enjoyable. Then the band started to play the last waltz and everyone took to the floor.

Larry held Jessie close to him, his head against hers. The floor was crowded, but nobody minded, and at the end the dancers applauded the band, and then stood to attention as the national anthem was played.

A taxi waited outside to take them home. He helped her into the back of the vehicle, climbed in beside her and took her hand. 'I do hope you enjoyed the evening, Jessie.'

'Oh, I did! It made such a nice change. The food was good, the company was enjoyable and I love to dance. I don't remember the last time that I did.'

'I'm delighted that you're so happy. I enjoyed it too.'

When they arrived at their destination, Larry paid off the driver and opened the front door. Once inside he asked, 'Do you want a hot drink before you go to bed or a nightcap?'

Shaking her head, she said, 'No, I'm really tired. If I'm to get up for work tomorrow, I'd better get some rest. You too, or we'll be late in the office and what would Helen think then?'

'Very well. Thank you for a lovely evening, Jessie. Let's hope it's the first of many.' He pulled her into his arms and kissed her until she was breathless. He stared into her eyes. 'I think we both should call it a night before this gets out of hand.' He kissed her fingers and led her to the stairs. 'You go on, I'll just check the house. I'll see you in the morning.'

Jessie walked into her bedroom, closed the door and leant against it. Larry had kissed her again! She waltzed around the room, singing softly to herself. She hadn't felt this good for a very long time. She now felt she could be happily married to Larry. How could you not love a man who'd saved your life, who obviously cared so much for you? He'd always told her she didn't know him, years ago when they'd first met. She now felt secure with him. He would always take care of her and she'd never have to worry about a thing if she was with him. How wonderful that would be!

Undressing and climbing into bed, the memory of the music and the dancing uppermost in her mind, she eventually fell asleep.

The following morning, Larry picked up the mail and seeing a brown envelope, opened it. He frowned as he read the contents. Jessie walked into the kitchen as he was still reading. She was about to greet him when he looked up from the letter.

'Harry Briggs's case comes up in court in three weeks' time.'

Jessie suddenly felt sick. She looked stricken. 'I'll have to give evidence, won't I?'

'Yes, I'm afraid so. Because when he was charged, he pleaded not guilty.' He walked over to her and put an arm around her shoulder. 'I'll get you a good solicitor. Try not to worry, it's an open-and-shut case, but it will have to go through the legal proceedings.' He gazed at her now-pale face. 'I'll be with you all the way, Jessie, and when it's over, we'll go away for a few days and celebrate! Now, you need some breakfast.'

'I couldn't eat a thing.'

'Rubbish! You *will* eat. You can't let that man win. Now sit down and do as you're told.'

'Yes, sir!' she snapped, but she knew he was right. She had to be strong and show that bastard Briggs he had picked on the wrong woman.

Before they left the house, Larry phoned his solicitor and made an appointment for Jessie to see him the next day. When he told her, he saw the worried expression and understood her anxiety. Not only would she have to give evidence, but she'd have to see Briggs as he stood in the dock. The whole terrifying experience would be relived once again.

Chapter Thirty-Eight

The following afternoon, Larry took Jessie to see Walter Cummings, his solicitor, who clearly remembered Jessie being abducted and Larry's rescue. It had been in the local paper for days. Cummings stood up and shook Jessie's hand.

'Please take a seat, Mrs McGonigall. I'm so pleased to see you are happily recovered from your ordeal, but I can imagine your anxiety now you will have to appear in court to give evidence.'

'Yes, you're right. I suppose I shut away the fact that this would happen after I was told he'd been caught, now I can't do that any more, but . . . I aim to make sure that devil is put away for what he did to me. Had it not been for Mr Forbes, I probably wouldn't be sitting here today.'

'I understand. I can't see any difficulty in getting the right verdict. There's no doubt that the man is guilty, but we must never take anything for granted. I've contacted a barrister friend of mine in London and he will be representing you.'

Jessie looked concerned. 'What do you mean "we must never take anything for granted"? Are you saying this bugger may get away with this?'

'Not exactly. But he may put forward a plea of not being of sound mind at the time, hoping for a lesser sentence. We must be prepared for every eventuality.'

'He knew what he was doing! He was perfectly sane, I can tell you that!' Jessie was fuming.

'Calm down, Mrs McGonigall! You have every right to be angry, but I must warn you that when you give your evidence, you must remain calm. Your barrister will school you. He'll lead your questions. You just answer them concisely, don't do more than that, and you must keep calm at all times or you may put your case in jeopardy. Now, when you go home you need to sit down and write out exactly what happened to you, from beginning to end. Tomorrow afternoon, Rupert Grantham will be here to go over the case with you. He's an excellent man, just do as he says.'

Jessie felt utterly deflated as she left the solicitor's office. Looking at Larry, she said, 'Well so much for being a done deal. I thought I would stand up in court, tell my story and watch that bastard being taken down to serve time! Now he could try and get out of it. That's not justice!'

Larry tried to placate her. 'It's the way the law works. Whoever is defending Briggs will try to do the best for his client.'

'Even if he knows he's guilty?'

'I'm afraid so.' He saw the stricken look on her face

and put an arm around her shoulders. 'Come on, darling, where's that fighting spirit?'

'Oh, well according to Mr Cummings, I have to maintain a calm exterior! That isn't me!'

'Not true, Jessie. Remember the fire? You were calm then and very brave, as I recall.'

'Oh, Larry! Is there no end to all these problems?'

He stopped her walking and held her by her shoulders. 'Look at me!'

She was so surprised, she did so. 'This is it! Once this is over, life will be so sweet you won't know you're born. We will be together. Your problems, if there are any, will be mine. Now stop being negative, this is *not* the woman I know and love.'

Jessie was shocked for a moment, then she started to grin. 'Oh, I do love a strong man! Of course, you're right. I was so angry at the thought of that bastard getting away with what he did that I was carried away.' Tucking her arm through his, she said, 'I will behave, I promise.'

The next afternoon when she and Larry met Rupert Grantham at the solicitor's office, Jessie was impressed by the barrister who was tall, with a cultured voice, well dressed. He had an imposing air about him and suddenly Jessie felt secure. They all sat round a table and she went through her evidence with him. He questioned in such a way that she now understood what the solicitor meant about him leading her, bringing out the important points.

At the end of the session, Grantham spoke. 'Well, Mrs McGonigall, if you do as well in court we will be fine, but please don't elaborate, just answer the question and do the same when the defence cross-questions you. Do *not* lose your temper but remain calm.'

She smiled at him. 'You've been warned about me, then?'

'I couldn't possibly say.' But his eyes twinkled with amusement.

During the days that followed leading to the court case, Jessie was naturally tense. Larry tried to take her mind off things as best he could, but in one way when the day came they were both relieved, wanting to get it over.

They arrived at the Crown Court and were met by Walter Cummings and Rupert Grantham, wearing his black gown and wig. He looked elegant and businesslike as he walked over to her.

'You and Mr Forbes will wait outside the courtroom until you are called to give your evidence. You will be taken to the stand where you will take the oath. Then I want you to take a deep breath and answer my questions. I'm there to take care of you, Mrs McGonigall, just trust me.'

'Thank you, I will.'

Larry led her to a long bench where they sat down. He took her hand in his. 'It's going to be fine, you'll see.'

She just gave a nervous smile in reply.

Inside the courtroom, the jury took their places after being sworn in and Briggs was brought up the stairs and into the dock, flanked by two policemen. Shortly after, the door opened and the judge made his appearance.

The clerk of the court stood up to say, 'All rise!' Everybody got to their feet until the judge sat down, then they too settled.

The judge turned to the jury to inform them of their task and what they were expected to do. They listened intently until he'd finished. Then they turned their attention to Rupert Grantham who, as the prosecutor, stood up to put his case to them, but before he could begin, the solicitor defending Briggs stood up.

'My Lord, forgive the interruption, but my client wishes to change his plea from not guilty to guilty.'

A buzz was heard from the spectators and the press. This was most unexpected.

The judge looked at the prisoner. 'Is this your wish, Briggs?'

Looking pale and haggard, Briggs answered, 'It is, My Lord. Guilty!'

'In which case, gentlemen,' he said to the two lawyers, 'that ends today's proceedings. The prisoner will return at a later date for sentencing.' He then left the court.

Briggs was taken down the steps and back to his cell and Grantham hurried out into the corridor to Jessie and Larry to convey the good news.

Jessie was confused. 'I don't understand.'

'My guess would be that Briggs has changed his plea because by doing so, they will reduce his sentence, but it means, Mrs McGonigall, neither you or Mr Forbes will have to give your evidence. You are spared from having to relive your experience.'

'But after this is over,' said Larry, 'I'm taking him to court for embezzlement, so he'll have extra years for that on top of what he's given.' He looked at Jessic. 'It's over. Done and dusted!'

She was still stunned by the news and continued to sit.

'Jessie! We can go home now, darling.' Larry took her arm and helped her to her feet. 'Come along, a walk through the park to the tram stop will help clear your head.'

Jessie turned to Rupert Grantham. 'Thank you so much.'

'I didn't have to do very much, Mrs McGonigall.'

'I know, but if we'd had to go into court, I know you would have done a good job.' She shook his hand and left the building with Larry.

It was a glorious sunny day as they made their way through the park and suddenly Jessie's spirits lightened. It was over! Briggs would be sentenced and she wouldn't have to stand in court, able to see him as she gave her evidence. Seeing the man stood in the dock listening to her had been her worst nightmare. She could still hear his cruel laugh as he told her he was leaving her to die. His words had chilled her and when she allowed herself to think about it, they still did.

'Feeling better?' asked Larry.

Looking up at him and remembering how he'd saved her, she beamed at him. 'Oh yes, much better.'

'Me too. When we get home, I think we both deserve a large brandy and tonight we'll go out and celebrate.'

'Could we stay at home and celebrate?'

'Yes, if that's what you want.'

'It is, I just want a quiet evening with you.'

He looked pleased. 'Then that's what we'll do.'

* * *

When they arrived at the house, Larry made a pot of coffee and took it into the living room, then poured two brandies into goblets and handed one to Jessie, then he poured the coffee.

Lifting his glass, he asked, 'What do you think we should drink to on such a day?'

Picking up her glass, she gazed at him for a minute, then said, 'We should drink to us!'

He raised his eyebrows. 'To us, Jessie? Does that mean you've reached a decision?'

'Why don't you ask me and find out.'

He took her free hand with his. 'Jessie McGonigall, indomitable woman that you are, will you do me the honour of being my wife?'

'Larry Forbes, the most intriguing man I've ever known, I will!'

He put down his glass, then hers and drew her into his arms. His mouth explored hers in a slow but deeply passionate way until he reluctantly released her. 'Oh, Jessie, I'm so happy you said yes. We'll have such a good life together. In the hospital when you were still unconscious I promised to take care of you, and I will.'

She gave a contented sigh. 'I know and I'm happy too.'

'Mind you,' he continued, 'I realise that I've taken on a load of trouble, but I'm sure that will only add to the enjoyment.'

Jessie started to laugh. 'You have no idea what you've let yourself in for!'

'Oh, believe me, I have but I'm looking forward to it.' And he kissed her again. 'Tomorrow, I'll take you to the jewellers and buy you a ring in case you change your mind.'

'You know I won't do that. You know when I take something on I don't back down.'

'I know that more than anyone. Remember how we met, me wanting to take over the cafe?'

They began to reminisce about their first meeting and what had happened along the way, bringing them to this moment.

Then Larry suggested, after they became engaged, they go to Bournemouth for the weekend to celebrate the ending of the court case and their engagement, and Jessie agreed.

When they arrived at the office the next morning, neither of them spoke about their engagement. They wanted to keep the news to themselves until they returned from the weekend, so during the lunch hour, they went to the jewellers, where Jessie chose an emerald ring, flanked by diamonds.

'Surely with red hair I have to wear an emerald,' she had said as they entered the shop. And that was what she chose, much to the assistant's delight. Larry put the ring on Jessie's finger and kissed her. Then they returned to the office.

It was when Jessie handed a file to Helen that her assistant noticed the ring. 'Oh, Mrs McGonigall! You weren't wearing that ring this morning. Does that mean what I think it does?' she asked, smiling broadly.

Jessie looked down at her finger. 'Yes, Helen, Mr Forbes and I are engaged. But we're keeping it quiet until next week.'

'I promise not to say a word, but congratulations!'

Secretly, Jessie was delighted that she could share her news with somebody.

Just before they closed the office for the day, Larry said he was going to call the hotel and book for the weekend. 'Do we need one room or two?'

She leant forward and kissed him. 'Do you really need to ask?'

Chapter Thirty-Nine

The two of them sat alone in a first-class carriage of the train as it journeyed down the coast to Bournemouth. Jessie leant back against the seat and placed her head against the pristine white headrest cover. First class! Why was she surprised? She was with Larry Forbes, who always did things with style – and it felt good.

Larry held her hand. 'Are you as happy as I am, Jessie?'

She looked at his expression of contentment. 'Absolutely! You know I feel as if I've come through a bad illness and suddenly I'm better.'

'Well, that's one way of putting it.' He laughed.

They chatted happily, watching the passing countryside, making plans for spending these precious two days together.

'While we're away, we must talk about the wedding. Do you want a big affair?'

Jessie looked horrified. 'Gracious, no! I would like it to be small, with just my closest friends and whoever you want to invite. A nice dinner somewhere. Yes, a small wedding cake would be nice, but not a big splash – if you don't mind?'

'That sounds perfect to me.'

Turning to look at him, Jessie asked, 'Do you have any family? Only you've never mentioned them.'

Larry didn't answer for a moment and Jessie saw the sad expression in his face as he seemed lost in thought. 'No, I have no family to speak of. I was an only child, my parents both died when I was nineteen. They were in a boating accident and drowned. It was a difficult time. I suppose I have relations somewhere, but I've never kept in touch with them.'

'You mean you've had to fend for yourself ever since?'

'Yes, Jessie, as did you, I believe. We are more alike than you realise. We are both survivors and ambitious, and we get things done. Let's face it, we haven't done badly, have we?'

'Put like that, no, we haven't, but you've done better than me. You're a wealthy man, not like me, a poor church mouse.'

'Ah, but I was left some money, so that gave me a start. You had to begin from scratch. There is a difference. But we were successful in our own way and it was harder for you, being a woman.'

They both sat back with their own thoughts, but Jessie could now understand even more why Larry said he was lonely and she felt sad for him.

They arrived at the hotel and Larry signed the register. They left their cases with the concierge to be taken to their room and then they walked along the seafront. It was a warm, balmy day and people were sitting on the beach in deckchairs, others were swimming. There was an air of peace about the place and little sign of the war raging across the Channel, unlike the constant troop movements in Southampton. They bought an ice cream and sat in two deckchairs.

'When the war is over, Jessie, we'll make plans for the future, maybe open another hotel.'

She looked at him and grinned. 'Do you still dream of having a chain of hotels?'

'Why not? It worked well before the war, why not after? It'll take time for the country to return to normal. Businesses will recover. The factory will probably close. The requirement for army uniforms will not be needed on such a scale, but I can find a use for it, I'm sure.'

As Jessie sat listening to him making plans, she was filled with admiration at Larry's business acumen. But of course, he'd come up the hard way, his success had been earned. She felt excited to think she'd be a part of such plans.

'Do you want children, Jessie?'

The sudden question caught her off guard. Of course she did! She *longed* for children, but now she'd have to tell him it wasn't possible. Things had developed so quickly in their relationship, a family hadn't even occurred to her. Would that make a difference? Would Larry still want to marry her? She was filled with dread, and suddenly her elation and happiness evaporated.

'What is it?' Larry asked, seeing the devastation in her expression.

'I can't have children. Conor and I tried, but I never became pregnant.'

'Did you consult a doctor about this ever?'

Shaking her head, she said, 'No. We just thought it wasn't meant to be. I wanted a baby so badly but, in the end, I just accepted the fact that it would never happen.' She looked at him. 'I'm so sorry, Larry. I would understand if this made a difference to our getting married.'

He looked shocked. 'I can't believe you just said that! I love you and I'm going to marry you. I told you, your problems will be my problems. We'll go to a doctor after we're married and see what he says, but if we can't have a family, it doesn't matter.'

She was overcome and couldn't speak. Being a mother was the one thing in her life at which she'd failed, and it hurt her deeply. But there were no words that could convey just how she felt.

Larry caught hold of her hand. 'Now, how about we find somewhere to get a bite to eat? This evening we could go to a show; there is a variety show on the pier that should be fun. What do you say?'

Relieved that the conversation had changed, she agreed.

They found a cafe serving fish and chips, and ate. The fish caught locally was in good supply, which made up for the shortages of food on offer. They tucked in with relish, then went back to the hotel to freshen up, but stopped in the residents' lounge for a drink first.

'I'd better hide my left hand,' Jessie said.

Frowning, Larry asked why.

'In case they notice I'm not wearing a wedding ring,' she said, her eyes twinkling mischievously.

'You're wearing an engagement ring, I'm sure no one is going to be that interested; besides, I'm sure we're not the first unmarried couple to share a room.'

They finished their drink and took the lift to their floor. The room was on the front overlooking the sea. It was tastefully furnished and Jessie looked it over very carefully, then she inspected the bathroom. When she returned to the bedroom, Larry had removed his overcoat and was sitting in one of the easy chairs.

'Well, Mrs McGonigall, did it pass muster?'

She started laughing. 'Sorry, I can't help it. I'm still a hotelier at heart and yes, it does pass muster!'

He pulled her onto his knee and kissed her.

'Ever the perfectionist.'

'Well, when it comes to business; other than that, I'm just a normal person with failings like anyone else.'

He started laughing. 'Believe me, you certainly are unlike anyone else! You are totally unique and that's part of your charm. Failings maybe, but we all have those – that's what makes you human.'

'Oh my, Mr Forbes, are you admitting that you have faults?'

'One or two,' he said with a broad grin. 'Now, let's freshen up or we'll be late for the show.'

By the time they reached the pier, they had time to play on the various slot machines like a couple of children, laughing with delight when they won a few pennies. Then they made their way to the theatre.

The variety show was good, with a man on a unicycle, followed by a sword swallower who made Jessie cringe as she watched the sword slowly lower into the man's gullet. In the end, she hid her eyes until he finished, much to Larry's amusement.

'Not always brave, then?' he teased.

A singer was the final act, and they sat and listened to the man who had a fine voice and sang all the latest songs, but when he sang, 'It's a Long Way to Tipperary', Jessie found tears in her eyes as she thought of the many troops who sang this song as they marched off to war.

Seeing her distress, Larry caught hold of her hand and held it until the show ended. They walked slowly back to the hotel and sat in the residents' lounge, where they ordered drinks and some sandwiches as they were not hungry enough for a meal after their lunch.

Eventually, Larry said, 'Time for bed, I think. Are you ready?'

Jessie looked at him and saw the expectancy mirrored in his eyes and she suddenly felt shy. Conor had been the only man she'd slept with and now she was about to be bedded by another. 'Yes,' she said quietly and rose to her feet.

They waited for the lift to descend, and then opened the gates and stepped inside. Larry pressed the button for their floor, then slowly drew her into his arms and kissed her softly. 'Relax, darling. You don't have to do anything you don't want to. You can just sleep in my arms, if that's all you want.'

The lift arrived and they went to their room. Larry took their coats and put them in the wardrobe. 'You can have the bathroom first,' he said. 'I'll sit on the balcony and have a cigarette until you're ready.'

Jessie changed into a simple cotton nightdress and had a wash, then cleaned her teeth. She took the pins out of her hair and brushed it, letting it flow free, then she called to Larry and climbed into bed.

Eventually, Larry emerged from the bathroom and walked towards the bed. He looked at Jessie, who was trying not to laugh.

'What's so funny?'

'I was wondering if you were going to be wearing a nightshirt! How stupid of me, I should have known you would have silk pyjamas, they're much more your style!'

He climbed into bed. 'A nightshirt? I think I'm insulted! I thought you knew me better than that. I hope you didn't picture me in a night cap as well?'

This was too much for Jessie and she was convulsed with laughter.

'Mrs McGonigall – soon to be Forbes – this is supposed to be a romantic moment in our lives and look at you, tears of laughter on your cheeks! You are supposed to be overcome with love and lust for me!' But he was smiling, too.

She stopped laughing and wrapped her arms around him. 'Oh, my very dear Mr Forbes, forgive me. But laughter is a necessary thing between two people. It's what will get us through any bad times and, for your information, I am full of love and lust for you, I promise.' She leant forward and kissed him passionately, undoing the buttons on his pyjama jacket so she could caress the firm chest beneath her fingers.

Soon they were both naked, exploring each other, finding out how to please one another, enjoying this new experience, taking their time until they lay in each other's arms, satisfied and complete.

Larry gathered her to him and kissed her forehead. 'Oh, Jessie, for a trial run that really was very satisfying.'

Snuggling into him, she sighed. 'I know. I can't wait for the real thing!'

They both started laughing. 'You really are a wicked woman! Now, let's get some sleep or tomorrow we'll be too tired for anything.'

Chapter Forty

They returned to Southampton, having enjoyed the break and their new intimacy, but when they had unpacked and were sitting together in the living room, Jessie turned to Larry. 'It'll seem strange to sleep on my own tonight after being able to snuggle up to you in bed.'

'What are you talking about?'

'We have to consider Mrs Jenkins. We don't want to shock her.'

'Mrs Jenkins is employed by me, she's not my keeper! She's been with me long enough to know her place.'

The note of dismissal in his voice reminded Jessie of the days when they were at loggerheads. It made her realise that there would be times ahead when they would clash, but now she was more at ease with that. It would be part of their lives. Two people with such strong personalities, such a thing was inevitable. But then she and Conor certainly had their moments, yet the making up afterwards had always been spectacular. As they climbed into Larry's bed that night, Jessie was relieved that they would be gone in the morning when the housekeeper arrived, so there would be no embarrassment on her part, at least. Harry Briggs appeared to be sentenced for abduction and attempted murder. The judge sent him down for fifteen years. It was a great relief for both Jessie and Larry. Now they felt they could move on.

Six weeks later they were married in Holyrood Church. Jessie wearing a silk gown in a pale rust, which brought out the colour of her hair, worn in a chignon, surrounded by a band of tawny feathers and carrying a small bunch of tea-coloured roses. Larry, sporting a suit with a frock coat in dark grey, with his best man dressed in similar clothes. Daisy was her maid of honour and the two boys, in smart suits, were her pageboys – to their delight and that of Maisie and Percy Williams the proud parents. Nancy and her husband joined a few of Larry's business partners which added to the small wedding party.

The bride arrived and was amazed to see a crowd gathered outside the church. She recognised several of her customers from the cafe. The dockers all called out to her, wishing her well. She was overcome by this unexpected show of affection.

Bill proudly led the bride down to the altar. Larry stepped forward and, looking at her, said quietly, 'You look beautiful.'

As they emerged after the ceremony, they were showered with confetti. They stood while a photographer took their pictures, then the wedding party walked the few yards to the Dolphin Hotel for the wedding ceremony.

Holding her hand firmly, Larry looked at his bride. 'Are you alright, Mrs Forbes?'

'Never better, Mr Forbes.'

Larry had called in a few favours and so there was food served that normally was in short supply, but as their party was a small one it had been manageable. Fresh crab and prawns on a bed of lettuce was served as a starter, followed by roast beef with all the trimmings, a thing that was hardly seen in the shops these days and much appreciated by the diners. The dessert was a meringue with fresh strawberries, grown locally, served with cream.

As the waiters cleared the table, Larry rose to his feet. 'Ladies and gentlemen – friends. Thank you all for coming to share this very special day with us. I'm a very lucky man to have such an amazing woman as my wife. Those who know our history will understand, when first Jessie and I met, or should I say crossed swords' – there was a ripple of laughter – 'no one would have envisaged our marriage today. Me least of all! But happily, those days are long gone and I would like you to raise your glasses to an indomitable woman. My wife, Jessie Forbes!'

They all stood. 'Jessie Forbes!'

Larry continued. 'There will be no other speeches. We both wanted a small wedding with our friends without a fuss. In a moment we'll cut the cake, but for now fill your glasses and enjoy the moment.'

* * *

The day went well. Everyone enjoyed themselves and when their guests had gone, the married couple retired to their room in the hotel for that night. They had decided not to take a honeymoon at the moment.

'Everywhere is so unsettled. Zeppelins are still bombing London and the war is still going on. If we wait, then we can do it in style,' Larry had explained.

Jessie didn't mind at all. After all, she was now living in luxury after leaving Union Street. Most of her meals were being cooked for her by the housekeeper, all she had to do was work in the office during the day and enjoy being married.

A month later, Harry Briggs was brought back to court to face the charge of embezzlement. Larry was there to give his evidence. This and the paperwork showing the discrepancies proved his guilt. He was sentenced to a further three years.

The time seemed to fly by to Jessie and here it was, the end of the year. 1915 didn't end well as the Allies had to retreat from Gallipoli after ten long months, and in January the government decided to bring in conscription. Single men first.

Jessie had breathed a sigh of relief on reading this. Only four months married, she dreaded the fact that Larry would have to go to war. But as he explained to her, he was overseeing things in the factory. Conscription meant that he'd had to hire and train new staff to work new shifts to increase the output and as he was working for the Ministry of Defence, he would be exempt, should they call on married men.

Jessie hadn't been feeling well, but had insisted that she still go to work, until eventually Larry made her stay at home and rest. After two days he asked the doctor to call on his wife and waited in the living room until he'd examined her. He was concerned as Jessie seemed to have such a strong constitution and this was the first instance, in all the time he'd known her, that she wasn't fit and full of energy.

At last, the doctor joined him.

'What seems to be the matter?' Larry asked with a note of concern. 'Jessie is usually so well. Did you find out what's wrong with her?'

'Sit down, Mr Forbes. Don't look so worried, your wife is still fit and well.'

'I don't understand.'

'Your wife is pregnant. Congratulations!'

'She is?' He looked stunned.

'You're surprised?'

'Jessie didn't think she was able to have children. She's a widow and in her previous marriage, she didn't conceive at all.'

'Yes, Mrs Forbes told me. As I explained to her, her husband may have had a low sperm count, but as they didn't consult a doctor, they wouldn't know the cause. Now I suggest you go upstairs to your wife, who is as surprised as you are.'

Larry shook his hand with some enthusiasm. 'I can't thank you enough!'

'I had nothing to do with it, Mr Forbes, apart from my diagnosing the cause. Bring her to see me in a month. I'll let myself out.'

Taking the stairs two at a time, Larry entered the bedroom. Jessie was sitting up in bed, a broad smile on her face. 'You're going to be a father and, at long last, I'm actually going to be a mother!' She burst into tears.

He put his arms around her and held her close. 'It's wonderful news, darling. Now don't be upset, it can't be good for you.'

Drying her eyes, she said, 'You have no idea just how much I've longed for a child. Every month knowing I wasn't pregnant was almost more than I could bear at times, until I buried it all in the back of my mind, but now . . .'

'I know. I'm as thrilled as you are, but now you must give up working in the office.'

She looked appalled. 'I certainly will not! I'm not ill, I'm pregnant. Yes, later I'll stop work, but not now. I'd go mad without something to do.'

'Fine, if you insist, but it's Thursday, at least take the rest of the week off and rest. Please.'

To pacify him, she agreed. 'But I will get up and sit with you in the living room. I fancy some tea and toast.'

He pretended to look horrified. 'Strange fancies already?'

'No, darling. I'm hungry, that's all.' She beamed at him and threw her arms up in the air. 'I'm going to be a mother!'

'Excuse me for pointing this out, but you didn't manage this all by yourself, you know!'

Putting her arms round him, she whispered, 'I do know, and I love you even more for the part you played.'

They sat together eating their toast and trying to come to terms with the change in their lives. 'I suppose, being a man, you want a son to carry on the family name?'

'Not at all! The sex of the baby isn't important to me as long as it's healthy. What about you?'

'I don't mind, like you, as long as it's alright, that's the most important thing.' She leant back against the cushions. 'My dream has always been to have my own home with a baby in a pram in the garden and I can hardly believe it's coming true. Did you have a dream, Larry?'

'Oh, indeed I did. I wanted success, because success brought security.'

'In what way?'

'After my parents died, I was completely alone. If I'm honest, I felt lost. I had the money to begin a business and if I was to be alone, I needed to feel secure, and money gave me that.' He gave a rueful smile. 'It sounds a bit cold-blooded putting it into words.'

'No, no, it doesn't. I can understand. Money was filling the gap in your life left by the loss of your parents. We all need something to strive for, you know. Now you will have your own family to fill that place.'

He let out a sigh of contentment. 'How wonderful is that. But I was an only child and I was lonely, I hope we have at least another to complete our family.'

'Good heavens! Do you mind if we have this one first before you start building a dynasty?'

He started laughing. 'Sorry, darling, but you know me, always planning for the future!'

'That's all very well, but let's not rush things, alright? In the meantime, just keep your mind on mundane things, like another cup of tea?'

'Certainly, Mrs Forbes. Anything you want, all you have to do is ask.'

'Now that's dangerous talk. Just give me a moment to think.'

'Oh, Jessie, you are far too clever. I'd forgotten. Here, drink your tea and behave. I'll take tomorrow off and we'll spend it together and make plans. Our lives will change and we need to be prepared for it.'

She looked at her man and smiled to herself. Larry would always be looking ahead, making a plan, but that was his security and now it would be hers. She thought of Conor and hoped that he would be happy for her. She felt that he would be with his love of life and people. How fortunate she'd been in so many ways to have known two such men and now she was starting a family of her own. Her life had been a battle ever since she'd been alone as a young girl, staying in Southampton when her widowed mother had returned to Ireland. There had been so many highs and lows throughout her life. Running the cafe, then seeing it burnt to the ground. Her elevated position as a manageress of a hotel, then its closing. Her abduction. She shivered as she thought of that and hurriedly pushed it out of her mind. But Larry, this man whom she'd hated when first they met, had saved her, and she had ended up being his wife. What a story she'd have to tell their children! They wouldn't have to battle in life as she'd had to, but she would make them realise that you must appreciate what you have.

Hopefully, when the war came to an end, life would return to normal. Larry and she would open another hotel, maybe more. No one can ever be sure of the future, however much you plan, but at least this time she wouldn't be alone to face any problems. She and Larry were a great team, that she knew. Together they would fight to succeed. She, Jessie McGonigall, now Forbes, was never a woman to run from a fight and the Forbes family would prevail. That was a promise!

Acknowledgements

My gratitude to all those people who gather facts and figures, who write about world events, history and oddball happenings that I can find for my research when I click onto Google. Thank you, thank you, thank you!

My thanks also to my daughters, Beverley and Maxine, for their never-failing love and support.

JUNE TATE was born in Southampton and spent the early years of her childhood in the Cotswolds. After leaving school she became a hairdresser on cruise ships the *Queen Mary* and the *Mauretania*, meeting many Hollywood film stars and VIPs on her travels. After her marriage to an airline pilot, she lived in Sussex and Hampshire before moving to Estoril in Portugal. June, who has two adult daughters, now lives in Sussex.

junetate.info